MADAME GRAY'S GRAVEYARD OF BLOOD

Compiled & Edited by Gerri R. Gray

Graveyard photos by Gerri Gray Photography

**A HellBound Books LLC
Publication**
Copyright © 2023 by HellBound Books Publishing
LLC
All Rights Reserved

Cover and art design by Timmy Fred
For HellBound Books Publishing LLC

**No part of this book may be reproduced, stored in
a retrieval system, or transmitted by any means,
electronic, mechanical, photocopying, recording or
otherwise without written permission from the author
This book is a work of fiction. Names, characters,
places and incidents are entirely fictitious or are used
fictitiously and any resemblance to actual persons,
living or dead, events or locales is purely coincidental.**

www.hellboundbooks.com

Also by Gerri R. Gray:

The Amnesia Girl
Gray Skies of Dismal Dreams
The Graveyard Girls
Blood and Blasphemy
The Strange Adventures of Turquoise Moonwolf
The Toilet Zone: Number Two
The Toilet Zone: The Royal Flush
Madame Gray's Creep Show
Madame Gray's Vault of Gore
Madame Gray's Poe-Pourri of Terror
All My Not-So-Pretty Ones

CONTENTS

INTRODUCTION
By Madame Gray

Madame Gray's word of the day is "coimetrophobia." This is the clinical term for a persistent and irrational fear of graveyards. While it might not be a commonly used word in most circles, it is, without a doubt, a fairly common fear among adults and children alike. Those unlucky enough to suffer from this phobia are known to feel overwhelmed by intense anxiety simply upon entering a graveyard. Just the very sight of graves, tombstones and mausoleums can evoke feelings of panic, dread and distress within them. Other symptoms they might experience include trembling, shortness of breath, nausea, a rapidly beating heart, profuse sweating, and even fainting.

But one doesn't need to be diagnosed with coimetrophobia in order to perceive a neglected, out-of-the-way graveyard as a truly dreadful, morbid and disturbing place... a place filled with untold perils and worthy of avoidance at all cost. Saturated in an atmosphere of gloom, it's an ideal place for the dark side of one's imagination to run wild.

It is human nature to be afraid of the unknown, with death being unequivocally the ultimate unknown. Therefore, for most of mankind, the thought of dying can be a source of fear to varying degrees, and nothing symbolizes death more than a graveyard. These shadowy places where the decaying remains of the non-living lie in their rotting coffins can serve as a reminder of our own mortality. For some, graveyards chill their blood because they believe them to be inhabited by the restless spirits of the dead who seek to possess or take their revenge on the living.

To say whether or not such beliefs have any merit is an impossible task.

Playing on these innate fears, horror movies frequently portray an old, foreboding graveyard as a portal to some hellish destination or a place where zombies, demons, and all manner of monsters seek out their victims. Such locations have long been fertile ground for the horror genre. And *Madame Gray's Graveyard of Blood* is no exception. In this fourth anthology in the HellBound Books' *Madame Gray* series, I proudly present to you twenty terrifying graveyard-themed tales, each guaranteed to elevate your fears to a whole new level.

Of course, such fears are totally irrational. There's absolutely nothing to be fearful of in a graveyard, except maybe for tripping over an unseen marker or twisting your ankle in a gopher hole. After all, we all know that ghosts really don't exist. The dead don't come back to life and claw their way out of their graves. And nightmarish things of a supernatural nature don't lurk among the gravestones, under the shroud of night, hungering for souls or the taste of human flesh.

Or do they?

MADAME GRAY'S GRAVEYARD OF BLOOD

GRAY

THE COFFIN BELL RINGS
By Charles Robertson

Jefferson coughed, a deep hacking that came from the pits of his lungs. "When my time on this earth is over and they bury me, make sure the coffin bell works. The last thing I want is to be alive when they put me in the ground. You are not such an imbecile as to forget that, are you, boy?"

A profanity-laced response formed in Carver's head. He swallowed and kept it inside, however. He was still in his father's will. Better to hold his tongue a little longer. Just a little longer, then the old man would be departed forever. "No, Father."

Carver sat on the concrete bench facing his mother's headstone. The etching read: 'Hilda Tubbs, January 9 1798 to April 2 1854. May God grant her eternal peace.' This was a relaxing place when Father wasn't there to shout his constant put-downs and expletives. Rose bushes ringed the cemetery plots and Aunt Darlene's newly-installed wind chimes hung in the oak trees over his head, waiting for a gust of wind to activate their heavenly sounds. To the left, Father's gravestone had already been set, needing only a date of death to be complete. That day couldn't come up soon enough for Carver.

The coffin bell apparatus, an eight-foot pipe, leaned against Father's headstone, waiting for a gravedigger to install it. At one end of the device was a brass bell with a string tied to it. The string ran through the pipe, which would be attached to the coffin through a hole drilled in the lid. The occupant, if he were still alive, could ring the bell and call attention to the fact he was not dead. It seemed a silly device. After all, why would anyone bury a man if they weren't sure he was dead?

"Just to make sure, I told the same thing to your Aunt Darlene and Aunt Henrietta. No way would I ever depend on you alone for something as important as that." Jefferson leaned forward in his wheelchair. "I'll bet you think I'm dabbling in unfounded fears. But remember your Great-Uncle Silas. They decided to disinter him a few days after his funeral and found the most horrific look on his face when they opened the coffin. His fingernails had been ripped off from scratching at the lid. A truly awful way to go. No way would I ever want that to happen to me."

"I will not forget, Father."

"Now, *boy*, take me back to the house. The smell of these leaves is going to choke me to death." Jefferson's voice was particularly hoarse.

Boy. Carver despised the word. The old man never called him 'Son' or any other name of endearment. Just 'lazy, worthless, good-for-nothing boy.' Carver took his time navigating the old man's wheelchair around the gravestones of the family plot and over the fallen autumn leaves as he headed to the house. He made it a point to run over some extra rocks and exposed roots on the way.

The wheelchair hit a particularly large rock. Father reached out with his cane and swatted Carver on the leg. "Watch it, boy. Are you trying to kill me before my time?"

A smirk came to Carver's face as he wheeled his father through the doorway to the kitchen. If only the old man knew the truth.

Jefferson coughed twice. "Push me to the dining room table. While you're at it then, get me a glass of the spirits. And light the kitchen lamp. Can't you see it's getting dark?"

Carver parked his father's wheelchair at the table. He retrieved the whiskey from the top shelf of the cabinet in the kitchen and filled a shot glass. As a special touch, he sneaked the bottle of arsenic out of his pocket and sprinkled in a few grains. It was so tempting to dump the whole bottle in, but he had to be careful. It needed to look like Jefferson was dying of a wasting disease. Just a few grains at a time. Sooner or later…

He secured the cap to the arsenic container and pocketed it. Carver plodded to the dining room and set the shot glass on the table in front of his father. "There you are. Drink up."

Father sipped from the glass. "I tell you, if it weren't for the pestering of your mother, God rest her soul, I'd never have left this estate to you. They say genius skips a generation. I hope in your case that's true. Maybe your offspring, if you manage to have any, will be able to run this place in the way it should be."

Carver squeezed the bottle of arsenic in his pocket, nearly breaking the glass. He relaxed his grip. The last thing he wanted to do was poison himself. 'Estate,' the old man called it. More like a desolate plot of land in the middle of nowhere with overgrown crops and thinning cattle. This had once been a fine farm, with a brightly-painted Colonial home and eighty acres of fat livestock and thriving crops. Keeping up this place and taking care of his father at the same time was more than one man could handle and the old man was too cheap to hire help. Naturally, the place fell into disrepair. The only thing that kept Carver from running off to the city was thinking of how much the land would fetch at auction when it was all his.

His father swallowed the rest of the whiskey and set down the glass. "Okay, boy, you can get me to bed now."

Carver wheeled his father to the staircase and climbed the steps backward, humping the wheelchair over one excruciating step at a time. Halfway up, his left hand slipped from the handle. The chair fell downwards a couple inches, but he managed to grab it at the last second.

Father twisted around to Carver. "Damn it, boy, you're as weak as you are stupid. I'm glad I won't be here to see what kind of a degenerate you grow into when I'm gone."

Sweat broke out under Carver's collar and armpits. Why couldn't he just have let go of the wheelchair and let it roll down the stairs? Maybe the old man's head would land on the oak floorboards at the bottom and split open. But if the old man didn't die in the fall, he'd know his son had dropped him on purpose. Carver would have to finish the job in a messy way and risk the constable's suspicion. No, it was better to stick with the plan. He'd put up with his father's constant tongue-lashings for the three years since Mother had died. A few more months wouldn't make any difference.

He lifted the old man onto the side of his bed and helped him into his night clothes. Father had deteriorated to the point where he wasn't much more than skin and bone. At least that made wheeling his miserable carcass from one end of the estate to the other easier.

Jefferson cleared his throat. "I'll have my cigar now."

Carver hated those things. Their stench was unbearable and the ashes were so hard to clean up. Why couldn't the old man forget about the foul-smelling things just once? He opened the cigar box on the table beside his father's bed and stuffed a cigar in the man's mouth. He then took the cover off the lamp and held it in front of his father's face while he inhaled.

Jefferson wheezed out a puff of thick, gray smoke. "You know, boy, when your mother died, it took so much out of me. I never thought I'd end my life with whiskey and tobacco as my only pleasures. Darlene and Henrietta hardly ever visit me anymore. Without you, I'd hardly have any human contact at all."

The old man finished his cigar and crushed the stub in an ashtray next to his bed. He then blew out the lamp, leaving Carver to pick his way through the darkened chamber as he headed to his own bedroom. Another day down. He needed his sleep also. Tomorrow the old man would be yelling at him at the crack of dawn to get off his rear end so he could do the same thing over again.

* * *

The rooster crowed as the sun peeked above the horizon. Carver opened his eyes. In a moment, the old man would be shouting for him to get out of bed, shrieking louder than the rooster. Carver might as well rest as long as he could. Every second without his father's voice grating against his eardrums was a blessing.

Carver closed his eyes for a few seconds. When he opened them again, the sun had changed from ember red to a golden yellow color. A mourning dove cooed in the distance. No sound of Father, though. Could the old wretch actually be dead? It would be too much to ask.

Carver plodded into his Father's room. With the windows closed, the stench of his cigars lingered from last night. Jefferson lay in his bed, face up and unmoving. His mouth gaped open. Jefferson shook the old man. "Father? Wake up."

The old man remained motionless. Carver shook him again, slapped his face, and listened for a heartbeat. Father was dead at last. Carver danced from one end of the room to another, laughing. The torment of living with that wretched old man all those years was finally over.

* * *

The pastor stood at the head of the open grave. Jefferson's coffin rested at the bottom with his corpse inside. A pile of black, fresh-smelling dirt lay at one side of the hole, with Carver, Aunt Darlene, Aunt Henrietta, and the rest of the extended family on the other.

The reverend closed his Bible and held it over his chest. "We now commend Jefferson Tubbs to the earth from which he came. May he rest eternally in peace next to his beloved spouse, Hilda. Amen."

One by one, the relatives filed past the open grave and dropped in a handful of dirt. Carver wanted to deposit a mouthful of spit, but threw in more dirt instead. His crime had been so perfect, he didn't want to cast suspicion on himself now. The reverend and the relatives went on their ways, leaving only him and the gravediggers, who were filling in the grave. The fine, loose dirt required only a few scoops as it fell so readily into the pit. He laughed to himself as he watched the men assemble the coffin bell, first by attaching the pipe to the hole in the lid of the coffin and then attaching the bell to the post at the head of the grave. Carver was certain the old man wouldn't be needing it. After all the arsenic Jefferson had ingested, he had to be quite dead.

* * *

The fire blazed in the fireplace, illuminating the parlor in a flickering yellow-orange glow. Carver downed one more glass of his father's spirits. It was amazing how serene the house could be without the old man screeching, "Get me this. Get me that. Do you know how stupid you are, boy?"

Carver's eyelids became heavy as bedtime approached. As he had done every day for the past three years, he climbed the stairs, only it was much easier this time without having to drag a wheelchair behind while listening to his father's unending tongue-lashings. Carver started toward his bedroom and paused. Why was he about to sleep in his own bed? He was master of the house now. He should be using the master bedroom.

The lingering stench of his father's cigar smoke forced its way up Carver's nostrils when he entered the huge bedroom. He opened all the windows and let the gentle, cooling autumn breeze circulate through the room. He crawled into the canopy bed and relished the fluffy mattress and soft blankets around him. A smile came to his face as he took in a strong whiff of the crisp night air and drifted to sleep.

* * *

Ding ding. Ding ding.
Carver raised his head. He thought he'd heard something, like a bell in the distance. He had to be dreaming. The trauma of all those nights when his father was still alive must have been replaying in his head. Carver lay back down and shut his eyes.

Ding ding. Ding ding.
Carver sat up. That couldn't be a dream. The sound was real and it was coming from outside. He stumbled to the window. At the top of the hill before him, the moon cast its ghostly blue light on the cemetery plots. The dinging in the distance could only be the coffin bell. Dear God, the bastard was still alive!

Carver shot out of bed and snatched a robe from the closet. He slipped on his shoes, then stopped. Why was he rushing to save his father? Carver had suffered for years under his father's constant berating. Now it was the old man's turn to suffer. It was time to pay back his father for all the years of Father treating him like mud under his wheelchair, and this was the perfect way to do it. He lay back in bed and let the gentle *ding dings* of the bell serenade him to sleep.

* * *

Ding ding. Ding ding.

Carver awakened to the sound of the coffin bell. Heavens above, the old man didn't give up, did he? How long could he possibly survive buried alive? Wouldn't he have run out of air by now? But then maybe air was circulating through the pipe that connected the string with the bell. He'd eventually starve, but that could take weeks. The livestock couldn't live more than a few days without water, however. That had to be true for Father. If nothing else, he'd be dead of thirst in a couple days.

* * *

As Carver dressed, the morning sun was already warming the room. The day would be a hot one for this time of year. As he descended the stairs, his throat was dry from thirst. He grabbed a cup from the kitchen and went to the backyard to work the pump. The trickle of cool, refreshing water filled the vessel. He held it to his lips. "Here's to you, Father."

That afternoon, Carver started moving Father's things out of the house and into the barn. The land and the old man's possessions would fetch quite a lot at auction, probably enough for him to move to New York, maybe even London. The bell rang again. *Ding ding. Ding ding.* It was so annoying. If it weren't for that confounded bell, this would be the perfect day. Then it occurred to him. All he needed to do was rip out the bell.

He stumbled up the trail to the cemetery plot. Why hadn't he thought of this before? The bell sat at the top of the post. He yanked it loose from the string and stomped it into the soft ground covering the grave. It sank easily. Then, he stuffed a handful of soil in the pipe to cut off any air going to the coffin. He slapped the dirt off his hands and went back to the house with a smile.

* * *

Carver settled into bed, thinking of what he'd do the next morning. He'd have to ride into town to put the advertisement in the newspaper and hire an auctioneer. His eyes had hardly been closed a minute before he heard a sound in the distance. *Ding ding. Ding ding.*

He lifted his head. It couldn't be. That sounded like the coffin bell, but he had already dismantled it. Maybe it was his imagination. After all, he had experienced a lot of changes lately and the strain of everything that had happened lately had to be building on him. He rested his head back onto the pillow and stared at the bed canopy above him.

Ding ding. Ding ding.

The tone rang again. Carver pressed his hands over his ears and found a reprieve of silence. After a moment, he let up on the pressure. *Ding ding.* He held his hands over his ears again. More silence ensued, save for the sound of his pulse throbbing past his ears. He held his hands there until his arm muscles burned and quivered. Finally, he let go.

The bell was no longer ringing. Nothing came from outside except the serenade of the tree frogs and night insects. Inside, the swaying of the pendulum on the clock in the hall gave a gentle, relaxing rhythm. Then it chimed, one time. One o'clock in the morning. Peace followed. Maybe it had all been a dream. Carver expelled a breath of relief and fell back asleep.

* * *

Ding ding. Ding ding.

The bell awakened him again. He turned his head toward the cemetery. "Go away!"

Carver had heard stories about phantom pain. Someone loses an arm, but still feels pain as if the limb were still there. The old man had tormented him for so long, he was now embedded in Carver's psyche. He buried his head in his pillow. "Get out of my head."

Carver lifted the pillow from his face and listened. The clock struck three. The night was two-thirds over and he'd hardly slept at all. Then, the sound returned. *Ding ding. Ding ding. Ding ding.*

He turned over and buried his head in the covers.

* * *

Carver opened his eyes to bright sunlight spilling into the bedroom. His head felt as if it had been shattered into a million pieces. The radiant sun's rays that should have cheered him up instead made his eyes hurt. He pressed his hands to his temples, but it didn't do anything to alleviate the pain.

And the bell continued to ring. *Ding ding. Ding ding.*

Carver shambled down the stairs and into the parlor. He examined himself in the mirror on the wall. Thick purple bags hung under his bloodshot eyes. Scraggly whiskers grew from his face, but he didn't dare shave them in his condition. For all he knew, he'd slit his throat with his unsteady hands. If the ringing didn't end soon, he would go insane.

Ding ding. Ding ding.

Carver held his hands over his temples. "Noooooo!"

As long as his father remained in that coffin, either dead or alive, Carver would not know any peace. He had to do something. A thought materialized in his head. He would dig his father up and let the buzzards deal with him. He would then crush the bones and use them for fertilizer. That would get rid of him once and for all. Carver grabbed a shovel from the shed and scurried up the trail to the cemetery, shouting, "I'm coming for you, Father."

He stumbled into the plot, panting for breath. "I'm here. What do you think about that?"

There was no answer, but he didn't expect any. He'd soon have the old man exhumed and be able to destroy the corpse once and for all. A bed of soft, loosely-packed soil covered Father's grave. He jammed the shovel into the dirt and watched it sink into the ground with the slightest effort.

He scooped a shovelful of soil, depositing it on the side of the grave. He threw out more lumps. Soon, Carver had dug out a knee-deep hole. The coffin lid couldn't be far below. He deepened the hole until he was waist-deep below the ground. A few minutes later, the shovel struck wood. He'd reached the coffin.

Now he would have to widen the hole enough to open the lid. He threw up scoopful after scoopful of dirt, building the mound now far above his head. The steep pile started slipping. For every two scoops of dirt he removed, one fell back on top of him. After a while, the dirt started sliding in as fast as he could dig it out. Carver stopped to catch his breath. The entire mound of earth gave way, falling on top of him. He held his hands over his face and screamed as the soil encased him in darkness.

*　*　*

Darlene and Henrietta sat on the stone bench in front of the gravestones as the funeral guests departed. On the other side of Hilda's grave, the earthen smell of freshly-dug dirt rose from Carver's final resting place.

Darlene admired the beauty of the roses growing around the cemetery plot. "They tell me the look on Carver's face was one of sheer horror."

Henrietta wrapped the dark shawl of her mourning outfit around her. "It must be awful to be buried alive. I can't possibly think of a worse way to go."

"All I can say is, he is at peace now." Darlene sat back and took in the serenity of the place. A gust of wind rose and rang the wind chimes above her.

Ding ding. Ding ding.

NIGHT DIGGING
By Eddie Spohn

The headstone was an upright piece of midnight black granite flecked with silvery specks of mica. It had been set there early this morning, as the interment hole was dug out with a small backhoe, before the rains came to make the afternoon burial a soggy affair. Now the flowers at its base sagged with the weight of collected moisture, the petals shaken now and then by a light breeze. Just past the flowers the casket was suspended over the interment hole by straps connected to a metal framework equipped with a winch. Drops of rain studded the polished mahogany surface of the casket like clear crystals.

As it was an atheist's funeral, one of the deceased's friends recited a memorized eulogy of times gone by to a small gathering of the bereaved, who stood in a circle around the burial plot, holding umbrellas and shivering in the dampness even though it was a muggy August afternoon. The storm was mild but it had turned the sky gunmetal grey, hiding the sun and stealing the color from the landscape; everything, no matter how bright and flashy under normal circumstances, was subdued, shaded in greys and blacks. Much like the mood of most of those gathered here.

The perfect setting for a funeral, some might say.

Or the start of a horror movie.

With the eulogy over, the groundskeeper was given the signal. He pressed a button and the winch let out a high whine as it lowered the casket into the hole. The casket touched ground ten feet below, its rounded lid just an inch under the required six foot depth (though compliance was a strictly moral thing; there were no graveyard police checking such things). Once it was settled in, the straps were removed and the funeral attendees leaned over the edge to drop flowers, tears, and mementos into the hole.

Two men stood back a bit, at the scene but not joining in the proceedings. Their presence did not arouse any suspicion, although it should have because no one knew who they were. Neither did they know the deceased or her bereaved, but they knew *of* her.

They stayed at their spot, umbrella-less and soggy figures, nodding in commiseration whenever they caught the eyes of departing grievers. Now the final attendees of the service, they watched for a bit as the grounds crew disassembled the winch framework and set about burying the casket with the small backhoe. Some of the crew might have recognized the last two men from other funerals had they bothered to look then or now, but, as usual, they were focused on what they were doing and oblivious.

"This is gonna suck," said one of the men to the other. His name was Bram Cooper. He was rail thin from a diet of amphetamines and other marvels of modern chemistry. His appearance was deceptive; certain of these substances gave him incredible strength and endurance. Helpful for someone who did night digging.

His companion, Roger Milgram, was shorter, stouter, with the look of a faded powerlifter. He knew exactly what Bram meant. It was hard enough getting in and out quickly and undetected. Wet dirt made things heavy and twice as difficult. However, rainy weather was ideal for covert activities, as any criminal knew. Less witnesses out and about, and the falling rain muffled sounds. There were pros and cons to everything.

"We'll live," Roger said, and the two of them returned to their pick-up truck. They had a few hours to kill (pardon the pun) until nightfall, and they needed to rest up before returning here, so they drove out the entrance of the cemetery and down the long road leading to Leesburg, the town in Georgia where they rented a ramshackle apartment on the shore of a polluted creek. The cemetery and the accompanying crematorium were visible from the town, its smokestacks poking to the sky like a long ago survivor's nightmare, the minute points of the multiple headstones skeletal fingers extended in accusation.

The small room they shared smelled of feet and body odor. It was not much different than the cell they had shared back in jail. They had been released from Georgia Correctional within weeks of each other and found themselves assigned to this place, where they could live on the government's tab as long as necessary. Roger made himself comfortable on the mattress beside the opened window. A half dead window fan blew fresh air from outside into the stuffy room.

"You better get some rest," Roger warned, but knew already that was not going to happen. Bram, as usual, had burned through his half of the proceeds from their last haul. He was as fidgety as a squirrel in hawk country. Roger, who did not share in his companion's bad chemical habits, reluctantly handed over a quintet of twenties. "You need to quit this stuff," he warned.

"It helps me work," Bram said, thankfully taking the money.

That was very true, Roger had to admit. When Bram was primed up on his favorite stimulant, he worked like a machine. He left the room to go score and Roger closed his eyes. When he opened them again, a glassy eyed Bram stood over him as the bedside alarm clock blared. "Rise and shine," Bram said, every cell in his body wired and firing on all cylinders.

Time to dig a hole.

* * *

The weirdo who needed freshly dug up bodies had come into the Maidenhead Tavern six months ago at a time when Roger and Bram were sneaking around to local towns and doing home break-ins while the owners were out at work. It was risky work with small reward, as they were not exactly in an affluent area, and out here people were well armed.

He came up to their table in the corner of the bar and sat down, a middle aged and well-dressed man with skin as dark as the midnight sky. The two of them immediately thought of rolling him but there was something absent from his eyes that made them think twice before discarding the idea as unwise. They had seen similar absences in the eyes of jailed serial killers. It was also the cool gaze of a predator upon prey, a skilled fighter, or a scientist studying a vivisected specimen with measured detachment. There were very fine lines separating these things, and it was hard to tell which one this man was.

"Milton Dobbs," he said. "You fellas looking for work?"

"You got some?" Roger asked with interest.

"Sure. How are your backs? You know how to dig?"

They'd done some digging during their stay in jail. Neither were much interested in making an occupation of it, no matter how much they needed the cash.

"Not even for a thousand dollars? For one night's work?" Milton Dobbs asked.

Well that was a different story. Of course there was a catch. Milton Dobbs told them what it was over a few beers, and left them to think it over. He paid their tabs and gave them each a hundred dollars for their time, along with a number to call if they decided to take the job.

"But don't wait too long if you're onboard," Milton Dobbs warned them. "I need this done Thursday. If you do good, I'll have more work for you."

"What do you think?" Roger asked when Milton Dobbs was gone.

"I think he might be one of those necronfeelias, dude."

"What the hell is that?" Roger asked.

"You know, has sex with corpses." Bram grasped invisible hips and thrust his own under the table.

"You think?"

"The world is a strange place with a lot of weird people in it," Bram said.

Roger had a sudden idea. "Maybe he's harvesting organs."

Bram got a kick out of that and burst into laughter. His knowledge of the word 'harvest' extended only to farmers and crops, and he had an image in his head of an old guy driving a combine across a field of plants adorned with breathing lungs and pumping hearts.

"What you laughing at?" Roger asked him.

"Nothing."

"A thousand bucks for a night though. He supplies the tools and gets us a work vehicle. I mean, who cares what he does with the bodies? They're just dead meat. We're still alive."

"True," Bram said, grasping the ends of the crisp hundred Dobbs had given him and stretching it between his fingers. He liked the look of Ben Franklin in the dim light. This was before his addictions took over and turned hundreds into an ephemeral liquid he could not hold for long. "Let's give it a shot."

They called Dobbs that night as they were walking home from the bar and left a message saying they would give his proposition a try. The following morning Dobbs called them back and told them to pick up their *work* truck in a parking lot in town. It was a late model Dodge Durango with the ignition key resting upon the front driver's side tire. It had license plates and the proper stickers, along with the paperwork in the glove compartment. Digging tools and rolls of burlap were in the covered bed.

Dobbs called and instructed them to attend the funeral of one Martin Nordtrom that afternoon, which they did. The purpose of this was to help them get familiar with the layout of The Restful Acres Cemetery, which was situated on a hill overlooking the part of Leesburg where Bram and Roger lived. It was a cool but sunny February day, and Mister Nordtrom had a lot of people at the ceremony. The two gravediggers returned later that evening. By then the air had cooled and there was a coating of frost on the ground. Once the freshly laid sod was peeled back and that initial crust broken through, it was surprisingly easy to dig down to the recently interred casket and remove the body of Martin Nordtrom. They wrapped the corpse in burlap and put it into the bed of the Durango, and Roger drove to the instructed drop off place while Bram stayed behind to refill the hole and put the sod back in place. The idea being to make it seem as if this whole thing had never happened.

Dobbs met Roger at the back of a dilapidated metal structure out in the woods a mile from the cemetery. Dobbs was in lab whites and he and Roger went around to the back of the truck. Dobbs was overjoyed when he removed the wrappings from Nordtrom's head and the young man's face was revealed in the flashlight beam. "You don't realize it but you and your friend are part of something that will change the world," Dobbs said. He beckoned Roger to follow him.

Roger hefted the wrapped body over one shoulder. Dark splotches on the burlap reminded him of an overripe banana peel, and he felt a cool wetness on his shoulder and back. He preferred not to think of what the stuff might be, though the words *dead juice* popped into mind.

He hasn't been dead long enough to be rotten yet, has he? Roger wondered. They advised you not to eat meat products left out in room temperature for more than a few hours, but that was due to pathogenic bacteria, not actual decay. How long before meat began to liquesce?

Who cared? It was Dobbs' problem now. Roger followed the man through an opened door and into some kind of lab. The building's decrepit exterior gave no hint of the immaculately clean space inside, filled with glittering chrome equipment and examination tables. Trays of medieval looking dissection tools were everywhere. There was a bank of microscopes and screens where slide images were projected. Atmospheric scrubbers hummed from secret places, vents created a gentle cross breeze of disinfectant-scented air.

Another person stood by a nearby table, hands on hips, the full lab whites unable to hide the curves of a woman. She was as hidden from view as an Arabian wife, only her eyes visible between her hair net and the circle of a face mask. Her eyes were large and dark, seemingly without pupils, outlined with mascara and oddly beautiful, though as devoid of emotion as Dobbs' were, as dead as the corpse over Roger's shoulder. "Here," she said with a muffled voice, patting the shining chrome of the adjacent exam table with one gloved hand.

Roger looked to Dobbs, who nodded confirmation. Roger laid the body down and was immediately whisked out of the lab by Dobbs. Roger had an over-the-shoulder glimpse of the woman stripping the corpse of its burlap mummy wrappings before the door shut behind him and he was out in the darkness. At the truck, Dobbs handed him an envelope. "No offense, my friend, but time is of the essence," he said as he sprinted away.

As promised, there was a thousand dollars in the envelope.

The following day, as evening approached, Dobbs called him again to dispose of the body.

"What do you want us to do with it?" Roger asked.

"Rebury it, I guess," Dobbs said. Understanding the silence at the other end, he said, "You'll be paid, of course."

Reburying a body was just about the same as digging it up in the first place, the two of them figured. And it kind of was, except that when they were halfway down to the casket Roger said, "We don't need to put it back inside the damn thing. No one's ever gonna know if we just put it here and cover it over."

Bram leaned on his shovel. The two of them were standing in a four foot deep rectangle, a pile of dirt and sod to one side, the stained burlap-wrapped body of Martin Nordtrom on the other. The Georgian winter sky overhead was speckled with stars. Owls hooted in trees. Both men wore forehead mounted lights that gave off a red spectrum perfect for covert operations at night because it was nearly invisible at a distance. The light glowed at the center of Bram's forehead like a fiery cyclops eye as he responded, "I don't know. It seems disrespectful. Bad juju, man."

"We dug this guy up and *now* you're worrying about being respectful? He's dead. At least we're making the effort to put him in the right spot. And we'll get out of here a lot quicker. Yeah?"

Bram weighed these facts in his mind. "You got a point," he agreed.

They buried Mister Nordtrom at half his original depth. And so it was with each of the other bodies these two gravediggers disturbed and then laid back to rest over the next six months until the rainy August night they dug up Marina Tresso.

* * *

Milton Dobbs worked as a pathologist for the State of Georgia Crime Lab.

He also had certain interests he could not pursue at his place of employment. Over time he had used several side hustles to finance his little backwoods lab. The occasional sale of a pilfered organ or two from autopsy specimens paid off well, and gave him a bit of a budget to work with. Sometimes bodies came in with usable items that would only go to waste, and if he was alone (or with his trusty accomplice Marissa) it was no big deal to put them on ice and unload them to his Asian contacts. He didn't go crazy with it, of course. Just a sale here and there, with long stretches of time between. Only dummies got greedy, and being greedy led to being caught.

And if he got caught, he would never get to pursue the great work.

The idea for the great work came to him during an overnight alone at the state morgue. He'd been taking a break from an autopsy, having a slice of pizza (that, by the way, looked very much like the interior of the opened chest cavity of the corpse on the table). The subject was a 29-year-old man who had died of an apparent drug overdose, though they were still awaiting the results of the toxicology report for final confirmation. The major organs, already detached and weighed by Dobbs and resting in the chest cavity like a pile of giblets, showed all the signs of long term drug abuse, and Dobbs would have bet his life this was another case of Death by Chemical Misadventure.

With a creak of stressed vertebrae, the corpse sat upright, spilling its organs onto its lap. The eyes opened and studied Dobbs. He had heard of such things happening during rigor mortis, when muscles stiffened and contracted and bodies sometimes sat up or appeared to breathe. But there were time constraints, a well-known cycle of events following death, and this was not the proper place in it for such things to occur. Rigor mortis was done and gone.

After fifteen years, this was a first for him. He dropped the pizza and the corpse's eyes lowered to look at the food on the floor. An arm raised and extended an index finger to point at it. The finger then pointed to a dead mouth that was stretched into an undeniable smile. It was as if the dead guy was signaling that he wanted something to eat.

Slowly, the corpse lowered itself back down and was dead again. Nothing Dobbs did could get any further response. He knew he had not imagined what he saw; he was much too analytical and unemotional for *that*. If Dobbs ever truly went insane, it would be the type brought on by the unbearable truths of the universe rather than hallucinatory bug outs. His would be the most boring and logical kind of psychosis; no talking walls and visual hallucinations for him, just the simple terror of knowing the things most people prefer *not* to.

He was convinced that what he had witnessed was not mere rigor mortis but a brief return to life. The life force, the soul, whatever that might be, had come back momentarily. Maybe just to mess with him.

Which got him to thinking about eternal life and how one might resuscitate the dead.

Marissa was the only one he ever told about the incident, one night during a long and tiring series of autopsies when it was only the two of them in the morgue. She was his assistant and the two of them, although Dobbs was a married father and she was engaged, had a casual *thing* that being pathologists made possible. It was easy enough to tell partners you were doing an overnight shift or much longer.

A mere physical attraction wouldn't have been enough to get Dobbs to stray. He really did love his wife and family. The cement of their relationship was Marissa's embrace of his hypotheses about the incident with the corpse…even more importantly, her *belief* in it. She had Dobbs' own form of cool and detached logic; he saw it mirrored in her lovely eyes. Her belief in his story on that tiring night had caused him to reach out and kiss her full lips despite knowing it was as professionally and morally wrong as it was fatefully so right.

Marissa was his partner in this quest for eternal life. They had experimented on sacrificed animals with various reagents and combinations of chemicals and electricity in an attempt at resuscitation. One combination appeared to bring about momentarily positive results, such as a dead guinea pig suddenly running across an examination table and plunging to its second death over the ledge. Dobbs and Marissa could never replicate this incident, but they were both witnesses and had video documentation of it.

Animal models only went so far. The two of them knew human specimens were necessary. An intact resuscitated human might be able to explain its state of being to the researchers. As a state official, Dobbs had access to death records and could further follow them to dates of interment.

He just needed to find someone to go in and retrieve the necessary specimens. The nature of his research and the modes of acquiring material meant that *employees* required a certain type of constitution not prevalent in most of society. He went to The Maidenhead Tavern because it was a well-known hangout for seedy clientele. He was a skilled fighter with a concealed carry permit and accompanying gun, so he did not fear venturing into the place. Most people knew not to mess with him just by looking at his eyes. Even the derelicts furthest gone had an instinct for immediate self-preservation.

Roger and Bram had given off the vibes he was looking for. Desperate enough to do anything if the pay was right. He started out with a low offer, prepared to go much higher if necessary. He was not surprised they had bitten, but he had not expected it to be on that initial offer of a thousand dollars. He would have paid much, much more.

They had served him well these six months, and he and Marissa were getting close to…*something*… in their researches. The last few corpses had showed signs of motion–sudden breaths, fluttering of the eyelids, clenching of hands. Always brief episodes that would not repeat themselves no matter what Dobbs tried.

"More potassium this time," Marissa said, raising a syringe over the newest corpse Roger had delivered on this rainy August night. Marina Tresso was stretched out on the exam table, her body nude and wrapped at the ankles and wrists with electric conducting restraints. Wires led from these to a floor-mounted generator, beside which Dobbs kneeled with one finger just over a green ON button. "And two more amperes," Dobbs said. The two of them spoke for the benefit of a tripod-mounted video camera recording their experiment.

"Go ahead," Dobbs advised Marissa. She punched the long needle into the corpse's chest and the still heart below and depressed the plunger, filling the aorta with the concoction. She pulled out and Dobbs put the generator on for a five-second cycle of the adjusted amperage. When the electrical burst ended, the corpse shivered and its eyes opened and looked up at Marissa.

"Milt, she's looking at me!"

Dobbs was up in a flash. "Marina?" he said. "Can you hear me?"

At the sound of her name, Marina's eyes widened and she began to scream. "No! NO! NOOOOOOOOO!" She wrenched one hand free of the electrical wire connecting it to the generator and thrust the sharp points of her nails into her eyes. They burst with a jellied pop and she thrust deeper, through the back of her eye sockets and into her brain.

Dobbs and Marissa were too late to stop her. By the time they pulled her hand free, the damage had been done and she was dead again, just a corpse with acai bowls for eyes and fingernails strung with brain matter. They had worked with other corpses for longer periods of time because their nervous systems were still intact.

This one was ruined now.

"Dammit!" Dobbs swore.

* * *

The only surprise this time was how quickly Dobbs requested corpse disposal. Roger had only just gotten back to the graveyard and picked up his shovel to help Bram finish up filling the hole when the call came.

"What the hell," Bram said. "This is ridiculous." He meant both the timing of the call and the rain, which was steadily increasing.

Roger was soaked already despite the rain gear he'd put on. "That was fast," he agreed. "All right, start digging down again. I'll be back in a little bit."

Bram did not respond. He had stopped shoveling and was looking off into the gloom. The beam of his red headlamp played over an ever shifting sheet of rain, within which was visible headstones and slow moving forms.

"There's something out there," Bram said.

Roger saw them now, pale forms within the rain, converging from all sides onto the site of the dig, bringing with them phantom whispers. *Why?* came the question. *We only wanted to rest. Why did you wake us?*

Roger had a .32 caliber pistol he'd purchased from someone on the street. He took it out from his waistband and leveled it at the nearest figure, a pale and bloated man who released puffs of decomposition gases from his anus with each forward step. Most of his face was worm- eaten but the gap in his teeth was familiar from one of the corpses Roger and Bram had half reburied. This corpse opened its mouth to speak, but because much of its throat and larynx was gone, it just farted out alien syllables at the two living men.

Not thinking of stealth any longer, Roger squeezed off six fear shots in rapid succession, blowing away this corpse's midsection in an explosive burst of septic entrails and subterranean insects and worms. The corpse's spine broke in half and its torso separated from the waist and fell beside them. The legs took one more flatulence-riddled step forward before they tumbled into the mud with a splash. The gun clicked on empty chambers.

The whispers were all around Roger and Bram now. Familiar corpses in various stages of decomposition closed in with outstretched arms, the chemicals and processes Dobbs had performed on them during his early research resurrecting the flesh after this delayed period.

They wanted to know why they had been awakened, pulled back into their rotting shells. But they were also hungry for the pulsing sacs of life within the two men before them, for the weird millivolts of life energy and the tangy liquid it propelled through the tubule ridden meat. This and this only would assuage that pain deep in their liquescing brainpans.

So they reached for it.

Swinging shovels with all their strength, Roger and Bram were still overwhelmed by the sheer number of advancing corpses that took them down, tore and rendered, and ate until nothing but bone remained.

Somewhat refreshed but still hungry, the corpses ambled forward through the rain and out of the cemetery, towards the delicious scent of the living in the town below.

Perhaps down there could be found an answer to their questions.

At the very least, a free meal.

CEMETERY ISLAND
By J Louis Messina

"We buried everyone there, rich, poor, young, old, didn't matter." Colonel Guerrier puffed on his cigar, leaned back in his chair, and pushed his mirrored shades against his face. "The Prime Minister had ordered political enemies shot for treason. No longer. It's forbidden to go there."

"Di Haitians call it Cimetière Île," Jocelyne said. "They avoid dis island like di devil. Soldiers buried dem with all their possessions, jewels and money, so as to leave no trace of dem behind. I so sure they took their share. My inheritance was buried with my parents, worth millions."

The colonel looked Jocelyne Montas over. Young and pretty, clothed in a sheer, black gown; her cornrow hair braids hung seductively over her slim, dark shoulders. When women had begged for their lives in exchange for their bodies, she was the type he loved. He'd taken many a girl that way. Some he let live; some he killed; some he sold into slavery. She had come to promise wealth in this destitute country. As much as he desired her beauty, he lusted after treasure more.

What more could a man want in life than wealth?

Guerrier wiped the perspiration off his forehead. "Do you have a map?"

"Map's up here," Jocelyne said, tapping her left temple.

"You said you haven't been there since a child."

"I never forget. The militia killed my family during a political uprising and buried dem on di island. They performed their voodoo rituals. Many politicians died. Graves filled wid riches. I hid in an empty grave, escaped to Jamaica.""Why should I believe you?"

"I saved dis sapphire from my parents' grave when I was five."

The colonel held the magnificent blue gem in his hand and examined it. He'd never robbed graves before. Bad juju. A relic belief taught by his superstitious, ignorant, poor parents. Nevertheless, it stuck.

"Why not sell it?"

"It's a family heirloom. I can't part wid it."

Sentimental rubbish, he thought.

"I don't know, honey." He tossed the gem on his desk and flicked his ashes. "Too risky."

Jocelyne braced her hands on his desk and arched toward his face intimately, flirtatiously, exposing her large breasts. He looked down her cleavage. Her nipples hardened, as did he. If it didn't pan out, he could collect his payment in other ways. Or both. Although he knew she enticed him with her sex, he didn't care. He had the upper hand physically, and he was a trained soldier.

"What you have to lose, Colonel?"

"Why me?"

"You have di boat, the authority to go, you've been there. No one question you. I promise to share."

Sharing her wealth with him was assured. He was only a poor corrupt official. He'd taken his portion of bribes, but the Haitians had nothing to offer but poverty and disease. Honesty was for fools, but dishonesty didn't pay enough.

"I'll commission the boat. We can leave tomorrow. And don't try anything funny or else." To prove his point, he mashed out his cigar in the palm of his hand. "Don't come here. We don't want to arouse suspicion. Meet at Port-au-Prince at the beginning of Mardi Gras. For your sake, there better be jewels there."

Jocelyne sashayed to the door and glanced over her shoulder.

"Maybe then you can afford yourself an ashtray."

* * *

Colonel Guerrier swigged a flask of whiskey. "They never stop, do they?"

"Two days of relentless Mardi Gras celebration. We Haitians do know how to party."

The Ghede, the spirits of life and death, the corpse of the first man, guardians of the cemeteries and lords of the erotic, dressed in black, purple uniforms, top hat, and mirrored sunglasses, poured libations around crosses and festooned tombstones with candles, skulls, and marigolds. Guerrier thought it funny and macabre. The humidity enhanced the putrid smells, brewing them with heat and despair. He fluffed his shirt, trying to cool the sticky sweat that pooled in his pits.

While they shunted through the swelling crowds and the graveyards, a Ghede possessed a peasant Haitian girl to come on to him with the dance of Guedeh La Flambeau, the flashing brilliance of the orgasm; she danced in her colorful garb and painted face, and writhed and grinded against his body; the people beat their drums and tambourines, danced wild and raucous, closed in around him and sang; he felt the fear rise within, the terror, the suffocation; as the pain throbbed in his chest, he struck her across the face, withdrew his gun, and fired over their heads. The crowd dispersed and shouted and protested. Jocelyne pulled him away before the crowd turned ugly, and they disappeared into the mass of stinking bodies. The impoverished residents that roamed the streets disgusted him.

"Why did you hit di girl?"

"Claustrophobic." He clamped his hand to his chest. "I panic in close spaces."

Jocelyne looked around. "Hope that won't arouse suspicion."

"Relax. They'll think it part of the festivities."

When they reached the sailboat, they scrambled in and set sail over the Gulf of Gonâve and through the Caribbean Sea. As night fell, the drums and chants thrummed low in the distance; the dots of candles floated like tiny, flickering eyes from Port-au-Prince.

A gust caught the sail and carried them swift and unseen across the sea. Fists of waves knocked against the hull. Jocelyne gazed into the briny deep.

"There was a massacre on Haiti, once," Jocelyne said. "Twenty thousand Haitians were murdered and dumped in di water. They say the hands of di dead are on di ocean spray."

Guerrier scanned the sea, as if half-expecting body parts to surface. He'd been there that night, gave the orders. He had some regrets, killing so many. But politics as usual. Taking another drink from his flask, he let it sooth his guilt.

Why had she told him that gruesome story?

Guerrier squinted at the distant fog. "Your terrible tale of woe moved me to tears. Leave the dead buried and forgotten. It's best."

"How far away are we?"

"There!"

A mist blanketed the humid mountains of Cimetière Île. Clouds smothered the tops. They landed and carried their flashlights and supplies inland.

As they climbed the steep mountainside, Guerrier panted and clutched his chest. The island climate, muggy as a steam room, poured a river of sweat down his body. His blood pressure probably hit 200. At fifty-eight, he had kept in shape, but the doctor said he had a weak heart. He would've been dismissed from the army but had threatened the doctor not to tell.

"Less than a kilometer away," Jocelyne said. "Di drums are pounding over our heads. Di mountain makes an excellent echo chamber."

Boom, boom, boom, like a cry to war.

"It's thundering inside my skull." Guerrier rolled his stiff neck and massaged his forehead. "What a headache. I'll need to rest soon, or my heart will burst."

They reached the peak and stopped. Guerrier gasped. Saturated in swirling fog, graves covered the ground as far as the eye could see. He'd forgotten how many had been dug. Cemetery Island had been well named. A mass of dirt mounds jutted from the wet soil like headless black bodies, stretched over the horizon, and fell off the face of the Earth. Vapors that rose from the mounds reminded him of spirits fleeing the ground.

"Where in God's name do we start digging?"

"They were buried over by those trees."

Jocelyne wound through the maze of graves and lurched over the stark landscape toward the aggregation of petrified trees. Guerrier skipped around them, as if a mere touch would infect him with death. The old superstitions his parents had instilled in him grew like a fungus in his mind. Memories from twenty years ago flooded in. He recognized this place.

"Won't be too bad," he said. "Most were chucked in shallow graves. Ones with coffins had to be buried deeper."

"Dig here," she said.

Gasping for breath in the heat, they removed shovels, struck soft dirt, and flung it. Guerrier tasted the muck in his mouth, smacked his lips, and spit. Six feet later, metal clanked against a rotted wooden coffin.

"Only the rich got coffins," he said, dabbing a handkerchief over his face. "They had to pay for them. Whatever we find, we split."

Jocelyne leapt inside the hole and pried open the lid with the sharp end of the shovel. Her wet clothes clung to her skin and revealed her flesh; Guerrier licked his lips. They uncovered fifteen graves, exposing white, cadaverous bodies, the emaciated and the foul, bones and dust, un-earthed silver and gold and stuffed them in a bag, but she hadn't found her parents' grave.

Guerrier rested on the nub of his shovel. Dark clouds scudded across the sky, bringing soft rain down in sporadic drops. He lifted his slack face to the cool water. The crack of splintered wood startled him; he peered down. Jocelyne rummaged within another coffin.

"Need help?"

Focused on her task, Jocelyne worked and searched, extravagantly quiet. Guerrier imagined Jocelyne uncovering one jewel after another, stuffing a few in her ample double D bra. No problem. He knew how to deal with her. When this was over, Jocelyne would have her own unmarked grave. After he had a taste of her body. Kind of kinky to do it in a graveyard. Although he'd had a few women that laid there like the dead, he wasn't into necrophilia. Who would find her in this godforsaken place? He knew the way back; he could navigate through the worst weather. Getting back to Haiti would be as easy as taking bribes.

"Find anything yet?"

"Yes. It's here."

Guerrier bent over to see what the girl had found. The flashlight lit her hand, and the glint from a round, metallic object caught his eye. Jocelyne held it with a maniacal glee.

"What's that?"

"The Jewel of Life. Natives call it Mort Vivant."

"Dead Alive? Is it worth a lot?"

"More than all di others. Took years to learn its secrets. Strong voodoo."

"Don't believe in that crap." He held out his arm. "Let me help you up."

"I know how you think, Colonel. Bury di body and grab di treasure."

"The heat must be affecting your brain. You think I want to be stuck here on my own? This place gives me the creeps."

"It didn't when you murdered my parents. I know it was you. I will never forget your face."

"Did you bring me all the way out here just to tell me this? Boo-hoo, pity me. Deal with it. This is the real world. Grow up. Bad things happen to good people, and all that New Age shit. You're young and about to get rich. Are there jewels here or not?"

Raising the jewel to her face, Jocelyne mumbled, as if speaking to it. Guerrier strained to hear what she was saying; but the tumultuous drums grew louder over the desolate land, drowned her words, and like a cancer of sounds, spread over the graveyard.

Boom, boom, boom.

He covered his eyes from the glowing object in her hand. A deafening grumble beneath his feet shook the ground, and he fell backwards, losing the shovel. He attempted to rise but slipped and fell again. The mud drenched his pants.

"What's going on? Earthquake?"

He looked around for his shovel to kill the girl and be on his way with the treasure. The hell with screwing her. The mood had left him; he'd need a bottle of Viagra to get going. The ground quaked again, and he slid heels-first into the grave.

The first thing he saw was the body in its coffin, unspoiled, the flesh almost alive. The eyes opened wide in terror, seeing but not seeing. The image didn't last long. Guerrier's eyes shrank from the undefiled head and ran over the thing as it turned meat-gray and putrefied. The flesh decayed and crumbled from the bone, the face caved inwards like ruins, and the marrow turned into dust. He caught a scream in his throat and his lips quivered; he stared at

Jocelyne in astonishment. She had not stopped ranting. As the close quarters of the grave fell in on him, a sudden, heart-pounding fear struck him. He had to get out. The girl was crazy; the dirt walls strangled his senses.

He grabbed her shovel, lifted it above his head, and brought it down on her. The blood splattered over his face; he swung it across her neck, nearly slicing her head in two until she collapsed in a bloody heap. He yanked the jewel from her death grip. Clawing and thrashing to the top, he scrambled up the muddy side. The slime oozed over him. At last, he lay on his stomach, wheezing for air. Clouds parted way for the moon, leaving intermittent drizzle. A pale blue light flooded over the darkness of the land, painting the graveyard in ghastly hues. Something stirred.

The Jewel of Life? He clenched it in his cold, soiled fingers. A chill tremored his body. What had she unleashed?

When he struggled to his feet, the repulsive stench of decay overpowered him. He clasped his hand over his mouth and nose and staggered toward an opened grave. He had to see, had to quench his curiosity; for the sake of his own sanity and peace of mind, he had to know. The dirt mound shifted. Something dug its way up. The moonlight had not caught the interior of the grave, and, trembling, he aimed the flashlight downwards.

This can't be happening. This can't be real.

All reason left him now. The hideous corpse stood and climbed upwards, staring at him with black, sunken sockets, grinning with shriveled lips that peeled back over its bared, yellow, decayed teeth. He emptied his gun into the body, but it had no effect. He threw the gun at its head, turned and ran; an unimaginable horror swept over him, beyond his wildest nightmares. He looked behind. The cadavers stuck their skulls out of the graves. As they rose, they shook the dirt off their tattered clothes, thousands of them, rising. Their skin hung off their bones like charred flesh.

Guerrier could see the bullet holes in their craniums. The ones he had ordered executed. They looked at him, as if they knew.

Guerrier fled the erupting graves, stumbled down the mountain, fell, and rolled to the bottom, thumping over rocks. He stopped and groaned. Shrieking like the final charge of an army, the dead alive tumbled down the side, snatched his feet, and dragged him back.

He screamed and thrust his shoe into the heads of the zombies to boot them off, jumped up, and limped to the shore, driven by a frightful frenzy. The cacophony of drums intertwined with the wailing dead. BOOM! BOOM! BOOM! it went as it kept pace with the thunder of his heart.

Amid the commotion, he barely heard his own inner voice encouraging him to go on despite his exploding lungs, the throbbing muscles, and the pounding in his brain. Fear was his savior, giving him enough fortitude and adrenaline to shove off the boat and leap inside. The things had reached him, but he paddled away.

He glanced back again at the loping dead things. The demons swarmed the beach and stopped at the water's edge. Their shadows flailed along the shore like barbaric creatures. But he could not rest until the grotesque apparitions had gone from his sight; he sailed desperately, praying they could not follow.

Once the shore disappeared from his view, he collapsed to the floor, letting the pain consume his body. Thirst compelled him to lift a canteen to his parched lips. His arm shook; his hand cramped. He drank too fast and felt sick to his stomach. Crawling to the side of the boat, he retched several times. The jewel glowed; the sea bubbled; something surfaced from the roiling deep. He was hours away from land, and he hadn't the strength to go on, but he knew he must, for the wind had died, leaving an eerie, stifling calm.

With deadened muscles, he lifted an oar and paddled on one side to get the boat moving. It felt heavy in his grip, but he rowed, ignoring every sane reason to allow his body to recuperate. He dared not look into the sea for what he might find there. But he didn't have to look far. Emerging from the deep, springing to the top, bobbing like barrels, bodies swam in the ocean.

Twenty thousand massacred and buried in watery graves, she had said, and she had called them all forth with the Jewel of Life.

The dead grasped his oar. Guerrier pulled them along. The unutterable horror strengthened his resolve. The sight appeared so loathsome he wished he could gouge out his eyes. The corpses seethed on all sides, obliterating the sea. He could have walked across the carcasses to shore. They banged against the hull to sink it. The boat plowed through the skeleton sea, cracking their bones, shattering their skulls. Rotting fiends, green and slimy, climbed port side. He kicked them off one by one, swung the oar, and batted more away. Their fragile remains crumbled. Fatigue gnawed at him. He had no way to fight so many, but his resolve couldn't be broken. If they boarded, he was lost.

Sweet Jesus, to rest would be heaven!

Then the miracle came. He'd been so preoccupied with his survival that he hadn't noticed he'd drifted straight into a storm. A gale blew down upon the boat and howled, spun it, and rolled it toward the shore. Torrents of rain poured down, flashes lit the sky, thunder rumbled, and the sea raged. A maelstrom as ancient as the monster Charybdis swallowed the devils. The mast crashed down and pinioned him. Battling with unconsciousness, he embraced the precious jewel to his chest. He couldn't, wouldn't close his eyes. If the ship sunk, the dead might prey upon him.

"Keep awake!"

Clinging to this thought as his only life-jacket, Guerrier's mind submerged into blackness.

* * *

The boat smashed against the rocks. Rain assaulted his face. Guerrier jolted awake. Bleeding and confused, he pushed aside the mast, scrambled from the wreck, and tripped onto shore. He had the jewel; he had his life. He looked at the wreckage. The dead had been sucked down into the sea. A sound moved his attention to the interior of the boat. Feet shuffled. Up from the deck rose the zombies that had survived. Eight of them.

Clambering up, he raced through the city. The things raced with him, faster than he'd imagined. The drums pounded, voices sang, tambourines and trumpets played. Guerrier ran into the profane revelers of Mardi Gras and squeezed into the mass of reeking bodies to hide. The zombies followed. People dressed and painted as skeletons and corpses hadn't noticed and paraded by their sides, as if they celebrated with them. A few handed the dead rum and whiskey bottles

"Great Mardi Gras, hey man?" The zombie moaned and drooled. "Nice costume!"

The press of the bodies mashed the zombies, and one-by-one, they fell apart. Feet trampled over their bones and grounded them into dust.

Safe! But the people swept him along, and he couldn't escape.

Crushed in the throng, Guerrier traveled from cemetery to cemetery. Like a great human flood, myriad clammy bodies ignored the onslaught of the storm and drowned him in the fanatical, urging, pushing mob.

"Not through the cemeteries! You'll wake the dead!"

"*Yes!*" they cried and blew their horns. "We must wake the dead. All must party tonight. Wake and join us!"

"No, you fools!"

He shrieked and shoved but could not raise his arms above his head; no one heard his pleas or his cries and screams over the jocular clamor.

Was the Jewel of Life glowing?

He couldn't see. If so, more zombies would pursue. The ground grumbled and shook. Bodies clawed their way up. Feet kicked their skulls like soccer balls into the rush and bounced around. Some corpses made it into the mob, but the crowd whisked them up, like a hurricane sucking debris.

A drunken Haitian man recognized a corpse in front of him.

"Cousin Amede! You been dead five years. You come to party with me like old times, hey?"

One cadaver from a grave seized Guerrier's leg; its arm broke off and held on; he shook it off, but couldn't escape the celebratory deluge of partiers. His claustrophobia had grown so severe, he thought he'd faint. Over the graveyards they tramped, one after another, celebrating death with death. Guerrier descended into insane insanity; into absurd absurdity; into stark, raving madness!

Finally, he spotted an opening, squirmed away, and completed his dazed peregrination at his home and reeled up to his room, locked the door, shoved his dresser in front, and flopped into bed. He slept until morning, tossing feverishly; he woke, shouted and cursed at phantoms, rolled out of bed, shivered, searched the room for corpses, and, satisfied the hellish journey had ended, ate and drank, as one who'd lost his hunger but required nourishment, and then slumped down in his chair, pondering.

The Jewel of Life was all that he had for his efforts. It had special powers, but he was only interested in its worth. He didn't know the chant to make it work, so it was useless that way. He'd sell it and make his way to the Bahamas, live a lavish lifestyle, wallow in drink and women, and forget this had ever happened.

The telephone rang; he sat up with a start.

"Hello?"

"Jocelyne is dead," said the husky voice on the other end. "You murdered her."

"Who is this?"

"Don't bother to deny it!"

"What do you want?"

"The jewel. Bring it at midnight to the cemetery."

"Which one?"

"The one you slapped the girl in. And don't try to leave the country or you'll be picked up by the authorities."

"How do you know all this?"

"Didn't she tell you she had a sister?"

Dressing, he slipped another gun into his holster.

* * *

Confetti and empty whiskey bottles littered the abandoned cemetery. The colonel sat on one of the old, gray headstones, perched black against the barren trees and oppressive night, like Poe's mournful raven. Waiting in the graveyard brought back recent, unsettling memories. But he knew nothing could harm him, that the jewel was dormant. He planned to leave Haiti before they found the person dead in the graveyard, if they found her at all. He'd dug up the grave behind him. After he killed his blackmailer, he'd stuff the body inside with the decomposed corpse.

A dark hooded figure approached. The garments covered her completely; the stranger stopped ten feet away and stood on a damp, brown-grassy grave, strewn with withered, trampled roses.

"Let me see it," hissed the stranger.

The colonel held the jewel up for the stranger to inspect. "Leave it on the ground and move away."

Guerrier slowly backed off. When the stranger stooped to pick it up, he produced the gun and fired twice, expecting the stranger to keel over. But the figure continued. He shot her again, this time in the head, but she refused to go down. After taking the jewel, the figure stood upright and removed the hood. Jocelyne's disjoined head leaned to one side. The blood had coagulated around the base, conjoining the neck to the body.

"The curse of di jewels can only be lifted when saying di sacred words. I escaped wid one di night my family was murdered."

Jocelyne whispered the primordial words of her ancestors. Guerrier heard a noise from behind his tombstone; he whirled to see a body rise from the opened grave. Countless more graves had been exhumed.

"I had to find dem, to put dem at rest. The jewel keeps di dead alive, buried in a horrific state of hibernation. It is how di soldiers damned those denizens that defied dem. My parents were about to expose di corruption when they were taken. It also controls di dead."

"I never believed in that voodoo nonsense the soldiers practiced. Just let them have their fun. Chicken bones, hair, and effigy dolls. Toys for children. Until now."

Corpses sprang out of the shadows and inched closer, surrounding him. Guerrier fired at them until the gun clicked empty chambers. He knocked one corpse down with the butt of his gun. Recoiling, he faltered backwards. His shrill cry fell on deaf ears.

"Stay away from me!"

The putrid bodies stretched out their bony hands to seize him; he shouted and grasped his right arm. A sudden look of clarity passed over his face, as if all the answers struck him simultaneously. What flashed before him was an understanding of all the money, pleasure, and lives he'd taken; however, before he could say a word, before he could denounce his actions, he fell forward, dead of a massive heart attack.

* * *

Guerrier's eyes opened in a fixed gaze of terror and watched the night sky. The soft clumps of soil thudded on top of him, and dirt covered his face. The enclosure was palpable. The jewel around his neck glowed. Dead alive, he lay paralyzed, unable to utter a sound, except for his screaming thoughts. No one would come with the words to release him from his ghoulish existence. He had his wealth and life. His body burned; hysteria rose in him. Close spaces.

He had an eternity to deal with it.

THE CONCEPT OF ZERO
By Paul R. Panossian

"Marcus Clay," I began, "was a gentle, wandering soul."

I raised my eyes to my audience. Two pale faces scowled across the crypt, huddled against the embankment as if it housed a great, smoldering hearth. A particularly merciless gust dispensed with the notion, and a shudder passed among us who had gathered atop the stone-studded knoll.

Even for the weather, this was a dismal turn-out. Exempting the priest and the undertaker, there was only Marcus' mother and his younger brother. What few friends and acquaintances Marcus had sustained would never have braved the unseemly association of attending his funeral, let alone the picket line whose angry din could be heard vacillating on the wind.

I could hardly begrudge them their absence. I'd had no intention of attending either, much less speaking at the service. I'd come at the behest of his mother, who had called the week before to allay any misgivings that she blamed me for his demise. As far as she was concerned, it was "that imbecile sheriff and his jumpy jackrabbit of a deputy." She'd waited until our conversation's close to introduce the idea of me speaking. "You two shared something special," she said. "Surely you can come up with some fine words for his service," and surely, I thought, I could, but the words I suspected she truly wished for her eldest son were "redeeming." Finding such words for a man branded a murderer and worse would be a somewhat greater challenge.

Yet I could not decline. My involvement in bringing about Marcus' fatal altercation with the police practically dictated it. So, despite the fiasco surrounding his slaying, and the spiraling disapprobation regarding his latent...practices, so to speak, I'd set to work crafting my old friend's eulogy.

The wind relented, and I carried on.

"If you spent time around Marcus, you came to know his long, searching gaze." His family nodded their assent. "For the unfamiliar, it could seem intense, but his intention was never to repel or intimidate; only to understand. It's what I believe he sought more than anything else in life: deeper understanding. Of the world, of its cycles and forms, of all its myriad intricacies. Nothing was too trifling or grand to escape his intrigue, from distant galaxies to minute ripples in a stream, but he was especially taken by living things and their experiences on this earth. Marcus had a profound veneration for consciousness, and it spawned an expansive, inquisitive empathy that he extended to every being he encountered. It became the cornerstone of his own personal philosophy of compassion that guided his every movement. He abstained from consuming animal products; he picked worms off the sidewalk when it rained; he left crumbs out for the ants in his kitchen. His benevolence defined him, and it became his life's work. He was truly a 'Light that shines in stone.'"

I paused to survey my audience. They showed no signs that anything was amiss. I might as well have quoted The Gospel. Marcus' brother sniffed, draping an arm around his mother who dabbed her misty eyes.

I concealed a pang of guilt. I'd had reservations about opening the speech by lauding the condition that had so crippled Marcus in life. It had felt disingenuous to write, and now that I'd delivered it to a favorable reception, I felt like a fraud.

In truth, Marcus' bottomless empathy had produced more than a vegetarian diet and some endearing quirks. The suffering world to which he'd opened himself had filled him up and dragged him down. The resulting creed was less a celebration of life than it was a debilitating abhorrence for the misery it entailed. Minimizing that unfortunate abundance soon dominated every aspect of his existence, and he developed a series of deleterious compulsions in response.

He quit driving because of the harm it wreaked on wildlife and people; he let weeds overwhelm his lawn so as to not disturb its residents; the morsels he left for the ants fueled an explosive cockroach population, which he refused to address on principle. He fell captive to bizarre ruminations like weighing a spider's hunger against the agony of the flies it devoured or the degree to which silverfish knew fear. His health flagged, his relationships suffered, and his presence on campus waned until all his professorial duties had been abdicated to his assistant. For a rising name on the tenure track, that latter made for an especially ruinous blunder, and he was soon forced to resign.

"Couldn't hack it," was the word circulating the halls, but I knew better. It wasn't the workload or the pressure. He had imbibed the world around him, and it had swallowed him in turn.

"We are giants," he'd said to me one late, restive night, "and our every footfall tolls disaster for the creatures beneath us."

"But what can you do?" I asked. "You have to live your life."

He didn't answer, only lowered his gaze to the dwindling embers. For a time, neither of us spoke. Outside, the wind crashed through the trees like a raging surf, and in that moment, beneath the creaking timbers with the darkness pressing in, everything felt so incredibly fragile.

All at once, I understood the great futility at the root of his sorrow.

It was that futility, I think, that ultimately drove him down those more precarious avenues of inquiry.

Now, standing before his few remaining loved ones, I wondered for the thousandth time how to reconcile that tenderhearted man with the abomination I'd found inside his shed.

I banished the thought.

I needed to focus to get through this.

"Those labors, however," I began again, "exacted a heavy toll. When the world bled, so too did he, and when its weight grew too great to bear, he sought solace beyond the corporeal. Marcus' spirituality was unique but elegant. He dreamed of higher states, untethered from the cruel, ramshackle architecture that binds us; of dreaming matter, and," I paused to examine the faces before me, "'divine ripples in the void.'"

There was no sign of recognition for the words I had spoken. His mother smiled tearfully up at me like I personally had delivered Marcus unto salvation. Her surviving son pulled her close.

Neither seemed troubled by my casting Marcus' "spirituality," as I'd put it, in a favorable light. That this most egregious distortion went unnoticed spoke for just how estranged they had become. To me, Marcus' sudden interest in the occult had represented an alarming metastization. By then, I'd grown so concerned I'd begun making regular visits to his house to monitor his condition. It was more than a year since his exit from academia, and with every passing week he'd appeared more withered, more exhausted, and less present as he wandered his cobwebbed rooms, agonizing over their wretched colonizers the way a parent would over a sickly child.

His deteriorating state began taking a toll on me, as well. I'd rumble up beside his decaying shell of a truck with an escalating dread that read doom in every detail. Were the cats out scavenging for lack of supper? Did the house seem too quiet this evening? Why did he take so long to answer?

It had reached the point that I needed to take several breaths before knocking to steady my racing pulse.

Then one night I arrived to find his windows black and his unlatched shed aglow with a spidery glimmer. Immediately I assumed the worst, but no sooner had I leapt from the car than he stood in the doorway with his shadow spread across the weeds. Behind his lean silhouette, an old workbench was piled high with books and dripping candles.

"I was wondering how this would look if you showed," he called out at me, "and now here you are."

"I must admit it looks quite mad, old chum," I said, but more perplexing was the smile I could hear, fluttering on his voice. A week ago, this man had struggled to rise and face the day. I wondered what had changed.

"Come inside," he said. "I promise it's not what it seems." When I made no move to join him, he clarified: "Inside the house," and closed the shed behind him.

Before the fireplace, bulwarked by his familiar clutter, I felt myself slipping into the comfort of routine.

Marcus, however, showed no such inclination. He was more animated than I'd seen him in years, perched on the edge of his seat like a gaunt gargoyle, or pacing before the hearth, gesticulating as he talked.

He'd had a revelation, he said. He was visiting the college library, perusing some arcane texts regarding the nature of nirvana when he was stricken by one monk's description of enlightenment.

"'Like a fern's quiet serenity unfurling its first frond,'" he recited, his eyes raised in exultation. "Plants pass their entire lives in nirvana. Alive and flourishing and yet spared from life's suffering."

"A beautiful thought," I concurred. My eyes followed his to the rafters, where moths wove circuitous routes about web-enshrouded eaves.

"It occurred to me then," he went on, "that if there could be life without consciousness then perhaps the converse is true."

A moment elapsed where the only sound was the crackling fire. An insect traversed the mantle and had reached the edge before I spoke.

"That is," I hazarded, "consciousness without life?"

"Exactly!" Marcus said, shaking an excited finger, "Think about it! Of all the matter in the illimitable universe, only an infinitesimal fraction is granted the privilege of experiencing it. So what of the vast remainder?"

"What of it?" I asked. "Consciousness isn't some mystical force, it's an emergent property of physiology."

"Perhaps," he said. "Perhaps. Tell me, old friend, how much do you know about koans?"

"Paradoxical anecdotes or riddles meant to assist Zen Buddhists in achieving enlightenment," I recalled.

"Precisely," he said. "Well in my rummaging, I managed to unearth the works of a rather singular Japanese sect, now extinct, who worshiped by reciting scripture infused with the most unusual koans. These koans hint at elevated states beyond nirvana, wholly unsullied by the karmic cycles of birth and death."

"That," I said, "is lunacy. And heresy, both against their order, and the laws of nature. It is no wonder this practice went extinct. Marcus, tell me you aren't seriously pursuing this charlatanry."

"Not as such," he said.

"And what you were doing in the shed was…"

"Merely meditation," he said, "but would you allow that there is more to this world than meets the eye?"

"Certainly."

"Then how can you be sure that in that vast sea of sleeping matter there might not be a permutation?"

"A…permutation?" I asked, examining the lines wrought across his face.

"A ripple in the void," he said, "An echo in the silence. A dream in the eternal night." Behind his jouncing outline, a moth swooped low and vanished into the firelight.

"Inert matter has zero structure," I retorted, "and zero capacity, so it rests."

He sighed, collapsing into his chair as if having expelled his passion in one exasperated exhalation.

"Come now," I said, leaning over far enough that I could have rested a hand upon his shoulder. "You yourself were speaking of nirvana. Is reverting back to how you were before birth really so terrible a fate?"

He didn't answer.

A marbled tabby, his favorite, materialized at the foot of his chair.

"Most run when I get near," he murmured distantly, "but this one came straight away." It nuzzled its nose into his palm, and he stroked its nape. The cat arched its back in delight. "A year ago she was just a stray, but now if one night she didn't return, I'd be inconsolable." He beamed down at the purring feline. "What a trap love is. Once you've felt it, you can't bear to let it go."

"But you will eventually have to," I said, again searching his face. I didn't care for this maudlin philosophizing or its implications. Had his deterioration finally encroached upon his objectivity? "All things fade, old chum. It's the nature of the universe."

He sprung to his feet. "The *observable* universe," he amended, "but imagine what secrets lie beyond these rudimentary senses we've allowed to shape our minds. Imagine what wonders await a liberated intellect! The spiritualists can't *all* be deluding themselves!"

Oh yes, my friend, I thought, *they absolutely can*, but what I said instead was: "I think you're mistaking the concept of zero."

He scoffed and shook his head. The tabby brushed against his ankle. He picked it up and folded it into his arms. The cat complied without protest, and he pressed it to his bosom, turning toward the fire while cooing into its marbled fur.

I didn't pursue the point. He'd made it clear the discussion was at a close. I might as well have reasoned with a stone.

I didn't stay long after that. His agitation was unwelcoming, and when I tried to shift his attention onto other subjects, I found the conversation lagging.

That was three months before our run-in at the library; three months before his killing. What radical transformations occurred between then and that disastrous confluence of fate I do not know. It wasn't like him to reach out, and I'd become interred with work. I suppose we both had. On the few visitations I did manage, I'd invariably find him engrossed in his "regimen," as he'd taken to calling it. Once drawn away, he'd be terse and reserved, and I got the impression I was interrupting something terribly important.

It was just as well, I thought. Classes were picking up, and my latest publication was finally attracting the right kind of attention. At least that's what I'd tell myself after long hours at my desk when my mind began to stray. I'd think of Marcus, shut up alone in the old tool shed, its white, windowless mass the sole deviation from the forest's encroaching gloom and ponder the strange ritual taking place behind its walls.

Perhaps, I'd think as the night wore on, it really was mere meditation. If he were able to find relief in Eastern religion, so much the better for him. For who would want to believe his share of eternity is but a fleeting dream when summers are so short and winters so bleak and lasting; when one's hard and lengthy toil amounts to so precious little, and every moment's respite comes at such incongruous cost? It seemed too cruel an irony that the idea of endless sleep should be so fearsome to one whose birth had become less a blessing than a curse. If this delusion was how he reconciled the hard facts of nature, then let him have it.

Thus I almost convinced myself that I hadn't turned my back. If only I knew how far he'd descend left to his own devices.

I remember I was browsing the stacks one morning before class when, through a gap in the volumes, I glimpsed an unmistakable flicker of disheveled hair and red-rimmed eyes. I peered into the fissure, and sure enough, it was Marcus, pacing the row in an aroused haste. At first, I was delighted to see this break in his seclusion, but that evaporated immediately.

There was something plainly and viscerally wrong with him. Never would I have described Marcus as a graceful man, but the cadence with which he now stalked the shelves looked almost inhuman. His muscles quivered, and his head reeled as he traced a grimy finger over the shelf's gilded titles. If I hadn't first recognized his face, I'd have taken him for a trespassing vagrant as his clothes were about as filthy as any I've seen. Clearly, he was in the throes of some severe episode and in need of urgent medical attention.

I called his name.

He froze in place, but did not turn. "Marcus," I repeated, my voice growing frayed, "what the devil has gotten into you?"

His head snapped back to face me, and his eyes latched onto mine.

Another beastly gale wrapped itself around our congregation, plastering garments to flesh in a permeating blast.

This time, though, I was grateful for the cover it provided. A chill had run through me of a coldness unmatched by nature.

I trained my attention back on the words at hand. "In these beliefs he was resolute," I read. My mouth formed sounds, but they had no meaning. All I could see were those awful, ringed orbs, lurid and feverish and utterly vacant. In them, I'd discerned no inkling of the kind, searching intelligence I had come to know so well. In its place was a fixed thousand-yard stare, peering through the gap in the books like one who has wandered so long across the desert, he has grown insensate to all but the immutable thirst that drives him. Even as he offishly pronounced the question of my name, his eyes probed mine as they would a well's black depths, and seemed to fill with pure disdain for the nothingness they beheld.

Then he bolted from sight, leaving me to stare on in stunned perplexity.

My vision refocused on scribbled text. From over the notepad, two expectant pairs of eyes regarded mine. I realized I'd fallen silent. "Whether..." I foundered, "Whether that resolve made him a fool or genius is not for those among the living to know, but I think we might draw certain conclusions from what Marcus omitted from his views."

I wished I'd been capable of such nuanced judgment that morning in the stacks. After scouring the aisles for a glimpse of shaggy hair, I'd stumbled through the library doors like one lost in a dream. Outside, the streets were as sleepy as when I'd arrived, and as the dawning sun lit upon the campus' desolate square, so too arose an even more odious presentiment.

A pall had descended upon the town that was, frankly, impossible to ignore. Rumors had circulated since the first boy's disappearance, but after the second had gone missing, a reptant paranoia had taken root that verged on full-fledged hysteria. All the local papers were amok with the most unbecoming conjecture, and missing person fliers hung from every public-facing facade in town. All I had to do was look up to see two gawky adolescents smiling down from the masonry on which their portraits were glued.

I hurried on. The notion was ludicrous. Marcus hadn't the guts to expel the cockroaches from his kitchen. He'd never be capable of committing a crime so heinous.

Still, what *had* he been up to these long, reticent weeks? The more I pondered the question, the more those youthful eyes seemed to track my movements, their rosy expressions appearing suddenly taught, like the photographer had pointed a pistol at their heads before telling them to smile.

I found myself back in the aisle where the morning's events had begun; apparently the Eastern Asia section of World Religions. I don't know why, but the knowledge that Marcus' obsession endured into the midst of whatever gripped him decided the issue. I canceled classes and departed for his home.

What I expected to find, I cannot say, but I spent the drive admonishing myself for the fool's errand I'd undertaken. I envisaged hammering on his door only to have some obvious but unforeseen circumstance make me feel like an ass.

The fledgling day seemed to agree. The sun bloomed overhead with the promise of winter's end, and daffodils rose from ashen lawns to meet the broaching season. The idea that some unseen malignancy advanced beneath the dappled greenery seemed far-fetched, but then the images of those missing boys would gurgle up to the surface, and no matter how I made the countryside blur, it never felt fast enough.

It felt rather like *I* was the one being sought after; like there were eyes drilling into the back of my skull, and my pursuer had but to extend his arm and grab me by the collar.

I'd gravitate towards the rear view mirror in expectation of those two kids' glazed-on grins, only now, I imagined, their eyes would be filled with a vast, alien emptiness that drew me in like the vacuum of space. I forced my focus back on the road. Marcus' turn was approaching and it wouldn't do to get in a wreck so near my destination.

As soon as my wheels left the lane for his drive's overgrown double-rut, I sensed a change. It had been months since I'd seen Marcus' home in daylight, so initially I attributed it to the buildings' blinding white paint and the yard's emergent colors, but there was something more, or perhaps more accurately, something missing.

It hit me the instant I killed the engine: everything was still. No breeze rustled the trees, no birds flitted about the canopy. I opened the door and stepped into a world so devoid of motion and sound, I had to fight the impression that I'd set foot into an intricate painting rather than an actual place. The landmarks were all the same: the porch sagged, his truck sank into weeds, and the shed stood with its featureless doors shut against the imposition of overarching trunks, but the vibrance that had so pervaded the property was gone. Even the cats, I realized with a shiver, had disappeared.

I tried the knob, and it turned without resistance, which came as no surprise. Marcus couldn't have arrived before me traveling on foot, but he'd never trifled himself with locks and keys when he left.

My first step through the door immersed me in darkness denser than the silt-stained waters of a stagnant bog. For a disorienting second, I moved untethered from any reference, lost within a noiseless turbidity, pristine and absolute. Then uniformity faded to dim contours, and I was fumbling in Marcus' foyer. I hastened on to brighter regions, but the house's typical disarray was touched with a conspicuous degradation endemic to forlorn places. Indeed upon closer inspection, a veil of dust clung to every surface, but how could that be? Its owner might have absconded, but what about the house's many other residents? Absent were the cats, moths, roaches, and ants. Even the spiders seemed to have been plucked from their webs.

"Absent," I conveyed across the crypt, "was a belief in heavenly retribution or any system of moral accountability. Marcus' creed placed no emphasis on such exacting devices; his was more humane, more forgiving." I swallowed a lump in my throat. Never had words felt so wooden as those that now mingled with the indignant intonations from the cemetery gates. How could I let myself participate in such sentimental pageantry?

The same answer repeated in my head as when I'd penned the speech: *You're doing it for Marcus.*

I forced more verve into my delivery to blot out the intruding chorus. "His was a belief," I nearly shouted, "in a sweeping cosmic amnesty for all upon whom this world has been thrust; a release into an endless reverie dipped in the virginal sleep of nirvana. Perhaps his optimism was naive or, or quixotic, but…"

But it wasn't, because Marcus was right. At least to a certain degree. In the end, the same silence consumes us all. Though that wasn't exactly right either, because he had found more than serenity awaiting him on the other side. What it was, I cannot say, but it had dogged me from room to gloomy room that day like a forest's leaden silence upon a predator's approach.

My inspection of the home terminated in the kitchen with an examination of wrinkling produce and, opposite his dish-filled sink, Marcus' telephone. I lifted the receiver, certain the line would be as silent as the alcove it occupied, but before it reached my ear, my vision aligned with the rear window. I placed the receiver back on its hook, and gazed transfixed through the dusty pane.

One of the shed doors had come ajar; not enough to see inside, but enough to allow a crack of inner darkness.

It is nothing, insisted the part of me that clings to the mundane. *The wind has blown it open.* Yet just as I accepted this as a valid likelihood, a primitive, more basal part forbade my withdrawal. I concentrated my attention on that distant sliver with abilities made available only by burgeoning dread. Pouring into the rift, I became increasingly confident, above all rationality, that something stirred within. I moved toward the window, and from tenebrous fluctuations there emerged definable forms: elongated curvatures, angled joints, appendages. I'd been looking at an arm! Its hand extended to the very cusp of shadow, then, haltingly, it came into the light.

It was a small hand of a complexion unblemished by the attritions of age, but so mortiferously pale, it shone silvery beneath the sun. Its exposure was brief; enough to snake into the open and beckon with three swift flutters of a serpentine wrist, as if to say "Come! Hurry!" before vanishing back between the boards.

For a moment, all I did was blink. Had I really seen what I thought I'd seen? Was it directed at me? Did the owner of that disembodied limb still watch from beneath a cloak of obscurity? I sifted through the beam of darkness, but it rested as flat and idle as an alpine lake. If someone did occupy the shack's interior, they'd receded beyond my senses' reach.

Why, then, come forward? I wondered. *Are they held against their will? Can there be truth to my wild cogitations?*

Marcus' vacant stare flared up from the dregs of thought, and I made for the back door.

"But we shouldn't be so quick," I spat into a gale that stung my rigid features, "to dismiss, or worse, condemn." I hoped my vehemence concealed the waver on my voice. An obscenity revolved behind my eyes, beginning with my charge across the yard.

"Is anybody there?" I'd hollered. "It's okay, I'm here to help."

Silence.

My fingers wrapped around the door. I flung it wide and fell back, aghast.

"For who can claim to know," I challenged the voices on the wind, "what crude impressions a lifetime's course might rend upon our molds of mind and flesh?"

The morning sun had bent a golden rectangle over the naked carpentry, igniting within its boundaries a rambling script carved into every available inch of wall. There was no sign of captives, nor of the tools that had once populated the spartan interior. Even the latterly books and candles had been cast to the floor to make way for the massive column of text.

Was this the final product of Marcus' "regimen" to which he'd been so arduously committed? If so, then why was its lettering nearly illegible? I leaned in for a closer look.

My eyes squeezed shut, but the memory persisted.

"Or whether," I murmured at the hewn earth, "those contortions might assume the form of saints or abominations."

The words leapt at me as if etched inside my eyelids.

They'd come first in disparate chunks: "The corvid snake stalks the yellow cur...one eclipse swallows the other...and we shall become like gristle in its teeth."

Were these the koans meant to usher him unto undiscovered realms?

What kind of enlightenment was that?

A familiar excerpt distinguished itself from the rest: "Divine ripples in the void." Marcus had spoken similar words that night he'd revealed his revelation. Had he been quoting some esoteric scripture? The line comprised the middle of three whose emboldened width and depth in the grain lent them prominence from the rest. I read all three in the order they were written:

"Light that shines in stone
Divine ripples in the void
Speak your silent words"

A haiku! But the koan within it struck me as less a riddle than an incantation.

I reread it. Then I read the next, then the following, and as those verses reverberated across the surface of my consciousness, the sunlight seemed to thin, and the yard fell away until my sight was consumed by the towering inscriptions. Deeper and deeper I traveled down their wreath of meaning, and the further ensnared I became in their logic, the longer my shadow seemed to creep towards the engraved monolith, blackening crumpled covers and broken spines, until my eyes were drawn towards a conspicuous swell in the debris.

It was the head of a cat, half-buried in the litter, with one cheek mashed cruelly against the boards. Its mouth hung crookedly agape in an eternal shriek, and its emptied sockets gazed through its papery sepulcher in a silent, unseeing plea.

Even through the matted stains, there was no mistaking the fur's marbled coloration. I slammed the door, but before I could sever myself from that arcade of horrors, I'd identified a paw, a once-bushy tail, and a human finger sewn into the refuse. Then the door clapped shut, and I stood in the sun with the daffodils about my feet.

Far off, in some dark recess of the woods, a twig snapped.

Just an animal, my rational half insisted, but I didn't linger to verify the theory.

Instead, I stalked back into Marcus' kitchen, picked up his phone, which issued a surprisingly steady tone, and dialed the police. I don't recall to whom I spoke or what words were exchanged, but I know I managed to stammer something about mutilated cats and missing boys. It was that last bit that got forwarded to the Sheriff and brought him and his deputy rushing over like sharks to bloody water.

Had I known I was putting them and Marcus on a deadly collision course, I would have acted more prudently.

That consequences of such gravity could hinge on something as arbitrary as the timing of a phone call has haunted me almost as much as the carnage that ensued. Whether I could have spared Marcus' life is dubious (I'm confident the justice system would have meted out a death sentence no matter how it got its hands on him), but if he'd been brought into custody, we might have been able to get answers. Several other body parts —both human and animal—were found in subsequent searches of the shed, and though some (a toe, a tooth, the lobe of an ear) were determined to have belonged to two separate children between the ages of eight and eleven, none were sufficient to be linked conclusively to the two missing boys. They remain missing to this day, and I can't help but blame myself for initiating that morning's incident. If I'd exercised a bit more caution, their families might not have been denied the closure they deserve.

I regarded Mrs. Clay, buttressed beneath the arm of her surviving son. There was one silver lining: aggrieved as she was now, Marcus' death had spared her the public spectacle of a trial. *Cold comfort,* I thought, *when one's relief is derived from the source of another's anguish.*

But what could she do? She had to live her life.

I shook it off. So, too, did I. My speech was almost at an end, and once Marcus was in the ground, I could go home to my desk, bury myself in work, and never see this miserable ensemble again.

I hurried on.

"Let us not then be prejudiced," I read, "against those whose actions seem abhorrent, for it is only their actions that we know and not the horrors that compelled them."

But what horrors, I wondered, *must have one endured to compel the ones Marcus authored?* It was something that had haunted me more or less incessantly since that scene in the shed. Waiting in my car, the question had whorled like a cyclone, funneling down into cryptic verses of crabbed shorthand that pooled in between temples until they throbbed like bleating sirens.

I opened my eyes. The police had arrived. The deputy approached my window, and the sheriff sidled out the driver's side.

We wasted no time with introductions. I briefed them on our way to the shed, and without further hesitation, they swung open the door. I turned away, but their reactions were made plain in a string of muttered expletives. From the corner of my vision, I saw the deputy reach for his sidearm.

So he sees it too, I thought.

The boards clapped shut. I unglued my eyes from the ground, and raised them on a long, gaunt shadow stretched across the weeds.

It was Marcus.

His eyes dissected our party with all the deliberation of a crustacean dismembering its prey, and even as the sheriff belted orders and the deputy drew his gun, their faces shriveled under his gaze like saplings in a conflagration. If Marcus absorbed their frantic gestures he displayed neither fear nor satisfaction.

"Are we to deny," I pushed on, "that the despicable among us are composed of the same strata?"

A vapid grin had stretched across his lips. The deputy shrieked for him to halt.

"Fearful of the same miseries?"

Words had spilled from his mouth like a noxious waterfall: "No fear in skin no pain in bones no thought in guts no joy in brains no love in nails no–"

"Deserving of the same compassion?"

Both officers had raised their guns. Though Marcus stood stationary in the weeds, his shadow streamed across the yard like a black rift in the canvas of the world. "no light in words no world in mind–"

"Marcus knew," I sputtered.

His raven outline was all I saw, his growling voice all I heard. He was right. His truth was as unavoidable as the shadow at my toes, and everything else—everything I'd ever thought or experienced—was a microscopic growth on the periphery.

"Marcus," I breathed, "understood."

All I felt was cold.

All I heard was his black mantra of truth: "nolifeinland-notruthinskynostrength"

"You've shown me a great deal, old chum," I gasped. "'Speak your silent words.'"

I don't know why I'd inserted the haiku. *You're doing it for Marcus*, I'd repeated at the time, and composed the final line.

"May you rest in–"

I never finished.

A piercing report had shattered the flow.

I wheeled in the direction of the sound.

Marcus lurched forward, a rosy patch blooming on his shirt. Another report exploded across the clearing.

The lid of the sarcophagus jolted against its latch. The priest offered an approving smile. The undertaker checked his watch. Neither reacted to the noise coming from the coffin.

The rear window had exploded behind him, but Marcus took no notice. The next four shots came in a volley. Of the three that hit, one passed through his deltoid, one shattered his hip, and the last struck him squarely in the abdomen. None succeeded in dropping their target.

I turned to Marcus' family. His mother beamed. His brother had circumnavigated the pit to guide me, arm over shoulder, into their midst. I looked to the coffin whose shaking nobody acknowledged. The brother said something, but all I heard was Marcus' voice drifting out in an unbroken whimper: "*Was that you, old friend? I heard you speak! Don't let them bury your old chum! Please! I didn't know what I'd opened up–that I was opened up–and then they had control! Please! I can feel them coming! Their touch is like ice! PLEASE! DON'T LEAVE ME WITH THEM!*"

I couldn't believe what I witnessed, couldn't move to stop it.

Fat streamers and inchoate syllables had run from Marcus' mouth. The shadow was gone, having retreated to its normal length the instant his injuries had stifled his speech, but neither deputy nor sheriff moved to restrain him. The former's pistol clicked. The latter steadied his aim.

Mrs. Clay patted me on the back. "You did splendidly," she whispered. The priest began his sermon. Marcus began to cry. He babbled something between sobs.

"With me," he was saying. "With me, *and they always will be!*"

I knew then that his mind had gone.

Everyone said amen.

"*No rest in peace, OLD CHUM!*" he shrieked.

The sheriff fired.

Marcus broke into a maddening giggle.

The undertaker slid the coffin over the hole. The shot mushroomed through Marcus' skull. He collapsed into the straw. His casket was lowered and swallowed by the earth.

In the deposition following his death, I was questioned about the events leading up to the shooting. Where I could, I parroted the sheriff's line that we had been subject to a vicious assault. When the questions veered towards motive, I simply repeated that I knew he had been unwell for some time.

Of course, even then, I had my theories, but how would they have looked at me if I'd explained that Marcus probably hadn't seen the killing as a sacrifice at all, but rather a service to his precious creatures; an act of mercy, regardless of the bestial ritual to which they'd be subjected?

As for the children, I suspected he had higher aims, though I'm sure he employed similar justifications. I thought it too coincidental that both youths were taken at an age when minds are blank and malleable.

I think he meant to teach them; to make them his disciples.

Soil slapped on pine. The undertaker had begun shoveling the fill into the maw from which Marcus' voice still emanated. By then, he had entered a state of convulsive hysteria beyond the range of recognizable emotion. A knot tightened in my gut with every shrill, animalistic note, but I couldn't compel myself to speak, couldn't overcome that part of me that knew what it entailed.

After all, I'd seen him die, watched the matter from which his consciousness was composed explode out of the back of his head.

So I stood there, watching the earth float into the pit. Farther and farther I followed it down, beyond the point where a coffin should have laid into a darkness so vast and deep, the surrounding hills were but a threadbare veneer, and as I peered into that black abyss, I became aware of a pervasive churning, as if the shadows were infused with the writhing coils of some immeasurable body. As if, in their anarchy, they tended towards coherence.

Something touched my arm, and my heart leapt. It was Marcus' brother, steadying me with a sure grip.

He and Mrs. Clay were leaving. They offered some kind words I barely heard, and she hugged me and told me I'd be in her prayers.

They all walked away, and in the end so too did I, but unlike them, I found no solace in withdrawal. Marcus' laughter sifted up from the ground and carried on the wind, hounding me through the gates with a persistence that has diminished with neither time, nor work, nor drink.

And so I stand atop the chair, facing down my last contingency.

For now I know that it was I who mistook the concept of zero, and as I fit the cord around my neck, that howl echoes as clear and raucous as on that frigid March afternoon when from the black, serried abyss, the outline of a man surged forth against its turning surface.

What might have befallen, I've often wondered, had I extended my arm into the pit? Could I, in taking one tendril-wrapped hand in mine, have extricated that tormented form from the black chaos that bound it? Or would I too have been dragged below?

Alas, I shall never know.

I stood there, watching in spellbound horror as two childlike masses reared up from either side like twin dread creatures of the deep, and, falling upon the body in their midst, were all three torn asunder. Only that damnable laughter remained, clinging like a stain upon my soul then and forever after.

Well, no more.

I kick the chair.

My weight bites down with the pull of a thousand arms. Through the pain, the world grows distant, but as eternal night comes to steal my senses, those monstrous verses writhe in my mind, and that hideous cackle seeps into nightmares.

IN THE HIVED CLIFFS OF SAL-MACADOR

By J. M. J. Brewer

For terrific compensation, Alazo the Deleterious had been tasked to watch this corpse the night through. Which meant he had six hours remaining. No, six and a half, because midnight had just passed, and the sun would not puncture this cave's filmed mouth until it had climbed half of the Hived Cliffs.

Alazo was bored. He was not one for waiting. Or patience. If anyone was ever a man of action, that man was he. Instead of running another lap around the cave, he leaned his chin on his club's cool silver head and balanced the other end between two stones. The butt shifted such that his teeth clicked together painfully.

Starlight blinkered diamonds onto the cave walls around him. It was as if he were inside his own bubble of galaxy. A disturbing experience, indeed, if one subscribed to the Salmacadorian belief system, which marked the vast spackle of outer-reality a dead heaven, the blackness being life's lack and the shining white stars the protruding tentacles of extra-dimensional monsters. Alazo did not consider himself a believer so much as one who made sure to shore up prayers and indications in the pursuit of being rather safe than sorry.

This starlight projection spawned through the cave mouth's half-translucent, sphincter-centered membrane. Alazo had very carefully squiggled through said sphincter. Afterwards, the sphincter contracted to a circumference no larger than his finger.

Inside this cave lay the body. The body lay exactly where Sage Ermin had promised. Sage Ermin, so intelligent that her very name proclaimed this truth, so gorgeous and so tall that she might be mistaken for one of Opherlion's

Winged Ministers, all decked in robes and wielding celestial harps.

The body couldn't have been fouler if it stunk. Which, thankfully, it did not, beyond a tinge like a toad's wet underside. Its foulness originated from its extensively tumored appearance.

Alazo did not know how this person had perished; it was hard to determine around the pustules, through which tufts of hair stuck like scrub brush. No yawning wounds or absent limbs. The head, bulging and blueish, remained attached to a swooped neck that ran tip to crown with bumps that looked like bird's eggs sewn beneath the skin.

Sage Ermin had not been forthcoming with information about this corpse. She'd given a single instruction: "Watch them until I arrive at dawn." This was trodden territory: Alazo had sat several death watches. Those had been for fellows who'd perished in conflict or battle. Alazo had waited in respect for them as well as in respect for himself, that he be first to avail of his companion's boons, doubtless reserved for him, anyhow. His club, silver-tipped on both ends, was a post-mortem gift from his friend, Gendledred Wolfbrainer, famed monster slayer.

But this corpse afforded no bounty. And in running his patron's instruction through his mind, Alazo learned a new worry. 'Watch *them* until I arrive at dawn.' Yet, here lay a single corpse. From an average mouth, Alazo would have assumed this a mistake in language. But Sage Ermin did not possess an average mouth. Rather, hers was plump and expressive and knew the shape of devastating, miraculous words.

Therefore, Alazo reckoned it would behoove someone—say, a mercenary with no payment up-front—to pay special attention to his patron's phrasing.

He waved the silver head of his club about so it caught and threw starlight. He cast light upon the corpse. The more he studied it, the more he began to suspect something was…off. He was reminded of connected pairs: trees that had grown together for decades, eggs with double yolks, rain drops on steel.

Well, no matter; whatever this corpse was, it was more dead than that.

So, he laid out his cloak for a blanket. He was seriously considering sleep when the corpse wriggled.

Could it be so? Sure enough, the corpse fidgeted. Well, not the entire corpse. Only the largest tumor, which pulsed aggressively from between the corpse's shoulder blades.

Alazo brandished his club. A wild part of him recommended poking the tumor but the rest revolted from this idea. And he needn't have bothered: at its apex point, bulging with the fervor of the wart-cum-blister which last year had haunted his heel, the tumor burst. Alazo vaulted away.

But not far enough. Gangrenous-smelling goo splattered his boots at five feet distance. He was wondering if it would be possible to wear the smell out, walk these tarnished waders in the wind and the rain until they did not smell like eight-day-old-ghoul-ejaculate, when a head rose from the untumored pustule.

"Sweet Superior," he swore. He immediately regretted the oath, throwing fingers and waving his arms to banish any curse bestowed by that most supreme and crochety deity, who was not to be disturbed except between lunchtime and afternoon's first zizz.

He did all this without taking his eyes off the protruding head. The head resembled an inlibleg's due to its surfeit of mouths, sharp teeth, and scimitar ears. It was attempting mightily to squiggle free of the corpse and this corpse-bound nature, combined with its diminutive proportions, proved to Alazo this was no inlibleg, at all.

The creature wasn't any bigger than two squirrels tied together. It had about a centipede's worth of arms all ringed around it on the same latitude and it used these arms to pry itself out of the busted tumor.

The creature—the squirrel—slid onto the cave floor. Alazo and the squirrel stared at each other.

Then the squirrel dashed toward the cave-mouth with a fierce propulsion. Its skittering limbs granted erratic trajectory.

Alazo was on it in three steps. The wide-end of his club clocked the back of its tiny head, which was disturbingly evocative of a child's shorn cranium. Blue-green blood pulped from the impact point as well as out of the squirrel's mouths and eye-corners. Alazo saw this all in slick slowdown, a state well known to the mercenary, and he took advantage by whirling the club around at its zenith to pulverize the squirrel's face.

"Foul beast!" he cried. "Never again will you sully the boots of Alazo the Deleterious!"

He leaned forward to investigate his kill. A headless squirrel, topped with a few bits and globules. There—a tooth.

Nonetheless, Alazo situated his back against the boulder so he could keep his eye on the corpse. He attempted to count the tumors. On the corpse's arms, its legs, the back of its ballooning skull. But the starlight confused his vision.

* * *

Two hours later and Alazo admitted he'd been wrong: the corpse had certainly become fouler as it stunk. Not exactly of rot, though rot did participate, but more like…mold. Mold so old, so foul, its odor was as black as its bodies.

Every few minutes a tumor would burst to ejaculate another squirrel head. Alazo clubbed their heads to spiraling freedom. They tried to ward his blows; he only swung harder. Their tiny arms snapped like wet corn stalks. Their tiny skulls ruptured like melons. Their puppet bodies sagged, still stuck in the root-corpse, which was not deflating despite its considerable output.

After a dozen such occurrences Alazo concluded that his job had never been a deathwatch. Rather, he'd been hired for his usual detail: engendering bodily harm to others. 'Watch them until I arrive at dawn' equaled 'slay tiny malevolent beasts until I arrive at dawn.' Simple. The way Alazo preferred it.

So whiled away the hours. He began letting them escape so he might practice his swing. By the time Alazo noticed that the stars were no longer refracted on the walls around him, he could barely step without crunching elegant, slick bones.

His arms and shoulders sang from the effort. His brain ticked away possible bonus payments dependent on creatures slain. His stomach grumbled, for nothing conjured an appetite like a job well-performed. Now he stood above the corpse and jabbed at any pulsing tumor, sidestepping the moment before impact that the goo be directed to the spot he previously occupied.

A line of sun began advancing through the cave. It was membrane-enhanced and sharp enough to shave by. All signs of discorporeal life ceased when this slow guillotine of morning passed over the corpse. The tumors sagged. One tiny blue-skull, just ready to breach, ducked back inside.

Alazo waited. Nothing stirred. The corpse looked much the same as it had before its disgorgement. Apart from the mucus and blood. He gave it a solid kicking. No tumors burst.

Thus satisfied, Alazo pressed his eye against the cave-mouth's sphincter hole. The membrane smelled like honey or maybe burned sugar and cut grass in ghastly curdle. Veins ran through as if through eyelids. Where the membrane met the cave wall there was nary a difference in texture or color until black rock encroached the stretched flesh. He half-expected the cave walls to start breathing.

Through the hole he could see clearly the vast plains of Salmacador stretching across the horizon, peppered occasionally with moss-back boulders tall as city buildings, wettened by intermittent marshes sprouting cattails, broken regularly by sandy expanses like miniature deserts. Crossing one of these: a person.

At this distance they were only a few interlocking shadows. Still, Alazo had no doubt of the figure's identity: Sage Ermin astride the long back of a tom gracip. Dawn broke behind the Sage as if she were backlit by Opherlion's Grand Lamp, setting fire once again to all the second born sons and feeding the third borns by their eldest brother's calf-meat.

Sage Ermin was not coming from the direction of Crindleshaftner, the frontier town Alazo had lately nested in, but rather from Aedelsbee, whose alchemical streetlights could be spied some thirty miles away.

Which meant Sage Ermin had been riding all night. She would doubtless need rest. The blankets beneath the gracip's saddle would serve as protection from the stone ground, and he could offer his clothing for her pillow. What she might be moved to pursue when confronted with his pearlescent flesh none could truly say. But Alazo prided himself on his tenacity, and no one had ever maligned him for lack of perseverance.

Alazo waited upon a boulder in what he hoped was regal repose. Scaling it had not been a distinguished endeavor, but he figured he could hop off rather gallantly.

Below, the bodies. Or to be accurate—a virtue Alazo held to the utmost whenever it behooved him—the body parts. He pledged he would not gloat over this demonstration of his virility. He would let the evidence speak for itself, as Sage Ermin was not the type who adored a brag-gadocio.

The Sage halted her gracip at the cave's mouth. Doubt-less with a lateral pull of the reins and, he fantasized, a firm clench of her leatherclad thighs on the chitinous flanks.

Her lips pressed to the sphincter. "Come here," she said.

Hoping the membrane would not impair her ability to witness his agility, Alazo leapt from the boulder. His sleeves billowed; his earrings tinkled. He landed in a crouch as leopardine as any panther.

Sage Ermin made no remark. Alazo could only con-clude she'd been struck to muteness. He strode to the cave mouth and boldly crammed his eye to the sphincter, hoping to contact her luminous skin.

But she'd retreated. Her face had all the edges of the costliest diamond of which Alazo could possibly conceive. Her hair was as illuminant as that stone. Wrapping her slen-der frame was a robe of blue velvet. Or a material kin to velvet, except sorcerious, possessing qualities beyond the ken of Alazo. Its fibers seemed to float at their own behest rather than that of their wearer or even the slithering wind.

"Widen the hole," she said.

"Good morning, Sage, how was your rest?" Alazo de-livered this with a twinkle in his eye, having planned the greeting over the course of his patron's approach. His hands were quickly moistening from his continual massaging of the membrane's edges.

"Stay," said Sage Ermin, not seeming to understand Alazo's ironic salutation. She tottered to the gracip's rear and untied the knots on her pack. Her arms were stick thin. Alazo made sure he frowned only when she couldn't see— the Sage had never been less than hale and hearty.

Her gracip's backsaddle was heavily loaded. The gracip's forelegs clasped sacks and the multitudinous fin-gers of its sub-forelegs were knotted around objects more mysterious. With the payout from this job, he hoped he could afford a creature so segmented, not to mention be-fingered, but he'd settle for a mare or even an unbroken jake.

Sage Ermin could not possibly carry this load inside on her own; he counted seven separate bundles, ranging from half his size to nearly hers. One looked suspiciously like a bedroll. Fresh Salmacadorian air swirled into his nostrils and the urge to be free of this cave struck with such ferocity he did not think before hiking his foot into the gap.

"Stay," repeated the Sage. Rather brusquely, Alazo re-flected, and in doing so lost his opportunity to reply before she ignored him again.

Sage Ermin instead addressed her gracip's ass. Or ra-ther the world nearest. She muttered a few things and sham-bled this way and that way. Her fingers made circles and triangles and other shapes he made sure not to study too closely. The gracip bellowed and, to Alazo's immense sur-prise, floated into the air. Sage Ermin tugged the gracip back to dirt before it had drifted more than a yard or two. She spat on its back legs. The spit impacted with greasy residue to tether the gracip. Nonetheless, the gracip gripped the ground with any available digits. Its eyestalks rolled cir-cles.

The gracip's load floated too. Sage Ermin handled the bundles with only her gloved fingertips, flicking here and steering there. Alazo caught the bundles on the cave side, where they became heavy again. He lined them along a far wall marred neither by blood nor pus.

"Can you extend your spell a few meager yards, Sage?" asked Alazo after the sixth package. His body, already sore from squirrel-culling, felt ready to revolt either by vomiting or collapsing.

"Last one," said Sage Ermin.

A seven-foot long and two-foot wide, pin-shaped object floated through the hole. It was shrouded in a long black veil. When it collapsed into Alazo's arms he was reminded of several occurrences, such as the day he'd earned his club after dragging a nearly dead Gendledred Wolfbrainer behind the stable.

"Let no light touch this," said Sage Ermin.

By the time he'd laid the corpse, Sage Ermin had made it through the membrane. He'd forgotten the spell of her presence. Part of this was her obscene height. Her head scraped stalagmites; she was taller than anyone he'd ever met. Part of it was undefinable. A product, he assumed, of her mysterious wisdom. She was exquisite as falling sheets of ice and possessed a similar androgyny—this always a weakness for Alazo, and it combined with his fear of her into a heady potion that made him inquire 'how deep' whenever the Sage said 'stab.'

Sage Ermin wobbled through the devastation. She scowled. "I said 'watch them.' I'll have to deduct your pay."

"I cannot believe my ears," said Alazo. He'd made serious misjudgment. Still, it was hardly his fault that she'd been unclear. He rakishly tossed the club over his shoulder and laughed. "A fine joke, madam."

"How many birthed?" She knelt by the prime-corpse and plunged exploratory fingers into the mess.

Alazo gave this some thought. "No more than six. Four, if I recollect the truth."

Sage Ermin appeared to be counting.

"That a lady of your caliber would make japes about my payment—"

"Shut up," said Sage Ermin. She closed her eyes and pinched the bridge of her nose. Her body language implied a storied feat of restraint.

"In the future, please refrain from violence. You need not harm the children."

"Imagine, for instance, a situation in which said 'children' are sprouting with ill-intent—"

"I am unsure where you got the idea that 'watch' meant 'massacre,'" continued Sage Ermin, as if Alazo had never spoken. "You are lucky I've had a fruitful month."

Alazo discarded those of Sage Ermin's comments which made little sense or besmirched his conduct. This did not leave him with much to work with.

"A boon of procuring my service, lady, is my ingrained quality of fortune. That you notice this trait speaks more to your sagacity than my luck, though of course it does also speak to my caliber."

"Let us then see your caliber of untying!" cried Sage Ermin. "And another test for my oh-so-competent hireling: show me your ability to be silent, that I might time your silence and present results afterward for your crowing self-appraisal!"

Alazo untied Sage Ermin's packages with catlike quietude. She was clearly exhausted from her trek and whatever adventure previous. She slumped her tatterdemalion body in the crotch between two stalagmites.

When Alazo finished untying the bundles—kindling, flint shards, a cord of wood, cooking pots, two wooden spoons, three clay jars of water, dried-clairyflower, sprouts, beans, jerked rabbit, salt, pepper, and a bedroll—Sage Ermin broke her silence.

"Put it next to the other," said Sage Ermin. She could only mean the original corpse, the squirrel corpse.

Alazo, loathe to get so close without bearing the club, was even loather to cross the Sage. He gripped the corpse beneath its armpits and dragged as hardily as he had on Gendledred Wolfbrainer's last day.

As soon as the body hit shadow it began rumbling anew. A tumor burbled. A tiny hand gripped his arm.

"Argh!" he shouted, and used his fear as a lever to toss the corpse completely into darkness.

His club leapt into his hands of its own accord. The spot where the squirrel had pressed felt itchy. "Touch not lest ye be touched!" he cried, springing forward, but Sage Ermin plucked the club out of his hands and tossed it across the cave before he could begin his swing. He followed his club a moment later.

Alazo breathed cave-debris and listened to the flat wet pop of breaching squirrels until he felt well enough to stand. He hoped he would not be called upon to speak before his wind returned. Under Sage Ermin's raptorial eye, he performed a vague bow by way of apology.

She'd risen. The squirrels rubbed against her robes. Two had crawled up the folds and now perched gargoyle on her rickety shoulders. He was horrified to realize that the squirrels quite resembled Sage Ermin, if she were eight inches tall, had four mouths, and a dozen legs.

The squirrels at her feet growled ferociously. One of them demonstrated the utility of his protruding organ for Alazo's benefit.

"Heel your homunculi, Sage," said Alazo, altering tactics. "Or I will demonstrate the origin of my surnom, 'the Deleterious.'"

"Self-proclaimed, no doubt," said Sage Ermin. And before Alazo could speak the Sage tossed a handful of riches to the dirt.

Among matin coins blinked the gold silhouettes of the Aedelsbeen ptarmigan and the triple-eye orozoros of Sungar-Lee. The azure hues of Piri Valley's etched gemstones cast oceanic shades onto the cave walls, comingling with the recursions of encapsulated lightning mined in the Floating Cities of Elsoon.

"Your payment, minus damages," said Sage Ermin.

This was at least quadruple his rate. He pocketed the riches.

"I admit, you drive a man hard, but such rigor produces positive repercussion. For this I offer thanks, Sage Ermin, that you've allowed me to pursue my purest potential in your service."

Sage Ermin had struggled to her feet in the midst of his proclamation. Now she overshadowed the betumored corpse. Her squirrels gamboled in her wake. Such was her pose that, for a shocking instant, Alazo expected her to make water.

Instead, she cast off her robe.

Alazo scuttled backwards in terror.

For Sage Ermin was nothing except a structure of sticks and bones, an incomplete skeleton buttressed by lengths of metal and polished hardwood and, in one case, a crossbow bolt. White sores seethed at the joins of these aberrant additions. The Sage's marvelous visage was now startlingly human in relation to its root.

"An entire brood remains," said Sage Ermin. Stacks of lightning capsules and etched gems sat in an interior shelf below her collarbone. She reached inside and tossed them in Alazo's direction.

Alazo, never prideful when it behooved him not to be, snatched the treasures. He made sure to keep his face perfectly frightened, which was a realizable enterprise, considering.

"I shall lose my voice in gratitude, dear lady, embarrassing me even more than does acceptance of your largesse. But I enquire: what is this further payment in relation to?" With one sleeve he surreptitiously wiped unclean matter from his funds.

"Oh, I'm hungry," said Sage Ermin. Below her the corpse shivered like a sick dog.

"Rabbit and clairyflower soup fills the emptiest well," he said, taking stock of the camping supplies.

Sage Ermin knelt. Her knees pushed into the corpse's armpits.

Alazo did not want to know what came next. "Now compensated, I will take this opportunity to abscond, leaving you to our own devices, with hope you will call upon me soon."

But he did not abscond because the squirrel-gargoyles on the Sage's shoulders hissed dangerously. And quietly, since their mouths and eyes were sewing shut. Not with needle and thread, but with films of inexorably expanding skin. Skin which coiled like so many flat snakes from the betumored corpse, up and through Sage Ermin's scaffolding, writhing with a wet efficiency to disperse droplets of hot blood and cold scale until the squirrels were not perched on Sage Ermin's shoulders, they *were* Sage Ermin's shoulders.

"Sweet Superior," said Alazo, only vaguely aware of performing the signs to ward off this ill luck.

Sage Ermin lay atop the betumored corpse. "Cease your nattering," she said. Her voice broke into an obscene moan in the statement's second half.

Once nestled intimately against the Sage, the corpse's swell found its fever pitch. Tumors exploded in calamitous sequence. Juice spattered through Sage Ermin's skeleton and painted the cave walls with the aesthetic of Morto Plenkutt's famed triptych of the Goddess Neth in Her Palimpsest Pool. The squirrels took to Sage Ermin's frame the way vines take to the trellis. One homunculus dug its teeth into Sage Ermin's rib and swung cleanly into the yawning space below. Its limbs grabbed bone at a dozen points, its skin already cascading to fill the larger body.

Alazo pointed the silver tip of his club at this developing monstrosity. Three particularly large squirrels swirled out of forehead-tumors to roost inside Sage Ermin's claw-hands. The homunculus-grown fingers were no less long or sharp than their skeletal armature, though they were more seductive.

When her reconstitution was complete, Sage Ermin covered herself with the robe. Alazo shifted uncomfortably. His thoughts raced down eerie and discomfiting labyrinths, far away from the apparatus of speech.

"Homunculus got your tongue?" she asked. She flicked a matin at him. The coin hit him in the tooth. He yelped.

"Watch you don't catch flies," said Sage Ermin. She stretched her arms and slapped the muscles of her thighs. She dragged the steaming husk of corpse into the sunlight, where it withered away into something akin to a man shaped snakeskin.

"Don't eat that," said Sage Ermin. She laughed. When she strode toward him, there was no wobble, no hesitancy, only the confidence of the full-bodied.

"I neither require nor desire incorporation!" cried Alazo. He had no place to retreat to, what with the cave-wall cooling his backside. And his club seemed like a chopstick compared to Sage Ermin's majesty.

But the Sage moved past him, past the supplies he'd so obediently arrayed, to the cave-mouth membrane.

"Fear commands even you," she remarked. Alazo watched her jawline as she shook her head: such magnificent disappointment.

"Preservation and apprehension may be confused for cowardice, then, by even the wisest," said Alazo.

"I never expected you to be half so smart as you appeared," said the Sage.

"I'm stung," said Alazo. "Yet, see how we play! What repartee!"

Sage Ermin snorted. She pushed her knuckles against the membrane. Leaned into it, her fingers stretching the film to soap-bubble translucence.

"I will follow you out," said Alazo. He gathered his pack.

Sage Ermin laughed. "You've at least a fortnight of resources. If needs pass time, do not leave, for I will be along immediately to spell you."

"I might resupply in Crindleshaftner," said Alazo. "Thus, saving you a trip."

"By no means will you leave this cave," said Sage Ermin.

"To be sure," he said. He would simply wait until she was gone—

"And if you leave, I will know, and I will come for you," said Sage Ermin. She was looking at him in a manner he did not enjoy. "Do you understand?"

Alazo pledged: "I understand acutely."

"Be safe, now," said Sage Ermin. She threw herself at the membrane with a sudden savagery. Again and again. Her teeth gnashed and claws dragged until in one final jump the membrane burst. Thin as it was, it spurted copious liquid in so wide a field that Alazo caught a spurt on his already-corrupted boots.

She stood on the other side of the cave mouth. In the free world. The membrane lay spent at her feet. Her pale skin was awash in dripping goop. Everything stunk of squashed worms rubbed directly beneath the nose.

She pointed at him. "Stay."

Alazo bowed. He did not bother hiding his scowl.

Sage Ermin hopped onto the gracip's saddle. She keeyawed and slapped the insect's mid-rump and the gracip shot off into the Plains of Salmacador. They disappeared into the first patch of swamp, but Alazo watched still more, because there was nothing else to do.

After a while, he made camp. He unrolled his bedroll and weighed the edges with stones. The shrouded body had already begun to swell. He had a fortnight until the squirrels—the homunculi—would sprout. Still, he eyed the knottiest bulge for any movement.

All while the cavemouth membrane knit itself back together, starting at the edges closest to the wall, from which spun a soft, wet, ribbon of skin.

* * *

By that night, the membrane was healed and sphinctered. Amber starlight reflected through, dancing on the cave walls as if Alazo were sitting river bottom while the golden hour colored the surface world. The stars were the same shade as his own dancing campfire. While he stirred rabbit and clairyflower soup, he wondered at the moons and stars blazing amber tonight instead of the death-white shade of extra-dimensional tentacles.

Alazo propped his spoon on the edge of the pot. He peered through the membrane's sphincter.

Toward the sky, where clouds blocked any sign of stars.

At the glowing outline of Aedelsbee, shining dimly to the north.

To the east, where curved the major expanse of the Hived Cliffs.

Into countless other cave mouths, each glowing with the light of campfire. What he'd mistaken for the stars, set to earth.

ONE FOOT IN THE GRAVE
By Gerri R. Gray

Dark clouds had been gathering since sunrise, slowly blotting out the sky and draping the uniformed rows of grave markers with shadows. A biting wind transformed a scatter of dead leaves into a swirling mass that spiraled into a dance of death before falling back to the earth to wait for another gust to send them airborne. It was only the second day of November–All Souls' Day– but the merciless chill of winter was already in the air.

A light drizzle began to descend from the heavens like weeping tears, darkening the mournful marble figures of religious icons and innocent lambs that stood in silent vigil over the final resting places of the dead. As the drops landed upon their heads and rolled down their cheeks, they gave the solemn stone faces the eerie appearance of crying.

Jerome Crippen paused for a moment to open his black, five hundred dollar, Maglia Francesco umbrella to shield himself from the rain. He then continued on his way until he arrived at the grave of his dearly departed wife, Laura. He had nearly forgotten where her grave was located. He had only been to it once, and that was on the day of her burial. He stood as still as the statuary around him and stared down at the small bronze grave marker before him, which bore his wife's name, along with the dates of her birth and death, the image of a cross, and the Biblical quote: WHITHER THOU GOEST, I WILL GO. He recalled that it was also raining on the day her body was laid to rest, and felt strangely amused by the coincidence of it.

Laura Crippen had died exactly one year ago on this day, leaving Jerome an enormously wealthy widower, thanks to a hefty life insurance policy that he had taken out on her several years prior to her passing. According to her death certificate, the cause of death was cardiac arrest.

Despite her demise occurring at such a young age, nobody questioned the certifying physician's opinion, for Laura was known to possess an enlarged heart resulting from years of untreated high blood pressure.

Jerome took a quick look around to determine if anyone else was in the cemetery with him. Confident that he was the sole person there–at least, the sole *living* person–he cracked a bit of a crooked grin.

"Wake up, Laura," he said softly, almost in a singing voice, to the bronze grave marker. "It's Jerome, your husband. It's been one whole year now since you've been gone. Time has a way of flying by, doesn't it? I hope you'll forgive me for not coming to visit you sooner, but you see, I've been rather busy enjoying that money your insurance policy paid out to me. I'm sure you'll be pleased to hear that you left me well provided for. In fact…" he paused to snicker, "I've been living like a king and enjoying the finest of cars, clothes, restaurants and women. Oh yes, especially the women!"

Another gust of wind swept through the cemetery and a miniature tornado of brown leaves that had dropped from the branches of some nearby tress during the previous month sailed past Jerome's Italian leather shoes. The rain felt like it had suddenly grown colder, almost icy to the touch, and was now falling harder than before, giving off a loud pitter-patter as it struck the grave marker.

"It's a bit amusing, don't you think," Jerome continued, "that you always told me I could never do anything right. Not even poison a rat. Yet, I succeeded in poisoning you, Laura, and I did it quite well and got away with it, if you don't mind me touting my own horn. Nobody suspected a thing. With that bad heart of yours, they all knew you had one foot in the grave."

Jerome chuckled to himself as his mind rewound to that fateful day when, after months of careful plotting and indecision, he finally mustered up enough courage and greed to see his plan through and spike the whiskey sour drink of his unsuspecting wife with a tincture of aconite root. During his researching of poisons, he had read online that a fatal dose of this plant, which is also known as wolf's bane, results in paralysis of the heart or respiratory center, with the only post mortem signs being those of asphyxia. It sounded to him like the ideal, and least messy, way to dispose of one's unwanted spouse.

Jerome remembered, with what only can be described as a fiendish fondness, the agonized expressions on his dying wife's face as the poisoning process inched her closer to death's door, and him closer to a world of freedom made sweeter by a half-million dollar death benefit payout. Laura had initially complained of a bad headache, followed by unpleasant bouts of nausea and diarrhea. In time, her mouth and face began to tingle and then grow numb, as did her arms and legs. A fiery sensation burned deep within her abdomen, causing her to double up in pain. Confused and sweating profusely, she struggled in desperation to catch a breath of air as her husband nonchalantly observed from the comfort of a tufted chair in the corner of their master bedroom, leisurely savoring a glass of imported cognac.

And then, nearly three hours from the time that Laura had unwittingly ingested the cleverly disguised poison, she let out one last loud and horrible gasp and her painful ordeal finally reached its deadly conclusion. Her body lay cold and still upon the heavy damask comforter of black and gold that draped the queen-size bed. Her pink peignoir was brown and sodden with vomit, and her lifeless eyes wide open and staring accusingly at her murderer.

A rumble of thunder sounded in the distance and Jerome looked up at the sky. It had formed into an ominous patchwork of gray, dark green and black, illuminated by random flashes of lightning.

"Well, my dear," Jerome sighed as he returned his gaze to his deceased wife's grave marker. "I believe the time has come for me to bid you farewell. Go back to sleep now, Laura."

He turned and started to walk away. But then, for some unexplained reason, an odd urge overcame him. He stopped and bent down to snatch up a rain-soaked wreath from a nearby burial plot. He then made his way back to Laura's grave with the wreath in his hand and tossed it onto the grassy ground that covered her remains. After blowing her a mocking kiss, he uttered, "I'll see you around."

With an explosive boom, a jagged bolt of blinding lightning suddenly struck Laura's bronze marker, shaking the ground like an earthquake. Jerome was knocked off his feet. Dropping his umbrella, he flew backwards and landed on his backside atop the wet and sticky ground that had been turned to sludge by the rain. A howling gust of wind lifted up his umbrella and carried off before his fingers could latch onto its curved cherry wood handle.

"Damn it!" he cursed.

As he struggled to free himself from the grip of the earthy-smelling muck, the unthinkable happened.

Like a scene from out of a horror film, or perhaps from the darkest of nightmares, the ground in front of Laura's grave marker began to tremble until a small fissure appeared, and from out of it emerged the foul and rotting limb of a woman. Its purplish hand turned in Jerome's direction and slowly opened like a blossoming nightshade.

Paralyzed by abysmal horror, Jerome recognized the gold rings on one of the corpse's fingers. They were Laura's bridal set. He felt a scream rise up in his numb throat. But before it could exit his mouth, Laura's bony, claw-like hand wrapped itself around his right ankle and began dragging him toward her grave.

Jerome's scream finally found its way up from his lungs, but was drowned out by another deafening crash of thunder. He fought desperately to free himself from the dead woman's powerful clutch, but her supernatural-infused strength won out.

The corpse had pulled Jerome's leg calf-deep into the grave when, all at once, he felt the terrifying sensation of teeth chewing on his ankle. Deeper and deeper into his bone they gnawed. The pain was unbearable and unlike anything he had ever experienced. He continued to struggle, and he bellowed out a series of hair-raising man-shrieks that reverberated in all directions, ricocheting off of tombstones and statues and the walls of mausoleums. The pain was tantamount to the most horrendous of torture and Jerome found himself drifting in and out of consciousness until the agony was mercifully supplanted by a numbness that raced up the entire length of his leg.

At last he was able to free himself from the hellish hole that had swallowed him alive. He yanked his limb from the muddy grave, only to discover that his right foot was gone. It had been completely chewed off and a gory hemorrhage was pouring out from the ragged stump at the bottom of his partially devoured leg.

His mind reeled from the horrendous sight and his thoughts swirled inside his brain like the dead leaves whipping in the wind around him. Soon, his vision blurred and faded to black. His body violently convulsed. The rapid-fire beating of his heart ceased and Jerome Crippen lay lifeless at the foot of Laura's grave, his blood staining the wet blades of dormant grass a ruddy color that not even the November rain could wash away.

LOVE NEVER DIES
By Sheldon Woodbury

The Leather & Chains was a desolate bar at the end of a long dirt road in a godforsaken patch of the Badlands. You had to know it was there because there weren't any signs to keep the tourists away. It was made out of rotted wood and rock with no view to what was happening inside. Buzzards flapped above for some unknown reason, cawing predators in the hot desert air.

I was there with the Hellfire Club, the scariest motorcycle gang there ever was. We were big and brawny, riding beastly bikes that spewed fire and smoke. We'd rumbled all day beneath a blazing hot sun that died a slow death an hour ago. Twilight was gone and the blackness of night was here, so it was time to have fun. We strode in like dusty dirt devils and headed straight to the bar. The music was heavy and loud, the lights low, with more murky shadows than anything else. The mysterious travelers who gathered here liked it that way. It was off the beaten track, a secret hideaway for desert nomads that didn't want their recreational pursuits to be seen by anyone who wouldn't understand.

I was on my third tequila shot when she strolled up, holding a shot glass too. Even in the murkiness she was something to see, like a vision I'd been waiting my whole life for without even knowing it. Nothing was said because we both knew what we wanted, and in here there were no boundaries to what that could be. We wanted to be naked and bloody, moaning on the floor, or slammed against a wall. It was like we could read each other's minds and there was no need for niceties or small talk. Like I said, this wasn't the kind of place tourists would like, unless they had a secret life that was shocking.

I was into the good girl gone bad look, so her pouty lips and wild hair were just what I wanted. Midnight black and tortured red were clearly her fashion colors of choice, a perfect match for the whips and chains hanging on the walls. She looked like a mythic enchantress from the bad side of town, and I was from that place too, hulking and tall, with steel studded boots.

I nibbled at the tattooed flesh of her neck and pulled her tight. What came next was exactly what I wanted, a crushing knee to the groin and a claw-like slap across my face. Right then and there, we were already in love, a violent match made about as far away from heaven as you could possibly get.

We gulped two more shots and stumbled to one of the private rooms in back where even more brutal devices were scattered on the floor. We assaulted each other with a fury that would have seemed way too wicked to those who didn't know that the strangest extremes are what life and death are all about. In this unknown haven of a desert bar, everything bad was why you came. It lasted for more than an hour, a writhing entanglement that was both a lusty struggle for domination and a quest to embrace unimaginable pain.

When we were finished, all the punishing toys had been used, and most more than once. We had similar tastes, but differences too, and that made it even more enticing. It was a private spectacle no one could witness or judge, as it was meant to be. We stayed on the floor and shared a few whispered secrets, feeling a bond that surprised even us. I told her who I was, the leader of the notorious biker gang that roamed the Badlands like legendary marauders from long ago. I recounted a few of our greatest hits, a mishmash of thievery, blasphemous mischief, and roadside terror.

She listened with an amused smile and a cryptic glint in her eyes. She'd covered her body with a tattooed tapestry of occult symbols and designs so there was very little left of her pale flesh. Her fiery red hair wafted up from the floor, and she told me she was the leader of a gang too, but didn't say anything more than that. I accepted this because mystery was always part of the game, the masking cloak we all wore to hide who we really were.

And then she was dead.

I can't remember exactly what happened, but round two was even more violent, both of us grabbing each other with a billowing ferocity that soared out of control. Screams became wails, wails became groans, and suddenly this glorious enchantress collapsed to the floor with a death-rattle moan. I'll never forget the look in her shimmering eyes when she gasped her last breath.

What have you done?

And I know what you're thinking: what the hell kind of love story is this? She was a really hot chick you said you loved and then you killed her.

But imagine how I felt from that moment on, because I'd met the girl of my darkest dreams and turned it into the worst kind of nightmare. There was nothing else I could do except stumble out of the room and tell the raspy old bartender what had happened. His weary nod made it clear this wasn't an unusual occurrence in this desert dive where outcasts could do whatever they wanted.

By the time I was dragged away from the bar, I was too drunk to ride, but that had never stopped me before. I'd mumbled what had happened to the others, but their boozy sympathy did nothing to quell the burning ache in my heart. We lived a desperado life, so there were plenty of dead bodies left in our wake. But this was different. I'd killed the girl I loved, and I knew my life would never be the same.

The emptiness of the desert outside made the emptiness inside me seem even greater. We rode away from the Leather & Chains with the grinding roar of our pumped-up bikes. They were giant, macabre machines that caused fear and dread even in the brightest light of day, with leering skulls, hellish creatures, and red-hot flames from some un-known beyond. Parents and kids in their boring cars would scream and point at our smoky stampeding horror parade.

We found the highway again and rode for awhile before veering off into the desert, bumping and swerving over the rough terrain. It was an eerie landscape, both primal and ancient looking. Craggy peaks and massive plateaus loomed like giant gravestones. We circled our bikes and turned off the grumbling engines. The howls of wolves and coyotes drifted in, a baying night chorus that never went away. This was where we always slept, out in the desert with just the wind and wild animals. And tonight the sky glowed with a monster's moon, when there was nothing else to be seen, no clouds, no stars, just a gargantuan orb that looked like a monster's glimmering eye.

Like all gangs, we had our private ways and customs. We loved the burning heat of the day, but the darkness of night was a more sacred time. First, we tended to our bikes, wiping away the dirt and grime. They were as much a part of the gang as us, snarling and mean, big and bulky, not to be messed with. If there were kinks or rattles that needed attention, Dirty Dave was our mystic mechanic. He never talked, except for a few guttural grunts, and that was usually to the ailing cycle he was bringing back to life.

And then it was time for our nightly ritual, sitting on tattered blankets inside the circle of beastly bikes. Slug was our medicine man. He looked like a leather-clad lizard, his face scarred and scaly from the burning sun. His eyes were strange too, like churning clouds before a storm. He took out his peyote mix and we passed it around, waiting for the tripping night journey to begin.

We were renegades who wanted a hell of a lot more than the civilized world could offer. There were way too many rules and restrictions, too much judgment and scorn. We were all about smashing through that and going where others were too scared to go. It was who we were, and nothing did that better than Slug's psychic battering ram. It smashed open locked doors and burned down barriers built by the normal world. And only then would we reveal who we really were.

The wolves and coyotes yelped even louder as we rose up and left the circle of bikes. The transformation was just one part of what was happening mostly in our minds. It was like curtains were ripped apart, revealing sights that seemed to have erupted from a fiendish underworld below. We howled too as the desert melted away from a fiery upheaval that reached all the way up to the monster's moon. And now there were other creatures too, misshapen and crusty, prowling through the sulfurous flames. It reached a crackling crescendo, a phantasmagoria of horror and fear. And then it faded away, as if the mind-blowing curtains had been slowly pulled back again. The others staggered back to their tattered blankets to end what was left of the night. It was always a deep and rumbling sleep that still sputtered and fizzled with burning flames and underworld horror.

And that's when I heard it, standing all alone beneath the monster's moon.

Love never dies...

Where it came from was a mystery, but not the source of the haunting voice.

It was my hardcore enchantress, the woman I loved and killed. I called out, again and again, but no answer came back. I began to doubt if it was ever there, or just a sign of my pain and longing. I waited beneath the monster's moon, hoping I would hear it again. But there were just the howls of the coyotes and wolves, which made it seem more like an illusion.

I continued to roam the Badlands with the Hellfire Club, but it wasn't the same anymore. Even the roar of our beastly bikes wasn't enough to drown out what I was feeling inside.

She was wicked and wild, spooky and beautiful, a good girl gone way beyond bad. I saw her in my dreams, and that made it even worse. She was gone forever, banished below where she'd end up as nothing but dust and dirt.

And then I finally heard it again, weeks later, standing beneath another monster's moon. It was the same haunting voice reaching out to me from some unknown place. But now I knew I had to find out where that place was.

So now I was in front of the Hellfire Club, going back to where it all began, the desolate dive for outcasts in a god-forsaken patch of the Badlands. I had to find out what happened after we left, where she was taken and buried. Maybe I was dreaming this too because I still couldn't believe she was gone. But I also knew we lived in a world that had no idea what secrets were lurking just out of sight. There had always been two worlds: one hidden and one not.

We were miles away when storm clouds suddenly took over the sky and rain began to splatter down. We kept going and finally reached the Leather & Chains with some of the watery night still left. We slogged inside and saw that nothing had changed. The music was heavy and hard, with a motley group of mysterious travelers lurking in the shadows. The drenching rain hitting the roof seemed like part of the pounding music.

I went straight to the raspy old bartender and told him why I was there. I needed to know where she was, the wild and wicked girl I loved and killed. He stared back at me and nodded, as if he knew I'd come back. Without saying a word, he shuffled out from behind the bar and went to the rotted door that led to the back rooms. Nothing had changed there either. I followed him down the grungy hall, past the private rooms. All the doors were closed, but I could still hear moans, groans, and louder screams, bringing back a rush of memories from the night that changed my life.

We reached the end of the gloomy hall and the hunched over bartender squeaked open a door that took us outside. The rain was still falling, giving the desert sprawl behind the bar a misty glimmer, like something not completely real. His gait was shaky as he trudged through the puddles and mud, and I was beginning to think he wasn't all there. He continued on and began to mumble to himself in gurgled words that were watery too.

Suddenly, something began rising up out of the rainy mist in front of us, a desert plateau that was low to the ground. Crude steps had been carved out of the dirt and rock. He staggered up, his hunched body huffing and puffing to the top. That's when I saw markers spread out in the soggy dirt.

"She's here," he croaked.

So this was a graveyard, but one hidden away at the top of this desert formation. But the markers weren't regular tombstones with names and dates. They were macabre statues and totems being drenched by the pelting rain. Some were creatures not of this world and others were bizarre configurations made out of scorched rock. They were markers for what was hidden below: the underground resting place for the dead and gone.

Then, I heard it again, louder this time.

Love never dies...

At a marker a dozen feet away, the graveyard dirt shivered and shook, and then broke apart, skeletal hands clawing up from below. The rain drizzled to a stop, revealing another monster's moon. The skeleton was now above ground, a trembling grotesquerie stumbling towards me.

And there she was, my one true love.

That's when she revealed her secret in that haunting voice: She was part of a gang too, a coven of witches that roamed the Badlands just like us, enchanted desperadoes using magic and sex as the source of their allure. The bartender shuffled away, leaving us alone in this hidden graveyard. As his hunched body reached the edge of the plateau, there was a flashing glimpse of what he really was, slithery tentacles trailing behind him. I shrugged away my disguise too, revealing my true form. I was ash and smoke, fire and brimstone, the leader of a motorcycle gang from Hell.

Yes, there are secrets lurking just out sight.

She staggered towards me, a skeletal temptress with barely any flesh left. I could see in the hollow holes that used to be her eyes that she was still mad at what I had done. But I also knew that didn't matter anymore, so I took her in my fiery arms and we tumbled down to the graveyard dirt. Beneath the glowing monster's moon, we both began to howl and moan, because make-up sex is always the best.

KING SOLOMON
By Hugh Alan

Long gray fingers with blackened nails traced the edges of the letters carved into the stone, *Edward 'King' Solomon 1789-1833, "Who saw them all to their rest."* Almost sixty years, he mused as his hand fell away from the stone monument. He took in the scent of the night air and looked around; it had been many years since his return to the old cemetery. Time moved differently in the Nightlands, and sometimes years could slip by unnoticed. It didn't look much different for all the years which had passed. Older graves crumbled away while fewer new ones were dug. It had become an old and unfashionable place, withering away to the inexorable crawl of time, even as the lives of those buried here disappeared from living memory. But, it was home.

Solomon turned away from the monument and instinctively dropped to a crouch, sniffing the air again as he cocked his head to one side. He could hear all the small sounds of the cemetery: the crows rustling in their sleep upon the branches, the rats as they skittered among the mausoleums, and even the worms as they churned the earth below him. He leapt to the top of a nearby headstone, scanning the night with wide black eyes long used to the darkest nights. Through the waves of mist that flowed languidly between the stones, he could see all of London spread out below the high hill where The Quiet Promise Cemetery stood.

He turned away from the city below and saw the great oak that stood at the top of the hill. Springing from the headstone, he loped across the distance on all fours, moving swiftly like a predator with the scent of prey in its nose. The shadows caressed his pale, grave-white skin, and seemed to cling to him. Even in the silver moonlight, they were reluctant to let him go. He passed among the headstones in silence. As silent as the grave, or so they say.

The old oak hadn't changed much either as he slipped into the familiar depression created by a timeless split in the thick trunk. Solomon laid his head back and closed his eyes, listening to the wind and relishing the feel of damp earth beneath him. A thin mist of rain began to fall, and with it a trickle of memories from long ago. He remembered the first time he had fallen asleep beneath this tree.

* * *

"I said, get up!"

This last was punctuated with a hard kick that brought a moan from Solomon as he rolled over onto his back. The stabbing pain in his eyes made him immediately regret it as he raised one hand to block the harsh light of the sun. His other hand fell to his chest where he found that his shirt was damp. The smell told him what it was without any need to look. Solomon sat up shakily as he brushed at the vomit clinging to his shirt and then wiped his hand along the dew-dampened ground.

"Disgusting," the man spat, this time prodding him with the nose of his shovel. "Go on now!" he yelled, "Before I summon the constable."

Solomon had nearly made it to his feet when a sudden wave of nausea washed over him and he fell forward, disgorging the meager contents of his stomach. When he finally managed to blink past the tears in his eyes, he found himself staring at the man's vomit-covered boots. One of those boots struck him in the head and he fell back against the bole of the tree.

"You God damn drunk, I'll—"

He raised his booted foot again and Solomon instinctively threw his hands over his face.

"Wait," a voice called from behind the other man. "Leave him be."

Solomon hazarded a glance between his fingers and saw an older man come to stand beside the younger. He was thin and silver-haired but still stood straight and unstooped. They both towered over him, looking down. One face was filled with fury while the other one held what? Pity?

"The filthy bugger done spoiled my boots," the younger man complained.

"Those boots ought to already be covered in mud," the old man said as he frowned, looking down at them. "There's three more been dropped off needs' burying."

"Dead of the fever, ain't they?" the young man said with a scowl, looking down the hill toward the city. "It's the king that's come back to London, and I ain't gonna touch'em. Sack me if yer gonna, but that's more than a dozen now this week. They can sit out here and rot for all I care—"

The old man raised his hands to soothe the other man's ire.

"Them dead still deserve a proper rest, King Cholera or not—" the old man began before he was cut short.

"—then you bury them!"

The old man sighed and brought one withered hand up to scratch at his thin beard. He paused as his eyes fell on Solomon again. With one hand, he took the shovel from the other man; with his other, he held it out toward Solomon. Slowly, Solomon reached up to take it and let the other man haul him roughly to his feet. He teetered for a moment and then made a sound that caused the older man to step back, taking care to keep his boots clear. He did not throw up again but instead stared at the two gravediggers with bleary eyes.

"What's your name then?" the older man asked as he placed a steadying hand on his shoulder.

"E—Edward," he replied with a tongue too thick and wanting to cling to the roof of his mouth. "Edward Solomon," he continued, "but most folks call me King Solomon."

"That's rich," the younger man guffawed, but the older man waived him quiet.

"My name is Joe," the older man said, smiling now. "And this is Reggie. How'd you like to make a few coins and help us out?"

Solomon's head turned slowly to look back and forth between the two men. He started to reply but was overcome by a coughing fit, which in turn led to still more retching.

The younger man skipped back a few paces in alarm.

"He's got the fever!"

"No," Joe said as he took a step forward, as though to prove the man wasn't sick. "He's just shit-faced."

The old man clapped him several times on the back until Solomon had, at last, recovered enough to stand up straight again. He pushed his prematurely thinning hair from his eyes as he stared at the old man. At his full height, he was taller than either man but weighed less by a good measure. He looked as though he had one foot in one of these graves already.

"So what do you say, King Solomon?"

Solomon cleared his throat until, at last, he could give a rasping reply.

"W—Whiskey."

"What'd he say?" Reggie asked, leaning forward.

"He said, 'whiskey,'" Joe replied with a sad shake of his head.

Reggie stepped forward, cocking his head to one side as he stared at Solomon. He took the shovel back from Joe and stabbed it into the ground in front of them.

"So yer sayin' you'll help us out for whiskey?"

"Whiskey," Solomon croaked as he reached for the shovel.

* * *

King Solomon teetered for just a moment and almost fell forward into the grave he'd just finished digging. He wiped at his mouth with the sleeve of his coat and, with exaggerated care, set the whiskey bottle on the headstone next to him.

He had very quickly lost count of the number of graves he'd dug, the number of poor souls he'd put in the ground. It had been five today, maybe six? There were more and more coming each week, and those that King Cholera hadn't taken were fleeing the city in droves. Reggie had stopped showing up more than a week ago, which just left him and old Joe. The gravedigger dug his share of the graves too but had a difficult time matching Solomon's seemingly tireless shoveling. They rarely spoke, but at the end of each day, the old man would nod his approval at Solomon's work and hand over another dusty bottle of rot-gut whiskey.

Solomon paused, thrusting the shovel into the pile of newly excavated earth next to the fresh grave. He took another long pull from the bottle before trudging back to the cart. He threw back the canvas sheet and reached in to retrieve the day's final burial. The body was wrapped in white linen and bound with twine, as they all were. Solomon had taken hold of the corpse's feet and was about to haul it from the cart when he suddenly froze. The body was female, but that was not what had given him pause—he'd buried plenty of women. Girls too. No, what drew his eye was the round protrusion of her pregnant belly.

He closed his eyes and sagged against the cart. His head began to swim from the whiskey and he had to take hold of the cart's side to keep from falling. He could still hear her screaming, and he closed his eyes even tighter, clenching his jaw at the sudden memory. In his mind's eye, he could still see the blood-soaked sheets. There had been so much noise: her screams, and then the shouts of the midwife. It was the silence that followed that proved deafening. The way no one would meet his gaze when he came into the room…

Solomon shook his head and roughly hauled the body from the cart until it crashed onto the ground at his feet. Taking hold of the feet again, he dragged it the short distance to the hole he had dug. Lining it up next to the grave, he shoved it with one foot and watched as it fell with a dull thump into the moist earth.

He stared down at it for several minutes before finally lowering himself down to sit on the grave's edge, his feet dangling into the hole. Solomon reached into his coat and pulled out the book he always kept there. The cover was worn and there was a strip of leather cord holding it closed. Unwinding the cord, he opened the book to a page marked by a bawdy postcard. He was up to Corinthians now. Solomon cleared his throat and began to read aloud.

He'd thought it a shame there was no one to say any words over these poor souls. Fear of the fever trumping any familial obligations. Solomon had no words of his own, but he had the Bible his wife had given to him on their wedding day. She had read from the Bible every day he'd known her. She swore to him that no man went to hell who read the good book in its entirety. Solomon didn't know if he believed that was true, but he also thought it couldn't hurt either. Besides, something should be said before the dirt was rolled onto these sad bodies—and what better than the Lord's own book? He didn't think it mattered which part.

It had become ritual. Over each grave, he read two pages, no more and no less before he tucked the postcard back in the book and took up his shovel. Tucking the book back into his coat, Solomon drank from his bottle and then began to shovel the earth back from whence it had come. As he finished and began to stamp the earth down, he heard something which caused him to whirl. It sounded like a whisper in his ear. Solomon cocked his head, turning from side to side, listening. All he could hear was the sigh of the wind through the oak trees.

Solomon shook his head. No one came to the cemetery while King Cholera ruled. It was just he and old Joe, and he'd seen Joe retire to his small shack more than an hour ago. He took a long drink from his bottle and then another, closing his eyes as he felt the fire work its way into his belly and the clouds begin to fill his head. He leaned against the headstone and felt the wind cool his sweat-dampened skin.

The wind slowly died, and in the silence, the whispers began again.

* * *

Joe had been sick with fever going on three days now. Solomon nearly gagged at the smell in the room. Joe didn't have the strength to leave his bed now, the vomit and diarrhea coating the blankets under which he shivered. Solomon tried to peel the blankets away, but Joe's hand shot out and pulled them back to his breast.

"Don't bother," he said in a voice barely over a whisper. "It won't be much longer now."

Solomon let the blankets go and instead reached for the tin cup on the table next to the bed. Carefully, he held the cup to Joe's lips so that he might sip at the tepid water. Joe coughed, and Solomon set the cup down, turning to go. Joe's hand caught his own in a feverish grip.

"W—Will you sit with me a bit?"

Joe's voice was tired, and when Solomon turned to look at him he saw fear behind his red-rimmed eyes. Solomon nodded and dragged a chair closer to the bed.

"How many today?" Joe asked.

Solomon paused to think a moment.

"Two carts today… seven bodies."

Joe started to say something but fell into a fit of coughing. It wasn't until Solomon gave him another drink from the tin cup that he was able to speak.

"Are they paying you your due?"

Solomon produced a whiskey bottle by way of answer and uncorked it. He took a long pull from the bottle and was about to tuck it back into his coat when Joe reached out with a shaking hand and took up the tin cup. He turned it over and let the water spill out, then righted it and held it out. Solomon was forced to put his hand over Joe's to keep it from shaking as he poured the whiskey into it. Joe sipped at it and began to cough, when the coughing had passed, he took a larger drink from it.

Solomon gave a dry snort of a laugh and took the cup back from Joe.

"There's something I want to ask of you," Joe said as Solomon set the cup down.

Solomon nodded, taken aback by the sudden intensity in the man's eyes.

"Don't put me in the cold earth," he said, reaching out to take Solomon's hand. "I spent too many years laying folks in the cold ground while I fought to keep from freezing to death in this old shack. I don't know what comes after, but I don't wanna be cold no more."

As if the very thought made him shiver, Joe's hand began to tremble.

"Burn this old shack with me in it, King Solomon," he said as his hand slipped away, the strength seeming to run out of him.

"Can you?" he gasped. "Can you do that for me?"

Joe's bloodshot eyes found his, and Solomon simply nodded.

Joe seem to relax some at that, some of the tension draining away as he sagged into the old straw mattress. Solomon picked up the tin cup again, but Joe shook his head.

"Can I ask you a question, Joe?"

Joe had closed his eyes, but he nodded his head.

"What is it that whispers in the graveyard?"

His eyes opened slowly as he seemed to consider the question. He turned his head but his gaze had trouble finding him.

"M—My granny called them the 'night folk'," he whispered so faintly that Solomon was forced to lean forward so that he could hear.

"The night folk?" he asked, laying a hand on Joe's shoulder, which seemed to help him find Solomon's face again.

"She said that they walk behind the stones," Joe said with a smile, remembering the long-ago conversation. "You don't have to be afraid though… they won't hurt you. They have no traffic with the living—"

Joe continued to speak but the words grew so faint and indistinct, Solomon could no longer make them out. Slowly, his eyes lost focus, and Joe only continued to stare up at the ceiling as his breathing grew haggard and shallow.

Solomon leaned back in his chair and drew the book from his coat. He was up to Job now, and he thumbed it open and began to read. He did not stop at the usual two pages but read deep into the night. He read as the wind howled through the cracks in the wall, and in it he could hear the whispers of the night folk.

When the wind began to abate, Solomon realized that Joe had long since ceased breathing. He closed the book and then leaned forward to close Joe's eyes. He rose from the chair and stared down at Joe for a long moment. With one hand, he pushed the oil lamp off of the bedside table and said his goodbye as the straw mattress caught.

* * *

Solomon's hands shook as he tried to read, and he could hear the tremble in his own voice. There had been no cart for three days now. No cart, and no whiskey.

He could hear the whispering voices urging him on. They no longer frightened him, and he instead found a strange sort of comfort in their presence. A companionship. Deep in the New Testament now, he could feel them draw nearer as he would read. Sometimes, he thought he could almost see them, dancing in the shadows of his peripheral vision. When he tried to see them head-on, they would melt away, just tricks of light and shadow. He could never understand what it was they were saying—but while they were saying it—he felt less alone.

He'd put it off far too long. He knew what he would have to do. He had no fear of the fever, no fear of King Cholera. No, what he feared most was the way people looked at him, the way it forced him to see himself. What he'd become. His skin crawled and the tremors would only get worse, it was the bottle-ache, and it hurt all the way down to his bones.

The walk down the hill seemed much longer than he remembered it. Each footstep jarring him until he felt like his bones were made of broken glass. It was the silence he noticed first. He kept expecting the sounds of the city's hustle and bustle, but the quiet remained resolute. The streets were all but deserted, save for the carrion crows and scavenger dogs picking at the bodies lying in the streets. Everywhere he looked were the signs of hastily boarded-up houses and empty shops, as those who had survived this long finally fled the city. Occasionally, there were signs of the few who remained, peeking down at him from curtained windows, refusing to meet his gaze. It didn't take him long to find what he was looking for.

The Pickled Plum Pub was boarded up, but it had been hasty work easily circumvented. Ignoring the tables with chairs stacked neatly atop, Solomon moved around the bar and pulled the sheet away from the shelves behind it. Gleaming bottles arrayed themselves in front of him in a tinkle of shivering glass as the sheet fell away. Solomon licked his dry lips as he reached out for one of the bottles. His hands shook as he removed the cork and took a long drink. He paused, took a breath, and then an even longer drink from the bottle. Solomon closed his eyes as he felt the fire ignite in his belly, and the dull ache in his head begin to subside. Gripping the bottle in one hand, he took down a chair and sat himself at one of the tables.

When he had finished the bottle, Solomon took another and stumbled from the pub. He had seen the cart by the side of the road when he had first come down the hill. With a heave, he righted it and began to pull it down the street, the clatter of its wheels on the cobblestones the only sound. He stopped at the first body he came to. Dogs had torn away much of the white shroud it was bundled with, but Solomon covered the body as best he could once he'd gotten it into the cart. Then he gathered a second, a third, and finally a fourth body before he turned back toward the hill. Carefully, he tucked the second bottle of whiskey in the cart and made his way back to The Quiet Promise Cemetery to fulfill his own promise.

* * *

Solomon had long since lost track of the number of times he'd made the trip back and forth down the hill.

Spring rains had given way to sweltering summer heat where the bodies would bloat in the sun until finding their way onto Solomon's cart. Now the autumn leaves were falling as one day blurred into the next in an endless parade of bodies, holes dug, and, of course, whiskey. As the weather turned cold, Solomon had taken to keeping an extra hole dug where he would hunker down for the night, pulling a piece of heavy canvas over it to keep out of the biting wind.

He continued to make his way slowly through his wife's Bible, always two pages for each corpse interred, and sometimes a little more in the evenings until the whiskey began to blur his eyesight. Always he felt, even when he didn't hear, the presence of the whisperers. They would draw especially near at night while he read next to the small fire he would make within his grave-hollow. They would listen as he continued to read, and often he would awaken with the open Bible still in his lap.

Every morning he would shake off what remained of the evening's drink and take his cart back down the hill. He would, on occasion, glimpse the brave souls who remained through the pandemic, and it was they who would leave their dead on their doorsteps, a bottle of whiskey beside them. Solomon didn't give them much thought, their relationship purely transactional in his mind. As autumn gave way to winter, the bodies became fewer and fewer. There were rarely more than one or two bodies now, and some days there were none. On those days, there was no whiskey, and he would not take it from the boarded-up old pub.

At last it seemed, the contagion had run its course. It had been days since there had been any bodies to recover, and Solomon had stopped going down the hill. The first snow had fallen and the bottle-ache was hard upon him. He could not tell if it was the cold or the want of drink that made him tremble, but he discovered one morning that he no longer had the strength to climb back out of his hole.

Rather than fear, he felt nothing but relief as he sank back down against the grave walls. There was just enough wood to make a fire he thought, and when it went out, so would he. It was just as well, he'd finished Revelation just the day before.

He dreamt of his wife that night, waking in and out of a feverish sleep. The whispers were there, and they were a comfort, even as he slept. Solomon awoke with a start. It was late in the evening and the fire had burned down to little more than embers. There was a full moon shining above, reflecting brightly off the freshly fallen snow. His chest ached terribly, and he was finding it harder and harder to catch his breath. The whispers were all around him now, much louder than he'd ever heard them before. It felt as though they were standing over him, darker shadows within the surrounding black of his hole.

Solomon struggled to sit up and froze when he saw something sitting just before what remained of the fire. It was a book. It was much larger than his pocket Bible; it was a ponderous old thing wrapped in flaking leather. He startled as it moved closer to him. With the palms of his hands, he wiped at his eyes, trying to focus them. He saw a thin pale arm emerge from the darkness as it nudged the book toward him, and he could just make out, *Canterbury Tales*.

Casting his tired gaze around, it seemed the hole had grown impossibly dark. In the darkness, he not only heard the whispers, but he could sense movement there too. Solomon rolled onto his side and reached out to drag the book closer. He pushed himself up to lean against the earthen wall and carefully opened its cover. With a trembling hand, he turned the pages, and the whispers grew suddenly still. Solomon began to read aloud.

He had only finished a page before a fit of coughing came over him and his vision began to blur, making the words on the page swim before his eyes. Slowly, the book slipped from his numb fingers. Something in the shadows reached forward and caught it before it could fall. Solomon watched as the book disappeared into the shadows and the whispering suddenly returned. He coughed again and could not seem to catch his breath. He felt a pounding in his chest, and he clutched at his breast with one frail hand.

A pale hand emerged from the shadows behind him, emerging from a space that could not be. It was slender and impossibly long as it reached toward him. It took hold of Solomon's hand, and it felt cool to the touch, but not cold. It squeezed his hand reassuringly. Another hand emerged and its slender fingers caressed his cheek as another took hold of his other hand. Slowly, more and more hands came from the impossible space behind him and each of them took gentle hold of him. The whispers were so close now, he could feel the breath of them on his ear. They gently drew him into the darkness, whispering to him how he would walk behind the stones.

TO BE ALONE

By Richard Farren Barber and Stuart Hughes

Over the previous four years, Abigail had grown to appreciate the challenge of breaking into well-secured graveyards. They occupied a wide spectrum, from the open plots nestled against the side of a medieval church to municipal acres of the dead, locked down with heavy gates and patrolled by guards and dogs. She came prepared; bolt-cutters, wire-cutters and a claw hammer settled at the bottom of her bag. She didn't usually need them, but she'd learned to hope for the best and prepare for the worst.

The target tonight was MountView. She parked the car in a country lane about half a mile away and walked back to the cemetery walls. A row of terraced houses backed onto the cemetery and only about a third of the street lamps were working, so the pale yellow lights burned feebly against the dark. The houses looked abandoned, cracked windows sealed with cardboard squares and overgrown lawns with clumps of wild grass.

She walked down the street, derelict houses on her left and open fields on the right. There was no sign of movement and so little chance that she was observed, but still she tried to look as small and insignificant as possible.

At the end of the road she turned left onto MountView Rise. Through the fence she could see the plots stretching back into the night. The familiar mix of tidy headstones intermingled with the occasional grand statement—usually involving angels or hearts—caused her own heart to ache.

The fence was at least ten feet high. She didn't want to think what would happen if she tried to climb it and got caught on the top, or toppled off to land awkwardly on the other side. A broken ankle would be the least of her problems.

She kept walking, looking for a weak spot.

A car approached, twin headlights burning away the night, and she pressed against the fence and froze. The figure inside the car was an anonymous silhouette and the vehicle didn't slow as it passed. When the road was quiet she started moving forwards once again.

Abigail reached the gates and tested them. They rattled against the padlock which held them together and she thought there was probably enough give to pop open the lock if she needed to, but for now she was content to search for an easier entrance. She continued walking to the corner where another street of terraced houses bounded the northern edge of MountView.

She cast a glance along the street: it was cold and empty. Up ahead, a feral cat mewled and litter rustled in the gutters, but there was no sign of anyone awake. Just as it should be at two in the morning. She switched her bag from her left shoulder to her right and continued on her way.

There was always a weak spot. She'd spent too many nights clambering over gates or squeezing through gaps in fences before she came to understand that patience usually trumped brute force. On this occasion she spied an opportunity in an alley between two houses. The wooden gate was unlocked and she pushed it open to enter a brick-lined alley that ran between the houses and the cemetery. The fence was not well maintained; the panels warped and loose. She tested some of the panels and eventually came to a point where the fence creaked and then shifted and she had enough room to clamber through, pushing her bag in front of her.

The soft grass of the cemetery absorbed the sound of her scrambled entry. She bent down and pressed a palm flat against the earth, feeling wet soil against her skin. The first grave was just a few feet away: a plain headstone of white marble and writing etched into the facing. She could make out the name Hannah Marie O'Connor.

Abigail sat down on the ground beside the headstone, the moisture from the earth seeping up into her clothes.

"Hannah," she whispered. "Hannah, can you hear me?"

There was no reply. No sound except the gentle breeze rustling through the trees.

"Hannah," Abigail whispered a little louder. "Hannah, please."

Nothing.

Abigail didn't look around. At this time of the morning there wouldn't be anybody about and… well, if there was, they'd be up to something as equally…*unorthodox*, as Abigail herself.

"Please, Hannah. I need your help."

Nothing at all. This wasn't unusual. It normally took a while for the dead to wake, and the longer they'd been dead, the longer it took. Abigail had become patient over the long months and years since…

Abigail's bottom was getting wet from the damp grass. She shifted position, moving first her right leg and then her left underneath her, until she was kneeling. She rocked back, her buttocks resting on her heels.

"Hannah."

She strained her ears and thought she heard something. A whisper of a reply or maybe just the breeze through the leaves again.

From her coat pocket she removed a penlight, pointed it at the ground and turned it on to summon a small circle of bright white light.

"Okay, Hannah," Abigail said, her voice rising above a whisper. "Time to find out more about you."

She shone the beam on the headstone and read the detail: Sacred to the memory of Hannah Marie O'Connor. A beloved daughter and sister. Died 1937. Aged 14 years.

"Oh, I'm so sorry, Hannah," Abigail said softly. Maybe it was an omen. "Nobody should pass at such a young age. You deserved a much longer life, Hannah, than you were blessed with."

Abigail heard something. She couldn't make it out, not clearly, not definitely, but there was something.

"Hannah."

There it was again. She shivered. The cold did not come from the night air or even the wet ground, it rose up from inside her.

"Hannah." Abigail shivered again. "Is that you?"

No reply, but Abigail closed her eyes and touched the fingertips of her right hand to her forehead. "In the name of the Father..." she said and touched her sternum "...and of the Son..." She touched her left shoulder, "And of the Holy..." and finally touched her right shoulder, "...Spirit." Slowly Abigail lowered her head. She kissed the fingertips of her right hand and said, "Amen."

Another shiver and then she heard it.

"Go… away…"

A slow, tired voice, but a voice nonetheless. Hannah's voice.

Abigail opened her eyes, a hint of a smile on her lips. She switched off the penlight.

"I need your help," Abigail said.

"Leave… me… alone."

Abigail leaned forward until the palms of her hands touched the ground to the right of Hannah's headstone. She dug her toes into the earth, and lowered her body until she was almost kissing the wet grass. She turned her head to the left, faced Hannah's final resting place, and said, "I'm looking for my daughter."

"Leave… me… alone…" Hannah said from her grave. "Let… me… sleep…"

Abigail lay on the ground and felt the damp against her cheek. She took a deep breath and slowly counted to ten, then reached out with her left arm and laid it on the ground above Hannah.

"I'm sorry to wake you, Hannah. I really am. I promise I'll let you go back very soon, but I need your help."

"Go… away…"

Abigail closed her eyes and said The Lord's Prayer. After 'Amen,' she opened her eyes and stroked the ground above Hannah.

"Nobody should die so young. Nobody."

She waited for Hannah to tell her to go away, but there was nothing. Was Hannah beginning to listen to her or had she simply gone back to sleep?

"My daughter's name is Olivia. She went missing four years ago when she was ten. Now she'll be fourteen, just like you."

Nothing. No response from Hannah. The wind blew through Abigail's long, dark hair.

"Please help me find my daughter."

Abigail lay in the cold and the damp, listening for a reply from Hannah. At first there was nothing. Not even the sound of the wind in the trees.

"I… can't… help… you…"

"Your mother would have been distraught when you passed, but she had somewhere to go and remember you. She probably came here and laid flowers on your grave."

"She came every Sunday after Mass," Hannah said, her voice rising from the ground like gas. "Every Sunday. She brought me flowers; nothing fancy. We couldn't afford proper flowers, just a bunch of whatever she could find growing alongside the road. Sometimes she came with my dad or my sisters, sometimes she came alone, but every

Sunday she came to check that I was okay. She told me what happened in the family. I watched the years roll past. I heard when my dad died from black lung and when my brother Archie never came back from the war."

"Your mother looked after you. That's all I want for my daughter. For Olivia to know that she is loved."

"Everyone should be loved," Hannah said.

"I need Olivia to know that. They say that there is nowhere left to search for her body. Such a cruel thing, to hide a child from her mother's love. I know they want me to give up my search and get on with my life. It's what the counselors have said, it's what my vicar has said. But how can I, Hannah? How can a mother abandon her child?"

"She came every Sunday. And then one day she didn't. I thought she had forgotten me. Maybe she had a new family with a new child to care for, a daughter who could laugh and smile and help her with the chores around the house. I cried until they told me that she had joined us. No room here so they put her on the other side of the cemetery."

"But they told you," Abigail said.

"I hope you find your daughter, Miss."

"You can help me."

"I don't know anyone called Olivia. Not anyone new anyhows. Not a girl. There's a woman over by the north gate, she's a mean old witch of a thing who's no better now that she's dead than she was when she was alive."

"My Olivia was the sweetest girl. When she smiled, the sun shone brighter, and the birds in the trees sang louder."

"I don't know your Olivia."

"But maybe there is someone here who would? Someone who can hear The Beyond?"

The long silence burned. Abigail didn't know whether the dead girl had fallen back into the deep sleep from where she had been summoned, or if she was thinking, deciding. In the past she had experienced both: the spirits who cared and those who were so caught up in their own loss that they had no empathy left for a mother searching for her beloved daughter.

"My search has cost me my husband, my home, my job. Olivia is all I have left in this world. I need to know," Abigail said.

"I can't help you," Hannah said, and Abigail felt that sick, sinking feeling in her stomach as if she had lost Olivia all over again. The sensation brought back the memories of the day when she had whirled around in a crowded market in Deerham and realized her daughter was missing. Or the empty hours spent calling her phone, praying for Olivia to answer, only to hear the soulless pre-recorded message inviting her to leave a message.

"... but I know someone who might."

The spirit fell to silence once more.

"Please," Abigail begged. She was conscious she was on her knees at the side of a grave, begging with the spirit. "Please tell me."

"I only know of him, and what I know is enough to frighten me. But if anyone here knows of your daughter it is Old Joe. He can listen into The Beyond."

"Where is he?"

"Over in the Gibbet Field. At the back of the chapel, beyond the stone wall of the graveyard. He lies in unhallowed ground."

Abigail cast around her. The graveyard was a field of shadows and darkness. She thought she could see the outline of a building which could have been the chapel Hannah mentioned.

"Thank you," she said.

"Old Joe is always angry," Hannah said.

Abigail bobbed her head without thinking. "Yes. I know." She thought of Olivia, about the chance that one day she might see her daughter again, in this world or the next. "Old Joe," she said. "Gibbet Field."

She started to run down the crooked path between the graves, heading toward the hulking shadow of the chapel. Too late she remembered to call behind her to Hannah. "Thank you," she said for a second time, but she was sure the child in the grave had already gone back to sleep.

The chapel was difficult to see, but Abigail ran on, stumbling, nearly falling. The bag smashed against her side and she knew that in a few hours she would have a large bruise there, but it didn't matter. She kept going. Ahead of her the chapel became clearer, and then she was upon it, running alongside it, running past it, her breath coming in short, sharp gasps, her heart pounding inside her rib cage.

The path was wider here, straighter and flatter. She picked up the pace, ran faster, her chest began to ache.

She ran on, fighting the excitement rising inside her. Before, she'd found spirits who'd ignored her and others who had woken up to speak to her, but she'd never found a spirit like Old Joe. Never found a spirit who knew how to listen into The Beyond. The chatter beneath the graves was a cacophony of voices raised in anger and sadness. It was hard to listen beyond this noise to the rest of the world.

Panting for breath, Abigail thought she could make out the shape of the stone wall: a long dark shadow, running the entire length of the graveyard.

Her hopes lay with Old Joe. She stopped short of the wall to catch her breath. It wouldn't help to rush in without thinking. She pressed her hand against the stones and, from the far side, she thought she heard the wailing of lost souls desperate to find their way into the hallowed ground. It was the last tragedy, the pain of the unconsecrated ground. A lair of murderers and petty thieves and unmarried mothers. She had entered such a place in Aitune and had been shocked by the pain seeping up from the unmarked graves.

Abigail forced herself to rest until her breathing returned to normal. She was aware her mind was a maelstrom of questions she needed answers to: Is Olivia in The Beyond? Is she safe? In pain? What happened to her daughter? Who took her? Why?

She cried out to still the voices in her head, and the low wail drifted across the darkened cemetery. She knew a few of the spirits close to her were aware of her presence, and maybe on the other side of the wall Old Joe knew that someone was coming to him.

She took a deep, deep breath. The early morning air was chilled and tasted of rotting leaves and dank stones. She'd never before managed to find someone who could search into The Beyond. In four years of searching she'd begun to accept that it was a myth perpetuated between the spirits trapped beneath their gravestones.

Her hands trembled through a mixture of cold and nervousness. She had one chance with Old Joe; if she got this wrong, she wasn't sure how long it would take to find someone else who could help her. Another four years? Maybe longer. Maybe Old Joe was the source of all the rumors and secrets she'd ever heard about The Beyond over the years.

She walked the length of the wall but there was no gate between the cemetery and Gibbet Field. It must have been deliberate; when they had started burying bodies outside the cemetery they probably didn't want anyone from that side of the wall to be able to taint their loved ones.

From everything Abigail could determine, the only way to enter Gibbet Field was to go out of the cemetery and back along the main road. She didn't have time for that. In a few hours the sun would rise. The spirits would fall silent. She could return the following night but, after searching so long, she couldn't bear the idea of postponing even for a day. No, she would find her way to Old Joe. She would get answers to her questions.

The wall was old and the stones weathered. In places, material had fallen away and Abigail found a spot where she could use handholds and footholds to raise herself off the ground. She tested a route and once she was happy it would suffice, she threw her bag over the wall and began to climb.

The tips of her fingers scratched against the rough stone. The muscles in her thighs were unprepared for the exercise and tightened like piano strings, shooting pain the length of her legs. At the top of the wall she peered into the shadows of Gibbet Field.

The stench of anger and desperation flowed up from between the rotting leaves and gnarled roots of the dying oak trees that dotted the field. It curdled in her stomach and passed into her bloodstream like poison. There were nubs of stones barely large enough to scratch a name; the rotting cross-ties of wooden crosses; and depressions in the ground with no marker at all, where bodies had been dumped and forgotten.

The grass was overgrown, knotted into a mat of weeds and brown mulch that strangled everything.

"For Olivia," Abigail said to herself and prepared to jump, but her legs refused to do her bidding. She heard whispered voices; they knew she was coming. Their words tickled the back of her neck and crept down her spine.

Shadows gathered under the rotting branches of the oak trees, as if the dead were rising up from their graves to challenge her. It was just her imagination, she was sure of it. The dead could not hurt her. She thought back to poor Hannah languishing in her grave, trapped within the confines of the cheap pine box her parents had found for her when she had been buried.

And the occupants of Gibbet Field were worse off than Hannah; tormented souls left to rot. Forgotten. Angry at their abandonment. There would be no compassion or empathy, but maybe there would be understanding, and perhaps that would be enough.

She dropped down from the wall and into the leaf mulch that immediately covered her ankles with slimy, moist vegetation. It felt like wet hands rising up from the ground to seize her and she gasped at the contact.

Unlike her experience in the cemetery, she didn't need to kneel down to the earth to raise the dead. They roiled like black snakes, slipping over one another, spitting and biting and searching.

Abigail stood up straight although the muscles in her legs trembled at the effort. "I want to speak to Old Joe," she announced.

Immediately a half-dozen voices laid claim to the name.

"I am the one you search for."

"I am Joe."

"Who comes looking for me?"

Abigail batted away the voices as impostors. They were weak, tepid souls. They did not have the strength to venture beyond the confines of their grounds. They were too desperate, too needy. No, although she had never met Old Joe, she understood him. He would be strong. He would exist in rage.

"Do not toy with me. I want Old Joe–the one who can speak for my daughter."

She glared into the darkness, attempting to project a strength she did not own. Around her feet the leaves shifted. The dead stayed buried, that was a primary rule. Their spirits may rise but their bodies rot where they lie.

A wind rushed through Gibbet Field. It pushed aside the leaves, dredged up a canyon of bare, black earth that pointed like an arrow from between two tall trees directly to Abigail. She trembled as it approached, and would have run, except that, after four years of searching, she was clear that the only one who could help her was Old Joe. If she wanted Olivia, she would have to confront his spirit.

The other voices within Gibbet Field were silenced. Even though there was nothing that Abigail could see, the electricity in the air betrayed his presence.

"Old Joe?" she asked.

The voice surprised her. It came not from the ground beneath her feet. Not from the shallow recess of a lost grave. It came from the air. From the trees. From everywhere around.

It was old. Old as the Gibbet Field itself.

And a woman.

"Who are you?" Old Jo asked.

"I am Abigail Wright. I am searching for my daughter who was taken from me when..."

"Silence."

Abigail clamped her mouth shut, almost biting off her tongue in her hurry to comply with the order. She stared into the shadows of the darkness that lay within the burial ground. The only sign of Old Jo's presence was the metallic taste of the air and the furrow of earth, cleared of all debris.

"How dare you disturb me."

"I'm sorry. I am searching for–"

"Your daughter," Old Jo said. "I know."

"Can you tell me where she is?" Abigail asked.

"I have heard of the woman who asks for her daughter. Who disturbs the sleep of the Many. By what right do you wake those who are sleeping?"

"The right of a mother," Abigail said.

There was no reply and Abigail wondered who Old Jo was. Who she had been and how she had come to be buried in an unmarked grave in a field outside the cemetery wall.

She had many questions, but only one that mattered. "Is my daughter in The Beyond?"

"You have nothing to offer me," Old Jo said.

"Mother to mother?"

The spirit laughed; a fearsome, humorless sound, and Abigail was certain she had made a terrible mistake. She stood on the edge of the abyss staring down into eternity and all that Old Jo represented. She could feel her mind unraveling under the strain. So many years looking for Olivia and now that she had found the one person who might be able to help, the opportunity was slipping from her.

"I am no mother. I am no longer even a woman. I am Old Jo. I am the one they fear."

"But you can help me."

"Why? Even if I could help you, why should I?"

"Because you hurt too," Abigail said. It was true, she could hear it in the woman's words. A sorrow knitted into everything she said. She pressed on before Old Jo had a chance to deny it. "Olivia disappeared four years ago when we were in Deerham. They told me to give up. They told me to move on with my life. I need to know. If she is in The Beyond–"

"Then she is lost."

"Then she is at peace," Abigail said. She felt tears on her cheeks. She had thought she had finished crying for Olivia. She thought she had no more tears left to shed for her daughter.

"And if she is not in The Beyond?" Old Jo asked.

"Then she is still alive. Somewhere. And I will keep searching until I find her."

"I cannot help."

"You must."

The wind whipped into a rage. Dried leaves scurried into a pile and then disintegrated. The branches of the nearby trees groaned as they shifted. Dust and grit filled the air and Abigail closed her eyes against the frenzy but held her place in the face of the battering. If Old Jo was going to force her to leave, then it would take more than that.

"I will not help you," Old Jo's voice thundered around Gibbet Field.

Into the maelstrom, Abigail shouted her response, unsure if her words were strong enough to be heard. "You hurt too. I can help."

"You can help?" Old Jo laughed. A terrible, dismissive sound.

"To be alone is a terrible pain," Abigail said. She opened her eyes although the grit scratched at the surface of her corneas. Within the storm the path was clear. She stumbled forward, her hand cupped against her forehead to protect her, staring down at her feet as she trudged along the path. She sensed Old Jo all around her, the spirit trapped between wanting to banish her and wanting to summon her.

The path through the field led her between two oak trees into a corner in the shadow of the wall, within touching distance of the consecrated cemetery of the churchyard. There was no headstone, nothing to mark the grave except for the shallow indentation where the earth had slumped. Old Jo was somewhere below and despite whatever crime Old Jo might have committed, her punishment was complete.

Abigail brushed fresh tears from her cheeks. She didn't need Old Jo to tell her. Not now. Maybe she had always known. From the moment she had turned around in the market to discover that Olivia was no longer by her side. Maybe even then she had known that her daughter was lost, buried in a shallow grave such as this.

"Where?" Abigail asked through her tears. "Where is she?"

"She lies in a field," Old Jo said. "She lies alone and afraid in a field on the edge of a town. Within sight of a tumbledown farm and a steel bridge that crosses the canal."

Abigail knew immediately. She remembered the place; a walk they had taken on the first day of the holiday; she, Rob and Olivia. The three of them walking along the canal tow path and arguing with Olivia about getting her ears pierced. She felt something cold and sharp slice through her chest, like an ice blade cutting into her heart. "All alone," she said to herself.

In time, she turned and began to walk out of Gibbet Field, through the shadows and out into the dawn. As she reached the car she remembered the bag of tools, left at the foot of the wall. She hesitated, but realized she would not need them. She had an appointment in a field on the edge of Deerham from where it was possible to see the old canal bridge.

And once that was done and Olivia was buried, she would return to lay flowers on the grave of Old Jo.

THE FOREST OF WOODEN GHOSTS
By Seaton Kay-Smith

The Earth, once green, had turned a silver-grey; the forests had become cities, the trees, buildings and soil had turned into concrete.

It has since turned green once more, but it is not a green to envy.

I walked along the highway this morning, my work clothes still dusty from the previous day, boots caked with dried mud, my head down. There were few cars on the highway—and fewer trees. For that, I was thankful.

I do not want to see a tree if I don't have to, even the old ones; I see faces in them, though I know there are none.

As I walked—hands plunged deep into my pockets like ostriches burying their heads in the sand—I remembered how things *had* been; a world of concrete and glass, made fat with the living, each of us breathing in oxygen and exhaling our carbon dioxide breath into an atmosphere which had long since lost the ability to cope with it.

I thought of death.

When we died, back then, we had a choice: dust and charcoal, ash and fire, or a body slowly breaking down beneath the soil, filling the Earth with our mass, in a small wooden box, waiting for our skeleton to emerge and be crushed by the mounting pressure of the dirt. We turned to shadow, but those we left behind had no way to sit beneath us.

I was almost hit by a car this morning. It drove right past me, practically clipping me. I felt the rush of air and adrenaline it left in its wake. Before I could even register what was happening, the car had already driven away. Perhaps they recognized me, blamed me for the current situation? "I only dig the holes!" I wanted to shout, "I tend to the plots, I don't have a

say over what goes in them or what comes out of them!" But alas, as I said, the car was already gone.

Though there are days when I welcome death, my brush with it this morning shook me, and as I stood—small and alone on the side of the highway—I felt, in that moment, all the vitality I'd absorbed from the morning sun suddenly leave me, my body preemptively tired from the workday ahead. I could feel the dread mounting. Keeping my head down, I continued to walk; I wasn't too far from the cemetery at this point, it was only a few blocks away.

Storms had lashed our cities, increased our mounting tally of the dead, as had heat waves, fire and pandemics. The Earth buckled beneath our 16 billion feet, our elbows in our neighbor's ribs, shoulders in their faces. We lived on top of one another, each of us adding to the weight that threatened to drown the Earth beneath its own waves. We'd called it 'progress,' our destruction of the Earth, and had convinced ourselves that all progress was good—a blanket statement, which we wrapped ourselves in so tightly, it became near impossible to breathe. The air had turned thick, acrid, as good as smoke, the sky tinged yellow, tucked beneath our blanket of progress and smog. We didn't have enough trees *then*; we'd cut them all down to make houses… for the living *and* the dead, farming the dirt until all that was left was sand.

As the living expanded across the earth and the dead beneath it, cemeteries grew, and more land was cleared to accommodate them. We found ourselves at a crossroads, and, as we all know from the stories, it's at the crossroads where we're most likely to meet the devil.

After my near collision, I left the highway at the same exit as always and turned down Hewlitt Road toward the cemetery. A dog barked at me as I did, and I stumbled backwards at the sight of it, its fangs dripping with saliva, its nose contorted with aggression, eyes locked on me, filled with anger and fear. I don't blame it, of course. It's just a dog. I can't imagine it was used to seeing people out on the street, even though I passed it every day.

You wanted a dog. Another mouth to feed, I remember thinking. Another pair of lungs to turn what oxygen we had into poison.

It seems silly now, my resistance; we no longer have that problem.

Why did I deny you such a simple normal thing that would have made you happy? Perhaps we *should* have gotten a dog. It doesn't matter; it's too late now.

When I arrived at the end of Hewlitt Road, I turned left. Having taken that route so often, I knew the way, the distances, *and* all the obstacles, from the sight of the pavement alone. The first day I walked this way, I didn't. *That* was an anxious walk.

People ask me how I can come to the cemetery every day, how I can make my living among the dead. "Aren't you scared?" they ask. "Doesn't it give you the creeps?" "How can you do it?"

"A job's a job," I always say, which isn't true, and, while I know I don't believe it—they probably don't either—I never tell them more than that. The truth is, I don't really know *why* I come, not really, but, if I didn't, I know that I would likely spend my days at home, inside, surrounded by silence and emptiness, which scares me even more. The faces on the trees might haunt me, but I see your face everywhere, anyway, plus, I needed work and it had been an easy job to get. There was no competition—I didn't even need an interview. I'm sure there was concern over my mental health, questions about my sanity, *what kind of a man walks into* that *every day*?

People were still dying, people still had to be buried, more so now than ever.

We've since returned to the old ways, of course. It happened after you were gone. We abandoned our short experiment into sustainability, we had to; an Earth bloated with corpses, suffocating in the carbon dioxide breath of the living might have its issues, but it is the better option in the end.

"Our intentions had been pure," came the apology from the then CEO of Remembering the Future Proprietary Limited, now buried in a plot in the East Garden, the guilt and shame finally getting to him, "We wanted only to find a sustainable alternative to the storage of our biological past," he'd said, using too many words, sanitizing them, "We were only thinking of the future, our future. We didn't know things would play out like this."

They had needed strength, so they began with the seed of an oak tree.

They needed perseverance too, a way for the seed to survive amidst the toxic chemicals that would inevitably fill the bodies as they decomposed, and so added elements of the humble dandelion, that persistent fast growing weed that rises from the cracks in sidewalks, standing strong, defiantly existing where it should not.

They also wanted it to be beautiful, to reflect the beauty in death and remembrance, saying, "To ignore this, or fail to allow for it, would do an injustice to the memory of those we loved so dearly."

As if an oak tree isn't already *beautiful?* Nevertheless, they added the genomes from sunflowers to the mix, and created a new seed; strong, persistent, and beautiful.

But something was missing…

To finish it off, the cherry on top of their cake of death, they added the DNA of the dead. It was the final step in the process. "A token," they'd claimed, "an inactive compound, designed to merely imbue the tree that grows from them with their spirit, so that when you visit their resting place, lay down your flowers and whisper your words of grief and loss, you will know that it is *their* shade that you are sitting beneath."

Hungry for a new way, starving, even, we ate it up. What choice did we have? We couldn't go on how we were. The science seemed sound, the need was great, and the ads were convincing: green canopies, dappled sunlight, images of young children playing in what looked like a forest, stoic adults with just a hint of sadness, each with teeth as white as snow. Not young, not old; attractive, but not sexy. They left their flowers; they touched their palms to the bark, and they shared gentle looks of grief with one other, smiling profoundly at their child's playful ignorance of death; 'Remembering the Future' showed us there was a better way, it showed us there was a more sustainable way; it showed us there could be a future.

What it didn't show us, however—not on the television commercials or the cinema ads, on the bus stops or highway billboards—was the technician in blue rubber gloves cutting open the chest of your loved one and planting the spliced seed, enriched with the deceased's DNA, into the chest cavity, into a small incision made in the heart. Not *too* dissimilar to how one might score a lamb roast and insert a sprig of rosemary. No one *needed* to see that, but you were given the option to.

Do I regret taking them up on the offer, taking your cold hand in mine and watching, bleary eyed, as they did it? No. Am I haunted by it?

"You're not burying your loved one," claimed the ad, "You're planting them so that a tree of remembrance can grow."

"The bodies," they'd said—*our* bodies, our lifeless husks—"would no longer be a waste product, or a relic of humanity's past, but rather, a vital element of humanity's future." We would be nourishment for the trees we would become; trees that would filter the air, cool the Earth, promote rainfall, and create shade for visiting mourners. Cemeteries would no longer contain blocks of marble or stone cut from the Earth as though they were tumors—barren quiet places of sadness and loss—but a living, breathing, forest, beautiful and full of cherished memories.

The initiative was a huge success. Like the spores of dandelions, the ideas of 'Remembering the Future' spread rapidly, not just in communities of keen environmentalists and humanists, but everywhere, as we scrambled to find a solution to not only our increasingly treeless existence, but to a better more sustainable way to honor the dead. A more unique way to say goodbye, to find in our loss, new life. The dead would rise to meet their ecological destinies; their deaths would not be in vain. They would allow others to live, countless others, along the expansive march of time, "Your grandchildren, your grandchildren's grandchildren…" They would create shade they would never be able to sit in. In death, a final, truly selfless, act.

I remembered this, as I traversed the leafy green sidewalks lining the cemetery's outer perimeter, and thought, *if I wasn't so terrified, I would laugh* at the absurdity, the hubris, the incompetency, theirs, *and* ours. It would have been a hearty laugh, a deep bellow, a soul laugh. I would have laughed like I used to, all those years ago. Like I did with you. But alas, the street remained eerily quiet.

Even the wind refuses to blow down that one.

Everything seemed to go according to plan at first: graveyards filled up with seed-infused corpses in what became known as 'Person Planting Ceremonies,' graves were dug, the seeds placed into that narrow incision in the chest, and the body, wrapped in a "Biodegradable Flax Funeral

Shawl" was rolled into a shallow pit. Dirt was thrown on top, the earth patted down and left to settle.

Things looked good for a time, as we waited for the first corpse-trees to grow.

We no longer needed coffins—so we were cutting down fewer actual trees as well—no quarries were mined for stone, and no embalming chemicals were buried in the earth. They *wanted* the body to rot. They wanted the flesh to slowly disintegrate and leach moisture into the soil so that it might provide food for the seed in their hearts.

Before we were trees, we were fertilizer, and before that..?

I didn't work here, then, but I was curious.

You asked me where I was going. To my shame, I simply said, "Out." *Why was I so short with you? Why did I not bring you with me?* What a fool I was to *ever* leave your side.

I battled through the peak hour traffic, in my oxygen mask and blizzard glasses, and joined the throng of onlookers, all wearing the same, and I waited like a vulture, perched on a tombstone with hungry eyes, oblivious to the misery around me, watching as gravediggers planted their shovels into the firm soil and dug holes in front of grieving widows and children. I saw it all happen, I saw the first sprouts appear in the individual plots, I saw the new leaves as they pushed their way through dirt in search of sunshine, I watched as they grew thick with time, fed by the nutrients of their organic casings. Watered by the rain, they grew limbs and climbed higher, their naked bodies roughening with bark.

We opened champagne that first night; we've been drinking harder stuff since then.

Every day I come to the cemetery, I make my way down the deserted highway, then wander down the quiet tree-lined streets, I unlock the gates and step inside.

I don't know why I lock them; no one really comes here anyway. Ever since the corpse-trees started growing, no one dares.

Something startling happened about a year after the first planting ceremony, something unexpected; the sustainable initiative intended to save us from climate disaster, became altogether, monstrous. As the corpse-trees grew, they began to resemble the people buried beneath.

Little by little, as the seasons passed, graveyards became a forest of wooden ghosts, full of the faces of those interred there, faces, unforgotten but terribly missed; their lifeless eyes, lips stretched across the bark, the limbs of the trees, as though human, hanging by their side, covered in a rash of scattered leaves. It was as though a sculptor had whittled from wood the person lying below the soil.

While not perfect facsimiles, they possessed as much of a likeness to the deceased, as if drawn by an amateur, yet highly skilled artist; a rough sketch of a loved one, small sprouting twigs and minuscule branches coming from their bodies, their cheek bones carved sharply, the thin skeletal kindling at the end of each branch, the fingers of the dead.

When I arrive at the graveyard, I leave my bag in the office, hang up my jacket and get to work; there are more holes to dig than I can achieve in a day and more requests come through each morning. We have never *been* so busy, and we have never lacked the resources to meet the demand so intensely. Bodies pile high in morgues across the city, mostly of those who could no longer take it, some who had been driving when they locked eyes with a long-lost love taken root on the side of the road, others who had simply been out walking.

Business is booming, and the boom takes its toll on all of us.

Understaffed morticians do their best to ensure the freezers stay cold and the smells are kept at bay—the diseases too—ever conscious that the shorthanded electricity department might make an error or lack the resources to respond quickly enough to an outage, and all their hard work will have been for naught.

It is not a debilitating smell, but you *can* smell it, when you walk the streets, if you are the type to do so. You can smell the dead.

You asked me once why I lit so many candles. This was the reason.

Leaving the office this morning, I collected my shovel and walked through the thick canopies of trees, avoiding eye contact with their wooden pupils. Every so often, I had to look up and each time it filled me with dread, to feel both so alone, in this quiet copse of trees, and so utterly surrounded by the staring eyes of these arboreal antagonists.

Another surprising thing, particularly surprising given the plants 'Remembering the Future' had chosen, was that these trees—these corpse-trees—when winter came, bore fruit; a plum red protrusion, bulbous and filled with sweet fibrous flesh, dripping fragrant purple juice when ruptured—the blood of the tree, sticky and warm. It attracted ants and *other* things.

There are those among us, who delight in the taste of these corpse-fruits, harvesting the produce each season to gorge on its flesh. Initially, it had simply been frowned upon; it wasn't long, however, until the practice became outlawed entirely, as those who consumed the fruit, found themselves plagued with diseases not unlike mad cow disease, losing their senses and acting irrationally. They still do it, these demons. They are not afraid of these wooden ghosts; they see no horror in those faded faces. They simply hunger for the blood red juice, with their insatiable appetites, resorting to violence when they are denied it. As I said, they lose their rationality. Some, whom I can sympathize with a little more, eat only the fruit borne from their loved ones. To them, it is a way to remember and feel closer to them. I can think of nothing worse.

Perhaps, most disturbing of all, however, was the way these trees managed to proliferate. Something they did with startling fervor, given perhaps the strong DNA of the weedy daffodil that made up part of their genomic sequence.

How had they not foreseen this? How could they not see it coming? It boggles the mind, but here we are.

It happened how you might expect it would, how any botanist might have suspected, one would think: wind strips the trees of their seeds, animals ingest fruit and deposit the seeds elsewhere, and new trees, born from death, once removed, begin to grow even outside the cemetery's walls.

In spring, the corpse-trees flower, and bees busily fly from wretched face to wretched face, pollinating these dendritic devils, often finding their genetic material for reproduction in the neighboring trees.

This led, as one might expect, to the creation of sapling offspring.

In many cases, where the corpses of lovers were buried side by side, in familial plots, resting together for eternity, this new tree bore a likeness to their children, in as much as an additional sibling. Occasionally, however, the pairing produced a tree that resembled, almost exactly, the still grieving child of the deceased parents.

Since working here, I have seen first-hand, the immemorial horror etched on the faces of devoted children, as they came face-to-face with their own face, on their own corpse-tree; glimpsing their mortal future, they find themselves among the plane of the dead, covered in bark, pulling nutrients from the soil before their time. I have seen them staring into their own wooden eyes, looking into them as though they are one and the same, not so much a tree grown from the communion of their dead parents, but a wooden prison they had somehow found themselves trapped in, standing for hours, paralyzed by this ghastly premonition, as the day gradually passed away and the trees trunk twisted slowly, so that it was always facing the sun—a quirk, perhaps, of the sunflower's DNA, that was spliced into their genetic sequence. Their dry timber eyes would gaze eastward as the sun rose, then following its arc across the sky throughout the day, they would watch it set in the west before finding a resting place for the evening, looking straight ahead into the deep darkness before them.

It didn't take long for the trees of the dead to begin forming entire forests. With the fervor of a daffodil, they found their way into built up areas. They proliferated in parks, in people's backyards, and along certain stretches of the motorway.

I remember reading a newspaper article about a young woman who had opened the blinds in her kitchen one morning after months of being a shut-in, only to find a corpse-tree standing right in front of her window, its dendritic fingers scraping at the glass, eyes staring coldly at her, lifeless, wooden. She didn't dare cut it down or remove it, recognizing the face, she feared the soul of her late uncle's neighbor might be residing within it, for, little did she know, her late uncle's neighbor was alive and well, and terrified of a different tree in a different neighborhood.

People began to spend more time indoors, their curtains drawn, doors locked. Mortality rates increased and life expectancy flat-lined. They locked themselves away from the sun and the air and the fear, knowing full well the existential dread they could expect to experience should they walk through a tree-lined street, where cold dark eyes seemingly watched your every step, staring silently at you as you passed their way, eyes wide in judgment, mouths, half open, parted in longing, resentful of the fact that you live while they do not.

Birth rates plummeted and the burden on the Earth seemed to lessen. Pollution decreased and the natural habitat flourished; notes were written, neighbors reported odd smells. Much of this happened after you were gone, that's when things really started to escalate. You must have been one of the last ones to be laid to rest in a 'Person Planting Ceremony.' We just bury the dead now, six feet deep in a wooden casket; no seeds, no incisions. A return to the old ways, unsustainable, but with fewer surprises.

Was it a failure?

In an odd kind of way, the trees achieved the goal they were created for, they did what they were supposed to do: they were a sustainable way to remember the dead. They stretched their branches skywards and absorbed the carbon dioxide in the air, turning it into oxygen for us to breathe. They brought balance back to our ecosystem and with that balance, more moderate weather patterns. The temperature of the Earth cooled, and the rising sea relented. Like sentinels, ever present, they stood on every patch of land they could anchor themselves to and made it impossible for us to forget that they were there. With their gaunt oak faces and lithe wooden fingers, it was impossible *not* to remember the dead.

I *could* remain at home, curtains drawn, doors locked, eagerly awaiting the day I would have the courage to join you, but instead, I come here, to dig holes and bury the dead in the cool shade of those that have come before me. I clear away the filth that amasses on the leaf-littered cemetery floor and chase off those who would come here, not to mourn, but to feast on the fruit of the dead, and I visit you. I trim your branches and water your roots, and I sit with you as you watch the sun make its long journey across the sky. I think about death, and I remember the life we had, the way we used to laugh, your confusion about the candles and your well-structured arguments for why we needed a dog, and I talk to you about what happened, and what is happening, and try to make sense of it; you are a good listener.

I'm proud of you. Your tree has grown so much in such a short period of time. It is chest height now, and already it is taller than you ever were.

A SHORT RIDE TO BOOT HILL
By Stone Wallace

Visible under the faint glow of a full moon partially shadowed by scudding, ghost-like clouds the stranger appeared, a silhouette riding his mount slowly at a steady, even pace across the southwest ridge that overlooked the sleepy, uncharted town of Dry Run.

The two old codgers taking their nightly ease on board-walk benches saw him coming. They watched for a long while, a lone shadowy figure on horseback, riding against the desert wind, his duster fanning out behind him like a phantom's cloak. They instinctively knew the rider would be heading into town, and while neither man spoke his thought to the other, each distinctly detected the arrival of an ominous presence, one whose approach carried with it a specific purpose.

In nervous anticipation, the two old-timers stood up from their porch chairs and stepped briskly into the saloon before the figure on horseback entered the town limits.

"Stranger's a-comin'," one of the men announced to those seated inside.

The town was so off the beaten path that it rarely was visited during the daytime. It was particularly uncommon for someone to be riding in at such a late hour, the hands of the ticking wall clock opposite the back bar reading 10:37. The announcement of an unexpected visitor riding into their dusty community immediately set a tone of suspicion among the few patrons occupying tables in the aptly-named Dry Run Saloon. The main grouping was at a center table where those seated were playing low-stakes poker. A couple other gruff citizens were off by their lonesome at far corner tables, content to concentrate on their whiskey. The assemblage was strictly male.

All went quiet for several minutes... until the slow, distant clip-clopping of hooves against the dry mud of the main street became increasingly more pronounced.

Then, a faint dismount... followed by the sound of slow, steady footsteps against the planks of the boardwalk.

To those patrons sitting at tables in the Dry Run Saloon, there was no mistaking that the man who entered the establishment was someone possessing a distinct presence. A man not to be dealt with lightly. Their initial perception was that, whoever he was, he was set and ready for a confrontation should the need arise. He carried with him an air of palpable menace. His physical size was imposing; his attitude intimidating. The stranger was tall, broad-shouldered and barrel-chested. His face was raw and red, weathered from long hours in the hot sun, but his features held an expression that was fierce and solid. His eyes were dark and almost unnaturally narrow. He'd fairly burst through the batwings of the town's sole drinking establishment, further making his entrance known by thrusting his big body forward aggressively, like a bull preparing to charge, walking with deliberate footfalls across the floor. The silence inside the saloon now grew heavy. Barely a breath was heard. While everyone present took note of this stranger's apparent determination, there was a subtle yet definite warning emanating from his person that it would be best for no one to acknowledge him directly. Eyes warily turned away as the stranger stepped up to the bar, set a boot on the foot rail and assumed a sturdy stance.

He spoke directly to the barkeep.

"I hear Jimmy McQuade's been in town," he said in a thick voice.

The barkeep knitted his brow, curiously. And he didn't respond. He turned his attention to wiping out a beer mug.

"You sayin' you don't know who Jimmy McQuade is?" the stranger said in a curious fashion.

The barkeep was a man not easily bullied.

"I never said nothin', mister. I just serve drinks."

He twisted his huge head and looked directly at the stranger and reacted with a faint start when he saw a cold ferocity reflected in the man's eyes. Of a sudden, the barkeep thought it best to adjust his attitude. He instantly understood that this man would demand an answer and that he'd likely do well to oblige him. At the same time, he shifted his eyes away from the stranger's steady gaze.

He said, "I know Jimmy McQuade; least I know 'bout him."

The stranger gave his head a slow nod. "That's good," he said with an enigmatic smile. "Then why don't yuh tell me what you know 'bout him?"

The barkeep spoke with a strained calm. "Really can't tell yuh much, mister. That's a fact."

"Yuh shoulda spoke that in the first place instead of makin' me scare it out of you."

"I wasn't a-scared," the barkeep declared.

"Sure you wasn't," the stranger said with the twist of a smile. "I don't figger anyone in this fine establishment is the scared type."

The barkeep eyed the stranger speculatively. "Do I know you?" he asked.

"You might," the stranger replied easily. "You just might."

"You ain't from around these parts, I take it."

"Not lately."

"So you..."

"I'll leave it to you to figger out."

The barkeep scrunched his face and shook his head. "I know I seen you someplace. 'Least you look awfully familiar."

"Been told that before," the stranger said.

"Well, can I get you a drink?" the barkeep asked, hands fidgeting on the worn surface of the counter.

"I'm thinkin' 'bout it."

"That's what I'm askin'. It's what I do here, serve–"

The stranger cut him off abruptly. "I already heard yuh." He let his eyes wander around the saloon. "Hear yuh also serve a mighty fine stew," he said casually.

The barkeep looked uncomfortable. "We don't... well, the kitchen's closed. The cook went home. He only works 'til–"

The stranger cut him off swiftly. "Suppertime?"

The barkeep nodded. "After supper's been served."

"Heard you often serve a late meal," the stranger commented.

"Only on occasion," the barkeep said.

The patrons remained silent, no one uttering a sound. The stranger suddenly slammed his gloved hands onto the bar and spun around to eye the customers, those men pretending to be minding their own business.

He focused on each man individually, as if studying them.

Then, in a raised, demanding voice: "Didn't none of yuh hear me? I said, Jimmy McQuade! Who here can tell me 'bout him?"

It was hard for anyone to detect whether the stranger was drunk or just stubbornly determined to get an answer. His surly, aggressive attitude suggested either–or both.

The barkeep coughed nervously and started to speak. "I–told you, mister–"

Without turning to look at the man, the stranger cut him off. "You ain't told me nothin'. Only that you serve drinks and it's too late to have a plate of your special stew."

"Don't know what yuh mean by 'special'."

"I heard tell," the stranger replied casually.

The barkeep spoke over a lump in his throat. "We're a peaceful town. We don't look for no trouble."

The stranger slowly pivoted his head to stare back at the barkeep. But there was another long silence before he said: "Not always so peaceful."

"Meanin'?"

"Meanin' what happened to Jimmy McQuade... and heard some rumors 'bout other folks who ride into Dry Run. Those who seem to... not be seen a'gin."

Beads of perspiration were now glistening on the barkeep's forehead though it was a cool night.

"Might wanta wipe off that sweat," the stranger suggested.

The other occupants sat or stood silent and motionless, remaining curious as to where this conversation was heading.

Eventually one of the card players spoke up. "You seem to want to know somethin', but you ain't tellin' *us* much."

"Shouldn't need to," the stranger replied smoothly, his back facing to where the remark was spoken.

The barkeep swallowed again. "Listen, let me get you a drink–on the house–and maybe that'll settle your spurs."

The stranger once again regarded the barkeep with an icy, slit-eyed stare–then, in the next instant, he swiftly withdrew his Colt revolver from its holster and swung around to the patrons, some of whom were beginning to reflexively lift themselves from their chairs. The ones standing took a few uneasy steps backward.

"Settle back, all of yuh," the stranger commanded. He clicked back the hammer of his revolver for emphasis.

The barkeep tried to placate him. "Okay, mister, no need for that. As I told yuh, we're peaceful people."

After a few tense moments, the stranger said coolly, "A man rode into this town 'bout two weeks ago. I wanta know what happened to that man. 'Cause I know for a fact he never rode outta here."

The ensuing silence draped over the saloon like a dark, malevolent shadow.

"Now there can't be a man here who can't tell me what I wanta know," he finished.

The barkeep spoke quickly. "Why's it so important to you, mister?"

"That's my business, saloon man," the stranger said curtly.

"If'n we could tell yuh more, we would," the barkeep said with a slight lift of his shoulder. "You come in here threatening us, demanding answers we can't give you 'cause you ain't providin' the questions."

The stranger squinted. "And by you sayin' that... it suggests to me you know more than what you're lettin' on."

"I really ain't tellin' you anything."

"Well, maybe so," the stranger said in a drawl. "But it ain't always just words I'm payin' attention to."

"I ain't brave, mister," the barkeep muttered. "But if'n you'd just speak straight without waving around that side iron of yours. This fella someone you got a specific grudge a'gin?"

The stranger merely smiled. Then: "Now why would yuh think that?"

The barkeep didn't answer.

"To my thinkin' I ain't said a word 'bout me holdin' no hard feelings a'gin him," the stranger said.

"I can tell yuh this much," the barkeep finally said. "Your friend, McQuade, or whoever he was to you... yeah, he rode into town, and yeah, he didn't leave here–alive. He was shot dead outside on the street. He asked for it, and he got it."

Several men in the saloon wore uncomfortable expressions, indicating that maybe the barkeep had spoken out of place.

"That's all you can tell me?" the stranger said in a flat voice. "That he was shot dead."

"Ain't no more to tell. Ask anyone here. We're a small town. Everyone knows what happens in Dry Run."

"Everyone knows everyone else's business, you're sayin'?"

"Can't keep much hidden in a town this size."

"Yeah, reckon not," was all the stranger said.

Silence.

After a while, the stranger slid the revolver back into its holster. He tipped the brim of his wide Stetson and spoke in a subdued tone. "What happened to the body?"

"What do you mean?"

The stranger smiled queerly. "Ain't a difficult question. Was Jimmy buried... or did somethin' else happen to it?"

The barkeep's eyes shifted past the stranger to his customers. "Why would you be sayin' somethin' like that?" he asked delicately. His tone got a little aggressive. "What're you aimin' at?"

Instead of providing an answer, the stranger said, "Y'know, I'll take that drink now."

The barkeep looked mildly relieved. He responded with a nod.

"Make it whiskey."

The barkeep grabbed a bottle of rye whiskey from the back bar and placed a shot glass on the countertop. In an effort to be convivial and keep the stranger's mood agreeable, he said, "On the house."

The stranger tipped the bottle and poured himself two shots that he tossed back quickly.

"Might want a beer to go with that," the barkeep suggested.

The stranger jerked his head in a nod.

As the barkeep poured the tap beer into a mug, he stated in a conciliatory tone, "We don't ask for trouble and we rarely get any. McQuade came through here and earned a bullet for his behavior. Again, that's all I can tell yuh."

"Yeah, Jimmy was always a wild one," the stranger said, speaking more to himself and sounding amused. Then his attitude shifted: "It's what yuh tell me, but it ain't all."

"Just drink your beer, mister," the barkeep advised.

The stranger raised his mug in a mock salute. "'Cause maybe it didn't quite happen that way."

The barkeep appeared both cautious and agitated, both moods clearly detected by the stranger. He knew something. The stranger could not be fooled.

"Plenty of guts," the stranger muttered through his teeth–and then, oddly, he tossed a wink to the barkeep.

The barkeep did not like what those words and that gesture insinuated. But he wasn't going to put up with this any longer. He reached under the counter and hefted a double-barrel shotgun, which he placed on the counter, close to where he could reach for it, if necessary. He didn't have to explain further.

The stranger just gave a slow nod.

"Have another drink on the house and you can ride out right after," the barkeep told him, emboldened now that he had the advantage.

The stranger accepted the drink by lifting a finger, which he again swallowed swiftly.

He wiped the back of his hand across his moist lips. "I'll be leavin' once you tell me where Jimmy McQuade is at. I'm trustin' he got a proper burial."

"That what you're interested in, his grave?"

"Maybe."

The bartender expelled an exasperated breath. "He's where all his type are laid out. Out on Boot Hill."

"*His* type?" the stranger inquired.

"Don't mean no offense. Talkin' 'bout strangers mostly. You just got me addled."

"Reckon different arrangements for the folks here," the stranger said, posing his words as a statement rather than a question.

"Arrangements?"

"For buryin'."

The barkeep gave a shrug. "We–take care of our own." He added almost as an afterthought: "We are a close community."

"Been around for a bit," the stranger remarked, again his words not intended as a question.

"Fairly."

The next words the stranger spoke, though delivered matter-of-factly, had a chilling edge.

"Good thing yuh told me... 'bout where McQuade's at."

"And why's that, stranger?"

"'Cause chances are, you'll have another visit tonight."

"You plan on ridin' back here?" the barkeep asked.

The stranger offered an enigmatic smile. "Not me. But I reckon Jimmy McQuade will be droppin' by. Unfinished business, yuh know."

The barkeep swallowed heavily. The other saloon customers were completely silent. The stranger again looked at each of them, then regarded the men as a whole.

"You might say Jimmy has a purpose for comin' back."

"You sayin' he wasn't killed fairly!" one of the men shouted.

"Likely the way Jimmy sees it," the stranger smiled.

"You tryin' to throw us some ghost story?" the barkeep asked, in an attempt to maintain a semblance of authority.

"No. Ain't hardly a ghost. 'Fact, it's a mite different when dealin' with a dead man who just might not cotton to bein' dead."

The barkeep frowned and he glanced about at the others in the saloon. "Now you ain't talkin' sense," he said quickly. "Maybe you've had enough–" He reached for the bottle of whiskey on the counter but the stranger clasped a gloved hand around the bottle and drew it toward him.

He grimaced, and then his expression relaxed. "You're right," he said as he pushed the bottle back toward the barkeep. "You'll be needin' this more 'n me tonight."

The barkeep lifted his hands, palms outward in a conciliatory gesture, and he stepped back, eyes gliding down toward the shotgun, easy within his reach. The stranger watched the shifting of his eyes and smirked.

"Wouldn't advise to be wastin' a bullet on me," he said. "Not that your shotgun will do yuh much good. You can't kill a dead man twice." His expression tightened. "I told you what to be expectin' tonight."

"Who was this Jimmy McQuade?" someone asked. "Was he kin?"

"Just let's say more'n kin."

Quiet prevailed.

The stranger spoke directly. "You think Jimmy McQuade is dead. But lemme tell yuh, he ain't dead, not the way you think, and you ain't killed him the way you think. You buried him, sure, but the grave won't hardly hold him." A brief silence, then: "Not tonight."

Once more, the atmosphere in the saloon was enveloped in a shroud of dread.

"You all know what I'm talkin' 'bout," the stranger went on. "This ain't no ghost. A walking dead man ain't a mere shadow on the wall."

One of the patrons said, "You sayin' to us that a dead man, one that we knowed is dead... ain't really dead?"

It was an absurd assertion that no rational person would take seriously–only there was a disturbing aspect: there was no hint or suggestion of humor in what the stranger was saying. He spoke earnestly–with conviction.

Another of the men said, bravely trying to conceal his smirk: "And might you be suggestin' that he–McQuade–will be comin' back here... to Dry Run? To settle some unfinished business?"

"He's got a score to settle," the stranger said again. "And I promise yuh all: Jimmy McQuade ain't the kind of man to let a debt go unsettled. Not when he was alive… and not when you think yuh killed him."

The barkeep instinctively closed both hands over the shotgun.

"So now I'm wonderin', I want a good man to ride with me," the stranger suddenly announced.

"A good man for *what*?"

"My business," the stranger said.

No one was quick to volunteer.

The wind was picking up outside, howling and kicking up dust that blew gray clouds in the street. Then a sudden gust swung open the batwings, giving the impression that something unseen and unnatural was making its presence known.

The ramblings of the stranger, coupled with the aggressive weather, looked to put everyone on edge.

Only the stranger ignored it. He said, "For what it's worth, I'll give yuh fair warning. If he is buried up on Boot Hill like yuh say, he won't be for long."

One of the men, agitated, shouted out to the barkeep: "You either better get this fella to leave or we'll kick his ass outta here."

"You talk brave," the stranger said. "Care to back it up by comin' with me?"

The man's bravado suddenly, if not unexpectedly, vanished. He slid back into his chair, wordlessly.

The barkeep now lifted the shotgun and started to position the barrel toward the stranger. "Listen friend, this is gettin' beyond reasonable."

"I hear some brave talk," the stranger said. "Reckon I'd like to see one of you back up your words."

"You still ain't offerin' a reason."

"Let's say I might need someone with me to prove that the fella you say is buried out in that graveyard is still there."

"And if he ain't?" the barkeep asked warily.

"Then God help all of you." There was no levity in the stranger's words.

"So how you plannin' to prove that he is?" one of the patrons asked. "You gonna dig him up?"

The barkeep spoke up briskly. "You can't be disrespecting the grave of a dead man, no matter who he is."

"No disrespect if he ain't in that hole," the stranger remarked.

"And that's really what yuh figger?"

The stranger paused before he answered straightforward. "That's what I *know*."

Another customer spoke up. "Let Lenny go with the man. We know it's all just crazy talk. Let's get this malarkey over and done with."

The man named Lenny showed his reluctance. He glanced about the saloon for support. No one sided with his silent objection. Instead, it appeared that each wanted an end to this nonsense and the only way that would happen was to have someone ride along with the stranger to Boot Hill and check out that grave.

Lenny finally said in a tremulous voice: "I–ain't no good for somethin' like that."

"No, I can tell you ain't." The stranger then cast a critical eye among the small gathering. "Anyone else want to volunteer?"

Then, faintly: "I'll come along."

A fellow stood up from his place at the table where shortly before he'd been playing poker. At full height he was about as tall as the stranger, but he had a slimmer, weaker build. He was youthful-looking, early to mid-twenties, clean-cut, wore wire-rimmed spectacles and was particularly well-dressed for this part of the country. The stranger quickly deduced that he was someone not connected with Dry Run; likely a passerby, born and bred in the city. Certainly no dusty cowboy.

"You been mighty quiet," the stranger said to him.

"Just listening," the young man returned.

"Well, maybe you lucked out, fella. The other weasel showed no backbone and just lost himself two hundred dollars in hard cash."

The young man was instantly impressed. "Two hundred dollars... just for riding with you?"

"That's what I'm offerin'."

"You mind if I see it. The money?" the young man asked timidly.

The stranger pulled out his billfold and opened it sufficiently for the young man to glance inside the leather.

The young man explained, "Just rode in earlier this evening. It was a long ride so I thought just a quick stopover to satisfy my thirst. See, I'm planning to purchase a piece of land just north for me and my wife to be settling. We both decided on rural life. So, yes sir, I sure could use the money. And I was about to take my leave anyway."

"Fella," the stranger said, "you mighta lucked out twice."

"Name's Robert Brandish, but everybody calls me Bob." And he walked over to the stranger and extended his hand.

The stranger gave a slight nod of his head but ignored the handshake.

"And you are?" Brandish asked, not showing offence at the slight.

"No need for introductions," the stranger said curtly.

The barkeep offered a final, solemn word directed at the stranger. "Lucky for you we ain't got no law in this town. A sheriff wouldn't take too kindly to havin' someone diggin' up our departed: coyotes or otherwise."

"Heard there used to be a sheriff," the stranger said.

"Just offerin' friendly advice," the barkeep said.

The stranger spoke pointedly. "In any case, barkeep, no lawman's bound to take issue when he discovers the truth about McQuade."

The barkeep spoke boldly. "Ain't afraid of ghosts... or a dead man."

The stranger merely responded with a vague smile. Then, with a sweeping gesture of his hand, he indicated for Bob Brandish to follow outside. Brandish downed the last of his beer and left the saloon.

Attitudes inside the saloon swiftly changed. The displayed attitude of naivety of the customers turned serious, features hardened even as a dark humor was exhibited. A heavyset man contentedly patted his ample belly. "Got me a little worried talkin' 'bout the sheriff," he guffawed. He stifled a belch. "Tough old bird, but he made a mighty fine feast."

"Yeah, well, I don't trust that fella," another said. "He was aimin' at somethin'... and seemed to know a little too much 'bout our goin's on."

"Not a concern," the barkeep said, his thick, flabby features shifting from a presumed joviality into a malevolent mask. "We did well. Now that we understand why he's come here with his outrageous claim, we can make our preparations. He'll ride back after the midnight hour... and we'll enjoy him... as we always do."

The stranger and Bob Brandish stepped outside into the gusty night. Brandish tightened his overcoat against the cold and blasts of dusty wind.

"I think we both picked a fine night to ride into town," he said with a shiver.

"Mebbe so," the stranger said lowly as he glanced upward to a sky that was glittering with distant stars. "But for me, it had to be tonight."

"Why's that? For that reason you stated inside?"

"Leave it be," the stranger advised him. "Where's your mount?"

Brandish pointed to a weathered old horse tethered to the hitching post outside the saloon.

"Don't look too sturdy," the stranger remarked.

"Got me this far," Brandish replied. "And for the two hundred you're offering, I can drive her on as long as I need to."

The two men mounted their horses, Brandish waiting until the stranger was sturdy on his saddle. The stranger rode away first. Brandish held back for a bit. He turned to look into the saloon and noticed how everyone had gathered to watch, some congregating within the batwing entrance, a few stepping outside. There was something about the expressions each was wearing that troubled him.

Brandish caught up to the stranger. He shifted his position on the saddle so that he was directly facing the man riding alongside him. "Just got me a feeling they're a strange bunch."

"Stranger than you think."

"Can't say I feel much different about you," Brandish admitted. "That was some story you were spinning in there."

"I don't spin yarns," the stranger said flatly.

Brandish frowned. "Well, I'll confess the money is my main motivation. But I'm also curious about this claim or yours."

"You sure talk fancy," the stranger grumbled. "Educated, huh?"

"Had some schooling, yes."

"College man?"

Brandish gave a self-conscious lift of his shoulder.

"Take that for a yes. That's a rarity 'round these parts. Yet you aim on bein' a farmer?"

Brandish didn't answer. He had a frustrated look pasted on his features suggesting his thoughts were elsewhere. He then said, "But as I think about it, I'm not completely sure you might have something else in mind and..." At this the young man emphasized his statement by withdrawing his revolver, which he aimed directly at the stranger. "Well, I think you can understand my point."

The stranger levelled his eyes on the gun held firmly in Brandish's hand. He wore an amused expression. "You thinkin' of robbin' me? Skeedaddle with that two hundred?"

"Just don't wanta be cheated," Brandish said. "Can't afford to be."

"You saw the money?"

"Not in my pocket yet."

The stranger said in an easy, confident tone, "If it'll make yuh feel more at ease, I'll ride ahead. You keep a distance behind with that gun aimed straight at my back. Gives yuh more than a chance if'n you figger I'm up to somethin'. Fair enough?"

"I suppose," Brandish said weakly.

"You'll get your money," the stranger assured him.

Brandish hesitated for a moment before he re-holstered his revolver. He then took a breath and said, "Maybe I got a little suspicious because I can see you're not exactly equipped for... what you say you might be intending to do. I don't see any shovel or any digging tool." He tried to joke: "You plan to use your bare hands?"

The stranger responded with an enigmatic smile. "'Less'un I miss my guess, McQuade's already clawed his way out. And he's waitin'."

The sarcastic smile on Brandish's face vanished.

"Likely there'll be somethin' I can use at the cemetery," the stranger said, adding: "If necessary."

Brandish eyed him warily.

The stranger noted his expression. "I reckon you don't disbelieve me as much you think you do."

"As I told you, I'm mostly interested in the money you've offered."

The night was unusually, if not unnaturally, quiet. The heavy blasts of wind had ceased, settling into a gentle breeze and the only sounds on the moonlit trail were a faint rustling of leaves on the trees that bordered the narrow stretch of trail and the steady and rhythmic clip-clopping of their horses' hooves on the pathway.

Neither man spoke for a while. Bob Brandish would not outwardly admit it, but with each step their horses progressed, he was feeling a mite unsettled. He formed the conclusion that despite the stranger's outrageous claim, he didn't seem an irrational sort. Someone to make up this kind of wild story. He had a determination that was hard to dispute. But it still didn't add up to Brandish. It seemed a known fact that this McQuade fellow was dead; those sitting at the saloon had confirmed it. For whatever offence he had committed, he was shot and killed by someone in Dry Run, his corpse carted off to Boot Hill for burial. Why was this stranger so insistent that McQuade did not die... or if he was indeed dead, that somehow... *somehow* the grave could not hold him?

No matter how Brandish churned this over in his brain, there simply was no way he could accept such an outlandish possibility.

Finally, he broke the silence and asked outright: "Why are you so stubborn sure McQuade isn't dead?"

The stranger didn't answer straight away.

"You owe me that much," Brandish said with impatience. "'Specially since I'll find out soon enough."

"I knowed the man," the stranger answered simply.

"That doesn't tell me anything," Brandish retorted.

The stranger released a long sigh. "Fellas like you look at death in a might different way than some others do. People who've had to live with it. Seen things that... well..." His words trailed off.

"What do you mean?" Brandish queried.

"You're just a kid. You ain't lived. Raised in comfort, I take it. Sorta dandified, meanin' no disrespect. This ride might be a learnin' experience for yuh. If'n you prove yourself up to seein' it through. Reckon I still ain't convinced of that."

"I'll see it through," Brandish said sturdily. "We have an agreement?"

"That what you think we have? An agreement?"

"You offered me two hundred dollars to be a witness... to something I'm still not even sure of."

"That's correct. Don't expect nothin' more of you. But can't give you no guarantee of what you might be a witness to. 'Fact, hopin' you might have some backbone. Some strong and sturdy blood pumpin' in your veins."

"Well, whatever, I'm not a believer in ghosts," Brandish said, speaking firmly, keeping his courage intact.

"Just so there's no misunderstanding, he ain't no ghost or no spirit." The stranger added, "'Fact, there's every chance we might meet him on the road 'fore we even reach the graveyard."

Brandish squinted his eyes and focused on the trail ahead of him. He barely suppressed a shudder that was not attributable to the chill of the night air. The path was dimly lit by the open moon and cluster of overhead stars. If someone were to come down that path he... or "it" would appear only as a silhouette.

Even for an educated, practical man like Bob Brandish, that was a frightening prospect. From that moment onward, he intended to keep mindful and alert for anything out of the ordinary that might show itself in the distance.

Brandish felt a little foolish for surrendering to such irrational apprehension but he suddenly felt the need for some continued conversation.

"What can you tell me about McQuade?" he asked the stranger, trying to speak casually.

"What d'ya feel you need to know?"

"Naturally, I don't know anything about him. Did he have a reputation?"

"Lived mostly outside the law," the stranger offered quietly.

"Like The Kid or Jesse James?"

The stranger chuckled to himself. It was clear his companion's knowledge of the West and its people exceeded no farther than dime store novels.

"Was he a murderer?" Brandish probed deeper.

"Meanin' did he kill people?"

"Yeah."

"Some."

"Was it... in self-defense?"

The stranger sighed.

"Did he kill them in cold blood?" Brandish asked, his tone more intense.

"Both."

Brandish sounded annoyed. "You're not telling me much."

"Just keep patient. Until it's necessary, best you not concern yourself with questions of that sort."

Brandish pushed out a breath and rested his hands on the pommel. "All right. Suppose I'll just content myself with the two hundred dollars."

"For now, that's all you need to be thinkin' about."

Boot Hill was just over a slight ridge. They were almost there and Brandish felt a relief–yet also a muted uncertainty. They'd come across nothing on the trail–dead or alive–and he fully expected not to encounter anything out of the ordinary once they reached the cemetery. But he remained adamant that if the grave was going to be dug open, he wanted no part in that morbid task. He wasn't going to disturb a man's final resting place for two hundred or even five hundred dollars.

They rode up the ridge and there was another slight grassy rise that would lead them to the gated opening on Boot Hill Cemetery. Once he passed inside, the stranger dismounted and removed the lantern he'd hitched to his saddle. He glanced about. Brandish remained seated on his mount.

"I do need to ask you one question," Brandish said. "Why tonight?"

The stranger raised his eyes skyward. "First full moon since Jimmy died," he replied in a distant tone. "It has to be tonight."

He began to walk away. Then he hesitated and of a sudden looked to be struggling with himself, as though he had something to say but was unsure about speaking it.

"You've got something you want to be telling me," Brandish said, a statement, not a question.

The stranger finally surrendered and turned his head toward his young companion. "You're right. I'll tell yuh this, and you take it however you want. But let me ask you a question first. How did you come by Dry Run tonight?"

"I–just rode into town. Wasn't planned. By chance, I guess you'd say. First place I came to after a long, hard ride."

"By chance? Well, maybe. Destiny is a funny thing. But here's a fact you might not want to know. Because of that chance you never woulda made it outta Dry Run alive tonight if'n you hadn't taken another chance and volunteered to come along on this ride with me."

"What're you talking about?" Brandish asked with a perplexed cocking of his head.

"Y'ever hear of the Donner Party?"

Brandish considered only for a moment, then with a tightening of his brow: "Yes, I have."

"Then you know the story of how they had to resort to eating those who didn't survive after they got snowbound in the mountains."

Brandish nodded his head, slowly.

The stranger drew a deep breath, exhaling slowly. "The thing is, some of those that survived actually developed a taste for human flesh following their ordeal. Realizing they couldn't live in so-called 'polite' society, they were forced to form their own community. An off-the-trail town where they could feed their appetite with strangers and drifters who happened to ride in."

"I still don't..." Brandish started to say.

The stranger delivered it straight: "Tonight you would have been on their menu. But now there's a different arrangement."

Brandish wore an expression of disbelief. He shook his head vigorously. "No, that's insane. How do you..."

"How do I know? I'll tell yuh. I was one of those survivors of the Donner Party. And... so was the fella called Jimmy McQuade." The stranger spoke as if outside himself. "He made the mistake of riding into Dry Run. You heard tonight, they said they shot him 'cause he was wild. Wild, yes, from what he had to endure. Never in his right mind after that. Still, Jimmy's not dead."

Brandish was so overwhelmed by what he was hearing he could not find the words to express himself.

The stranger fiddled with lighting the candle inside the metal frame enclosure of the lantern. Once he got the candle lit and sufficient illumination was provided, he moved slowly from the gate into the cemetery proper.

"Seems as if Jimmy hasn't come out yet. I'm going to check on him."

Of a sudden the wind whipped up again, as if in announcement of the stranger's presence.

Brandish instantly was consumed with a sensation of dread. He could no longer comprehend why he had ventured out to this lonely, desolate cemetery. The hour had to be approaching midnight. Something beyond his knowledge was about to occur; he instinctively knew that. The promised two hundred dollars no longer seemed important to him. His presence at Boot Hill had a greater significance, yet one that he remained fearful to consider.

Within moments, the stranger had ventured deep among the graves. All Brandish could see was the faint yellow glow of the lantern, moving and shifting, as if held aloft by invisible... perhaps even ghostly hands.

After what seemed like a long while, Brandish heard the stranger's voice echoing an exclamation through the blackness.

"I found the grave. *It's open*!" Then, shortly: "He's comin' out."

Brandish could no longer restrain the panic that overtook him. Neither could his horse, which of a sudden began to grow agitated, as if sensing imminent danger. He tried to steady his mount.

"You can keep your two hundred!" he yelled back into the blanket of night. "I'm riding out of here!"

He waited momentarily for a reply.

A reply that didn't come.

"Did you hear me?" he shouted again.

Quiet... A heavy, oppressive quiet.

"*We all heard you,*" finally came the reply, followed by a chorus of phantom voices issuing from the depths of the graveyard.

Brandish tensed in the saddle.

We?

Forms began to emerge from the black cloak of midnight. Shambling forward, some bodies appearing twisted, their gaits slow and awkward. With horror, the first shape he noticed he assumed was Jimmy McQuade. As the figure became more visible in the feeble natural light, Brandish experienced utter horror. The figure was carrying the lantern the stranger had taken with him into the cemetery, now swinging limply in almost skeletal, unsteady hands. Brandish took note of the cadaverous gray pallor, red bloodshot eyes, and, mostly, the predatory expression embedded in a narrow, triangular face. He saw that the dirt-encrusted shirt had a large tear where the discharge from a shotgun had blasted an ugly hole in his chest. It was at that moment the terrible truth dawned on him.

Though it was a realization impossible for a sane mind to accept.

Ambulatory corpses freed from their graves followed behind this grim reaper, some apparently fresh, others in various stages of decomposition, many with sections of flesh stripped from their desecrated bodies, organs removed to serve as meal items for the diners at the Dry Run Saloon, as the stranger had revealed. The ghoulish entities moaned hauntingly and joined together with the one who Brandish had once identified as the stranger, their assemblage creating a ghastly midnight tableau.

"All the graves are open," the lead walking dead that Brandish assumed was Jimmy McQuade uttered.

Before Brandish could react, cold, clammy hands reached for him and he was forcibly pulled from his mount by the other undead entities and his body stretched out and positioned on the ground. He lay there, helpless, petrified, unable to utter a sound.

"Now you can be told the truth," these words spoken to him in a voice subtly shifting into something dark and sinister, breathy, sibilant. "McQuade died but I brought him back. Because *I am* Jimmy McQuade."

"Y-you?" Brandish managed to stammer.

"Yes, *I*. I rode into Dry Run. They recognized me from the Donner group. They knew that *I* knew and they could not have their secret revealed and so they shot me dead. Or so they thought. They killed the body but they could not destroy my essence. Not my soul, as that was surrendered long ago when I was forced to do what I needed to survive. Up until this moment, what you and those who I'll soon be visiting at Dry Run saw was merely an illusion. What I made you and those others believe you saw. Why did I choose tonight to ride out to Boot Hill? I came on the night of the full moon to reclaim my body. It is the night of resurrection and with it the revealing of the true self. And out of your own free will to accompany me on this night, you will supply the nourishment I require for the long hours ahead. I require a different sustenance. You will not feed them your flesh as they'd planned, but you will feed me your life blood. For all among us have an appointment this night."

The resurrected Jimmy McQuade's jaws snapped open and his teeth were sharpened and elongated. Two rows of canine fangs were only briefly visible to Brandish before his throat was punctured and he endured just a moment of extreme physical pain before being overcome with an unimaginable bliss as the life fluid was drained from his body and his soul was consigned to oblivion.

McQuade raised his head; the transmutation of his essence into the vampiric entity he was destined to become as a result of surviving the ordeal of the Donner Party through the only means possible was complete. He and the others now resurrected sought vengeance against those survivors afflicted with the disease, who now killed to feed their obscene hunger... and to maintain their gruesome secret.

McQuade veered his crimson-eyed gaze in the direction of Dry Run. His words were expelled in a hiss. "You served humans among yourselves, foul flesh eaters. Now those you fed upon are coming to feast upon you."

THE CONSPIRACY AGAINST THE HUMAN RACE

By Carlton Herzog

She came to me every night with burning eyes and disheveled hair. Clad in tiger skin, she wore a skirt of human arms. Small fangs protruded from her mouth. It gaped wide as her fire red tongue lolled out. She was accompanied by serpents and a jackal. They drank the blood dripping from the head she carried. It was mine.

Yet, she called to me in sweet mellifluous tones, "Come to me Eddie Felson, come to me."

I could not rise to answer her siren call. After all, it was just a dream. One that recurred every now and then with greater vividness and intensity. Acid in my heart for all those I had butchered, or a grim omen of things to come. Back then, I could not say.

At the time, I was working as a second tier soldier for a third tier crime family, the Carbones. They ran a murder-for-hire business out of a funeral home and enormous private cemetery. For hitmen, graveyards provide a simple way to dispose of bodies while maintaining a respectable image in the community.

Things went south when I let somebody I was supposed to have whacked, live. Tear Drops Thompson had jacked a Best Buy truck and been less than forthcoming with all the loot: a thousand laptops. His boss contracted with my boss to send Tear Drops to hijacker heaven. When Tear Drops explained to me that his kid Joey had cancer, I took a step back and said, "I get it. I'm a father too. Let me talk to the boss, and we'll see if we can work something out."

Alas, in my line of work, soldiers such as myself do not have the authority to countermand a kill order or otherwise negotiate its terms. That indiscretion left Mr. Carbone livid.

He slashed my face with a broken wine glass. Then he called me a "rotten soldier, soft as cheesecake."

That was not the end of it. Later that night, my friends whispered in my ear. They told me that Carbone was sending Joey "Pliers" and Eddy "Machete" to put me on the elevator and send me downstairs. Since I was the funeral home's resident gravedigger as well, they would wait until I had dug a fresh grave. After that, they would toss me in and throw the dirt over me. If I dug my way out, then I would be back in Carbone's good graces. If not, then *c'est la vie*.

I thought Joey might do me a solid and pretend he and Eddy buried me. After all, I was best man at Joey's wedding. Years ago, I dated Eddy's frog-faced cousin, Lucia. There is ugly and then there is amphibian ugly. I kept waiting for her to have us stop at Tony's Tadpole and Cricket Store for a bag of water beetles. When I thought about giving her the brush off, I remembered that she had bashed in her mother's head with a bowling ball. Something about too much garlic in the sauce. And, as her mother lay there with the right side of her head collapsed into the left and still alive, Lucia pliered her mother's teeth and pawned the gold. A gal for all seasons. And, apparently, charmed since she evaded justice via two mistrials.

On the fateful night in question, I was providing permanent resting places for two mooks. No standard funeral for these two. From the looks of things, Eddy's machete had hacked off their arms and legs. Their lack of eyeballs, noses, teeth, and lips told me Joey had done the detail work. Gruesome as it was, there was an element of artistry to it. In both cases, the left arm was positioned at the right leg's stump. The right arm at the left leg and so forth. Mindless as those two were, they somehow had the good sense to use the fabric of life itself to create memorable works of art.

I heard my two would-be murderers approach, laughing and giggling as if Eddy was knitting and Joey was holding the wool. Nothing like a live burial or dismemberment to tease out the inner spinster. But alas, unbeknownst to all of us, the character of the cemetery had undergone a radical transformation since I had last dug graves. Neither I nor they knew that our cemetery had been seeded by meteors. But not your ordinary meteors. These bits were juiced with the same stuff that had gotten everything rolling from the Big Bang to life on earth. Small glowing rocks of pulsing blue light with the power to resurrect the dead. They were everywhere, but I was always too drunk to notice. The alcoholic in his cups as they say.

As Joey and Eddy approached the backhoe, a battalion of cadavers advanced toward us. They were not stumbling, bumbling cadavers hungry for the living. No, they were coherent remnants of their former selves. With the right cosmetician, some could—and eventually did—pass for the living. But most of all, they were people we had hit and buried here. I assumed they had returned for payback.

I rose to my feet and grabbed my shotgun. I pointed it at the undead. Jo Jo Gotti, his black suit covered in grass and dirt, said pointedly, "Hey Pisano, can't you see we are dead? By the way, I'll need a new suit. This one's fugazi."

"How are you alive and kicking? Rebecca drained your blood then flooded your veins with a mixture of formaldehyde, glutaraldehyde, and methanol."

"The *petras* that crashed into the graveyard. What you call all meteorites. They talk, you know. They woke us up. They said that they had tweaked the soil. Made it regenerative with something called the *vivi petram*."

This exchange between the living and the dead was lost on Eddy Machete. Dumb as a bag of hammers, he passed through the crowd of reanimated corpses and split one down the middle with his machete. Joey Pliers followed him. He drew his gun and shot the undead closest to him. But the numbers did not favor the two killers. The dead swarmed them. One went so far as to grab Joey's pliers and stab him in the throat. As for Eddy, he found himself on the wrong end of his own machete.

I looked at Jo Jo and said, "If what you told me is true, we can't bury these two. They'll just come back and make more trouble."

"Good question. Let me ask Mr. Bits."

Jo Jo dusted himself off and sat on a tombstone. His eyes rolled back in his head. He spread his arms as if they were wings and he was about to fly. Then he spoke in a slow, deliberate way, his voice no longer his. Something spoke through him; its powerful resonances made my hair stand on end.

"You," Jo Jo bellowed, pointing to me. "You killed a man on ground I sanctified with my minions. You did so without permission. Nonetheless, you were unaware of my presence here. Therefore, I grant you clemency. As for your two adversaries, I have no use for them. For that, they will be cremated to prevent their return to the living."

There was a long silence. I thought the transposition of minds was over. But Jo Jo continued in that deep baritone voice. His message indicated there would be a change of management. First, here, and then everywhere else.

"Your philosopher, Nietzsche, once said that man's stupidity would turn this world into the 'floating gravesite of humanity.' Fortunately, we are here to change that. From now on, Fast Eddie Felson, you will be my spokesperson for what comes next. I would use Jo Jo but he is somewhat the worse for wear. Now, it is time that we meet."

Glowing blue rocks exploded from the ground. They tumbled and rolled toward me, fusing themselves together. Larger and larger the mass grew. It shaped itself into a crude humanoid form with arms, legs, and head. The thing was enormous.

When it finished accreting, it spoke to me again.

"Find a reason to bring your *capo di capi*, Victor Carbone, and his bodyguards to this location. I will do the rest. If any stand in our way after that, I will send my minions to deal with them. Rejoice, Fast Eddie Felson, for this is the dawn of a new age."

I thought it odd that an invasive species would have such a profound interest in our business. After all, we were not a Fortune 500 company. We were gangsters who used a funeral home to launder money and dispose of bodies. But Mr. Bits sold me on the idea of selling resurrection plots at exorbitant prices. The clients would come in cold as ice and leave on fire with their second life. There would be no coffin, only an extended exposure to the rejuvenating soil. Nor did we embalm them because Mr. Bits said, "The process works better with blood than embalming fluid. The catch was: neither they nor their kin could tell anyone about the service, or their second life would end abruptly. I thought he meant one of the boys would be sent to whack them. But there was no need for anyone to get their hands dirty. Mr. Bits would telepathically remove his sustaining essence and *voila*, dead as a door nail.

To ensure the security was tight, Bits ordered me to use the sketchy-looking resurrected victims of our criminal enterprise.

"I am eager to comply. But most are sunken and withered. Maybe hiring an outside security firm would be better than using liminal criminals perched on the cusp between the living and the dead," I offered.

"No, what we do here needs to stay in house. I am confident that your wife Rebecca, our resident cosmetologist, can do the job. Besides, for a human she's a knock-out. Unfortunately, your mind tells me that she's also a strong-willed woman. She won't like taking direction from me. Best if you present the idea."

"Understood sir."

When I went to the morgue, Rebecca was more agitated than usual. She launched into one of her rants. On this occasion, her social commentary focused on obesity in America.

"Eddie, did you know that we are the fourth fattest town in America? Right behind Dallas, Tulsa, and parts of the Mall of America? The obese are impossible to fix. I need a hoist to roll them over. Their arteries are so clogged it's hard to get the blood out and the embalming fluid in!" she screeched.

"I hear you, babe."

"What we need is a diabetes telethon. We get the people to dig their chubby hands into their plus-sized pockets and donate generously."

"We could make a documentary. Call it: One Butt, Two Seats: The Widening of America," I said.

She laughed so hard she nearly wet herself. So, I struck while the iron was hot.

"Bits wants you to make the resurrected dead passable as security guards," I said timidly.

"Does he now? You tell Bits that will cost him a bonus. No, forget that. I'm busier than a hooker with two mattresses. I want a raise and a say in which bodies get picked for the security detail."

I went back to Bits and told him her answer.

"She's a live one. But not for long. Don't worry Eddie. I'll bring her back. Only she will be more manageable as a corpse. Take care of it, please."

I didn't blink. To be sure, I loved that her dagger-long nails could curl my hair and make my ass whistle. But she was an exasperating, demanding shrew. When Jo Jo complemented me for having such a trophy wife, I asked, "What contest in hell did I win to get her as a trophy wife?"

At dinner, I shot her in the head. Somehow, she stood bolt upright, even with the right side of her head gone. She kept calling for "Mommy, Mommy." I got up, walked over and shot her in the face four more times. My liminal maids cleaned up the mess. They buried her in resurrection soil. I dug her up a few days later, somewhat the worse for wear. Our relationship was never the same. She did whatever I told her to do without complaint. As for the sex, I was never one for necrophilia.

Whatever minor misgivings I had about killing my wife or throwing in with outer space monsters, never stopped me from admiring Mr. Bit's business acumen. He was to our graveyard what Mark Zuckerberg was to social media. Bits got rid of the broken and cracked headstones, the headless angels wrapped in weeds and fungus, and anything else that reeked of decay.

"Eddie my boy, I want to divide the grounds into four quadrants. In number one, I want a casino, a petting zoo, and a kiddie railroad. Homespun lures for prodigiously wealthy prospective clients. In number two, we will continue our resurrections of the newly minted dead and the recharges of our security soldiers. In number three, we will have our high end custom mausoleums. That's where we will make our real money. As for number four, I want to keep that a secret since it speaks to our ultimate goal."

I would soon learn that Mr. Bits had a talent for unique monumental architecture. Take the Gleaves mausoleum for example. With a diameter of fifty feet, it offers an exact representation of Walter Gleaves from neck to crown. The large, soulful eyes scan visitors to verify their identity and tailor their experience accordingly. That is followed by his trademark salutation: "I alone can make America great again." From there, the visitors enter a capacious skull. The inner surface of the skullcap is concave and presents depressions for the convolutions of the cerebrum, together with numerous furrows and granulations. The fresco in the skullcap is modeled on Michelangelo's *Creation of Adam* on the ceiling of the Sistine Chapel. Gleaves is depicted as God imbuing his son Foster with life. Memorabilia, such as Gleaves' bloody Coleman axe, his meat cleaver, and his collection of Russian poisons, are set in various fissures and cavities on the skull walls.

The lower teeth, which convert to soft recliners, function as seating for the movie screen on the rear wall. Visitors, be they family or otherwise, are treated to daily showings of a CGI generated movie depicting the major events of Walter Gleaves' life: *The Triumph of the Will*. They see him successfully dodge the draft, insult a Vietnam POW, purchase a gold toilet seat, steal money from charity, mistreat women, become President, and then try to overthrow the government after losing his bid for reelection.

To further personalize the experience, visitors are entertained by synthetic versions of Walter Gleaves' favorite entertainers serving drinks. Such luminaries as Shecky Collins, Wendy McFee, and Sally Anthony, all of whom are doing time for tax evasion, break bread with the guests. On occasion, the synths read from Gleaves' bestseller: *I'm Okay; You're Not*.

Mind you, such a monumental piece of architecture comes at a steep price, both monetary and human. It took one hundred million dollars to build the Gleaves' skull crypt. Annual maintenance runs an additional two million a year. But all the money in the world could not make that mausoleum possible without the sustaining life force of the *vivi petram*. It not only grew the head, it birthed the synths and infused them with a crude intelligence. Like any organism, however alien and weird, it must be fed. The Gleaves crypt and synths demand the regular infusion of a reanimating cocktail consisting of liquified human hearts, brains, thorium and *vivi petram* extract. To that end, we maintain eight annexes across the country dedicated to the acquisition of live humans. We transport our human cattle by train since there is a branch line that runs parallel to the cemetery.

As one might expect, megalithic head mausoleums appeal strongly to Russian oligarchs, former heads of state, and wealthy entertainers. Needless to say, they are a potent source of revenue as much from their initial purchase price and maintenance as from the admission fees from daily visitors who number in the hundreds.

Mr. Bits understood that human vanity had no limits. So, he introduced the heroic giant crypt. Here the deceased is entombed in a Greek temple providing the same features as a skull tomb. Standing next to the temple is a massive statute of the deceased. Our tallest ones emulate the Seventh Wonder of the World: the Colossus of Rhodes. They stand with one foot on either side of a *faux* harbor mouth with *faux* ships passing under it. Others emulate the size of such projects, but opt for the decedent's head to be affixed to a Thor, Iron Man or Black Panther. The typical cost for such a work is two hundred million dollars.

Although I was the only human who spoke directly to Mr. Bits, I had an overseer: Little Miss Tiny Bits. She stood four feet and presented as glowing blue rocks morphed into humanoid form. Where Mr. Bits was the Patron Saint of Bombast, she was the Mother of Snark. Our meetings were always weird and unpleasant.

"Well hello, Mr. Head of Security. Doing okay, are we? I don't suppose you heard about the attack."

"I haven't heard anything. I've been too busy rounding up the stiffs who keep wandering off the reservation. This time Jo Jo and his Funkadelic Parliament took over the local Waffle House. They don't get that when you die and don't come back right away, your taste buds turn to shit. But they keep trying. One day it's lobster, the next porterhouse, and now waffles."

"So, you've heard nothing. My God, man you are the worst assemblage of human flesh that ever walked the earth."

"I don't deserve that. I give body and soul to this operation."

"Get off your cross; we need the wood. Now pay attention: our Midwest body train was attacked just outside of Penn Station. Eighty-eight bodies were taken from the train, dismembered, and poisoned."

"When you say dismembered...?"

"Torn limb from limb then splashed with hydro-cyanide. Nothing could be salvaged. Moreover, the Blue Rock Brigade guarding it was disassembled, scattered, and de-energized. They are dead rock."

"Who or what is powerful enough to do that?"

"The metallarians. Our mortal enemies. They object to our colonization methods."

"Why am I just hearing about their existence now? And what do you mean by 'metallarians'?"

"Our Cosmic Grimoire teaches that after the Big Bang, the universe was one big energy stew. 300,000 years later it cooled, allowing photons to create atoms. Somewhere in there sentient energy forms were born. They had varying atomic affinities toward certain forms of matter. The borborgymites bonded with gaseous bodies, such as nebulae and stars. The metallarians bonded with metal. Rock became our sad clumsy lot.

When technological civilizations arose, war between the metallarians and us stones became inevitable. They wanted to possess all things metal that an industrial civilization had to offer. We wanted to possess the people to create biological and mineral hybrids. Hence war. As our soldier, your job will be to find and kill the perpetrators of the attack."

"How am I supposed to find these metallarians?"

"They will go where there is an abundance of loose metal. Wrecking yards are a good place to start. Technological graveyards where the obsolete go to be repurposed. Here is a list of them near the attack."

"How am I supposed to kill them?"

"You will be accompanied by the humanoids I have been growing in the Fourth Quadrant. I crafted them to be a weaponized adhesive. Something that will gum up the works, so to speak. You will also have back-up from three giants I have grown from mythological templates: Thor, Iron Man and Vision, with powers roughly corresponding to those of their cinematic counterparts. They will travel on flatbed train cars. When called, they will deliver the *coup de grace*."

"I don't get why you just don't bomb them. Thermite would turn metal to slag."

"You are pathologically stupid. The thermite residue would pique the interest of the FBI and Homeland Security. We are an invasive species. The last thing we need to do is call attention to ourselves in official or unofficial channels. By the way, I will be coming along to make sure you don't screw this up."

I expected to ride in silence but for a diminutive pile of glowing blue rocks, she proved to be a chatty Cathy.

"I was looking over your contract: twenty-five years of service for immortality with a touch of invulnerability. Clearly, Mr. Bits was in an excessively generous mood. After all, you humans are tools, mere instrumentalities, nothing more."

"Well at least I'm not a mouthy pile of fish tank rocks."

"Funny you should mention that, sad sack. My deal consists of a new body that is being grown even as we speak. Once it's ready, I will transfer my consciousness to it. A humanoid body that will never age or decay, imbued with powers far beyond your crude monkey mind's ability to imagine. And after all that, you will still be my footstool."

"I thought all that world domination chatter was just hype."

"Hardly. Consider that ours is not the only graveyard beachhead. We have franchises all over the world. The goal is straightforward: To turn our rocky selves into super beings: mobile, flexible, omnipotent. As for your kind, it will service us as our needs require. You were smart to pick our side."

The rest of the drive consisted of Miss Tiny Bits extolling her virtues and denigrating mine. I kept my mind busy searching the Web for signs of the enemy. After several unsuccessful visits to car graveyards, we came upon Scrappy Joe's Wrecking Yard in South River.

Scrappy Joe, the proprietor, was a toothless old coot. Afflicted with severe stenosis, he was so bent over, his back seemed nearly horizontal to the ground as he walked. But his affliction did not stop him from describing the unusual activity in his wrecking yard after dark.

"It was 'round about 2am when I hears a ruckus out back. Things banging around. Now my dog, Old Roy, he's a howling and a barking. Going plum crazy. So, I grab my shotgun and go out to take a look see. It's dark, and I don't see so good counta' my eyes ain't what they used to be. But I see shadows moving around, big things that look like giants. They're dragging scrap cars into the back. Making a mess of my wrecking yard. So, I says, 'Hey you motherfuckers. I don't know what you is, but if you don't knock it off and let me sleep, I'm gonna' give you both barrels.' They didn't take the warning but kept at it. I shot both barrels into the air. Next thing I know, a shit load of my old hub caps come whizzing by my head. I ducked. Then I yelled, 'Okay, do what you want, but keep the fucking noise down!' Whatever they were, they got quiet after that. Being careful to drag shit soft like to keep the racket down."

"Did you call the police?"

"And tell them what? That the cheese had slipped off my cracker and I was seeing Transformers? No sir. I said nothing because them metal giants weren't bothering me. Best as I could tell they were building stuff out back with my scrap metal. But I never went to see what it was. I didn't want to know."

"Mind if we look around?"

"Knock yourself out. Say, what kind of fellows you got with you? Them fellows with you got no faces. They look like pink Gumbies. And what is that pile of walking rocks?"

"Shut your pie hole, Grandpa Bunions, and get out of the way. Eddie, call the train cars and tell them to launch our back up. The rest of you follow me."

I made the call, then joined the legion of squishiness as it headed into the wrecking yard. No sooner had we made entry than we were beset by crab-clawed mechanical spiders. I ran for cover. The humanoids ejected a glutinous paste at the arachnid armada. Once the stuff made contact, it made for the joints and hardened. The metal spiders froze in their tracks.

That was just the metallarians' first salvo. Scrap metal giants came surging forward. The gooey humanoids stopped some of them, but the rest hurled cars at Miss Tiny Bits and me. She was slow on her rocky legs, so I tried to carry her, but she was far too heavy. I thought we were goners. Miss Tiny Bits conjured up a deep hole in the ground for us to take cover in. I remained at the lip to watch the outcome.

Then came the *deus ex machina*. Thor's hammer flew in and tore through the standing metal men. Iron Man fired repulsor blast after repulsor blast, turning scrap yard metal to slag. Vision's mind stone shot off arms and legs. The army of metal giants was finished, and it seemed that we had won the day.

The iron meteors that rained down changed my perception. They targeted our superhero knockoffs. The kinetic energy obliterated them, the humanoids and most of the scrap yard. Had we not burrowed into the ground, my tiny boss and I would have been dust in the wind. We stayed there through the night into the next day. After we thought the coast was clear, we made for the one salvageable car. I got it running and we headed back to headquarters.

Mr. Bits met us. He directed us to Quadrant Four where we would meet the big boss. We took a golf cart to a secluded stretch of cemetery adjacent to the neo-sapiens' birthing grounds. Miss Tiny Bits was uncharacteristically silent.

"Why so quiet, little Miss Muffin? Somebody eat your curds and waves?"

"Shut up. We are in deep. Three giants and half our humanoids are gone. Minimal casualties to our enemy."

"How were we to know we would get pummeled with meteors? How could they target our forces so accurately?"

"All that metal ramps up their ferromagnetic ability to target ground forces. We were sitting ducks, just like we are here."

"Meaning what exactly?" I asked.

"We have been called to the center of Her earthly power. There's no way we can escape. If she decides we failed Her so miserably, then we deserve to die."

"Her?"

"Her," she said pointing to a geological disturbed hillock up ahead. I watched the ground heave and undulate as if it some great creature were moving beneath it. And there was, for a moment later, the impeccably maintained lawn burst open and an enormous misshapen female head rose from the earth. As it did, I began to tremble. Little Bits looked at me and said, "Look at you, all special and such. You didn't know you were one of the chosen. They grafted Kali's sigils on you at birth. That might save us. Or get us eaten, I can't say which."

I dropped to my knees and vomited.

When the head emerged, I saw that it was similar to the one in my dreams. In this case, the other players were different. Enormous worms with purple heads and blue-grey bodies slithered from her cavernous mouth. They coiled around her as if waiting for something. That something was a truck loaded with bound humans.

I watched my undead security team unload the human cattle and march them toward the worms. The feeding was over in minutes. Uncoiling, the worms would open and expand their mouths, revealing serrated razor-sharp teeth. One by one, the worms would clamp down on the standing victims, rip off their torsos, chew them up, swallow, and then quickly digest their meal.

"I can see where they could eat me, but you're made of rock," I said to Little Bits.

"They wouldn't eat me. They would drain my essence and add it to their own," she replied.

Before we could say anything more, three faceless robed men emerged from Kali's mouth.

"Who are they?"

"The *Alma de-Yihuda*. They exist in the idyllic veil beyond this living reality. They are visionaries who reflect the true transcendence. They will judge us on Kali's behalf," Little Bits said.

"Are we fucked?" I asked.

"We'll know in a minute or two. The judging business involves reading the *Corpus Symbolicus*—the momentary totality which is perceived in a mystical now that includes all dimensions and times simultaneously."

"Sounds like a mouthful of authentic outer space gibberish to me," I snickered.

"Shut up. Here it comes," she warned.

"I don't see anything," I said.

"Will you please shut the fuck up? The instantiation is coming to me telepathically," she whispered.

I got silent. She got silent. The three *Alma de-Yihuda* wafted back into Kali's mouth. They were followed by the giant worms. Then the ground shook as Kali's head submerged.

"Do they live inside the earth?" I asked.

"No, they have returned to the Aleph, our interstellar portal."

"Okay, Miss Tiny Bits. What did they say?"

"We're going to be buried alive in the Fourth Quadrant."

"That's a fine how do you do. I work my ass off and this is the thanks I get!"

"Somebody call the pope; we have a new saint. Listen genius, they're burying us alive so we can get new bodies. We will be leading the charge against the metallarians. Our army will consist of five hundred neo-sapiens ripening in the ground below our feet. Now shut up and follow me."

Our escort consisted of eight zombie security guards all carrying shovels. Presumably, if we got cold feet, they would use the shovels to motivate us. We didn't go very far before we came to two freshly dug graves. I could never tell what Tiny Bits was feeling since her stone face did not register emotion. But as I stood over my open grave, the register of her voice told me she was laughing her ass off on the inside.

"Here we are, lover. Today we are the mundane incidentals of an uncaring universe; tomorrow, the first wave in the new order."

Before I could say anything, I felt hands on my shoulder, followed by a rough shove. I landed face first in the sweetest loam I had ever smelled. The ground bubbled and pulsed from a battalion of worms just below the surface.

"Shouldn't I be in a coffin?" I asked.

"Nope," said one of the zombie soldiers. "The soil has to infiltrate and co-opt your body's systems before it can make the necessary changes."

All I could think of was the irony. The guy telling me I had to die to be reborn was the same guy I had shot in the face nine months ago. "What goes around comes around," I said, spitting dirt out of my mouth as I turned over. Not a smart move since I was greeted by a shovelful of dirt. Then another. For no apparent reason, I got sleepy, and it was off to dreamland where I was greeted by non-other than my version of Kali. But this time, she didn't just call my name. She explained her larger purpose:

"Transformation is the essence of creation. It is the process which runs through all the visible and hidden worlds."

Then she sunk back into the earth.

I rose from the dead three days later. Mind you, I didn't dig my way out. I willed my molecules to rise through the dirt as if it were not there. Once in the light, I looked for signs of physical difference. There were plenty: my skin had turned to diamond. Where there had once been veins carrying red life, there were now titanium canals carrying I knew not what.

As for Little Bits, she was no longer little. Nor a thing of stone. Like me, she had come back diamond.

"I am no longer Miss Tiny Bits. You can call me Mistress Diamond, soon to be overseer of this world."

We watched as our diamond army rose from their graves, disturbing not a whit of soil. Getting buried alive was worth it just to see that bit of extra-dimensional theater.

"What now? I asked solemnly."

"While everyone else was transforming, I received our orders. Thus far, the only metal beachhead is Scrappy's. Iron meteors have been saturating the area there day and night. As one might expect, several scrap giants have been seen. Attempts by local human authorities to investigate matters have not gone well. Currently, the area is under quarantine and surrounded by the Fifth Armored Brigade. That's a problem since tanks and other armored vehicles can be repurposed by the metallarians to serve them."

"So, what will we do?" I asked.

"We neo-sapiens can reduce our mass to zero. Thus, we will place a ghost soldier in every vehicle to repel any metal attempt to control them. That will isolate their forces in the scrap yard. As for any meteoric assistance, it's hard to say. Ferromagnetic meteors are everywhere in the solar system. It's child's play for them to use the earth's magnetic field to draw them here. We'll have to keep our diamond fingers crossed that we can manage the numbers. We go now."

"Are we driving? Should I order buses?" I asked.

Mistress Diamond looked at me with pity in her glowing eyes as if I were a dog trying to play the piano.

"No. I will create an anti-gravity bubble to send us skyward. Then I will tap into the ionosphere—that shell of electrons and electrically charged atoms and molecules that surrounds the Earth. Those ions will be our propulsion."

With that, we made our heavenly ascension like a cadre of Latter-day Moseses. I had always been afraid of heights: Ferris wheels scared the living shit out of me. But my new eight feet tall body of grown diamond enhanced by perdurable metal made me fearless. As did Mistress Diamond's reassuring chat.

"I know what you're thinking, big boy. Don't worry. These bodies are designed to take ridiculous amounts of punishment. A fall from the stratosphere would shake you up, but anything broken can be regrown in one of the healing graves. So, quit your bellyaching. We have the fun job of sending the metallarians packing for good."

"Why not ghost myself to lessen the impact?" I asked.

"Once you go ghost, you stay ghost until your essence can find and possess another compatible body. We don't have time for that. Now shut up and fly, little birdie."

So, I did. There was something to be said for our dexterous, eagle-eyed view of the world. Everything looked so fragile and minuscule. Soaring above the clouds without wings, I felt like an archangel leading a heavenly host. "To the corners of the moon" or the "green earth's end" we "could fly" and never tire. Diamond hard men and women, the new gods of earth, soon to take what belongs to them.

It did not take long before we wafted high above the scrapyard. From our aery height we saw many giants making copies of themselves. Formidable monsters to an unenhanced human. To us, it remained to be seen. But Mistress Diamond made it clear: metal was no match for diamond.

"These are not celestial spirits. Your griding swords will wound them deep and they will bleed their life force. That nectar we must collect lest it find a new habitation. You all carry a diamond sword in your right hand to smite them; in your left, and on your belt, vessels designed to contain that substance."

She gave the signal to attack. Half our wingless angels descended on the machines of man to ensure they could not be used against us. The rest of us fell upon the metallarians like the unforgiving hands of God.

Things did not go as planned. If it had been a simple matter of goring ordinary metal, then the day would have been over quickly. But the metals wore an unseen suit of electromagnetic armor that repelled our death strokes. Time and again, we chopped and hacked and stabbed, only to be repelled. In contrast, their electrified metal fragments took a heavy toll on us. Once struck, those who sought refuge as ghosts found themselves unable to do so. The combination of heat and electricity disrupted their nervous systems, scrambled their brains, and made it impossible to focus on the mass reduction mantra.

Much the same happened to our ghost soldiers in the armored vehicles. They were driven out from their new host. Some joined us, but most were destroyed.

We retreated to the clouds. Powerful though they were, a good third of our host had been disabled. They lay twitching and writhing in the scrapyard as the metallarians set to permanently destroy their minds.

Mistress Diamond spoke to us all telepathically.

"Unless we can cut off their power, this will be a stalemate, and they will win the day. You neo-sapiens are super beings. Surely, with your superior brains, one of you has an idea," Mistress Diamond complained.

Two diamond soldiers drifted toward us.

"Mistress, I am *Gikatila*. This is *Orah*. We believe that the metallarians' individual shields are being fed from orbit. Most likely, there is a gathering of ironbound asteroids drawing on the solar wind—electrons, heavy ions, protons, and alpha particles—and redirecting it earthward. Perhaps, we could send a small contingent to attack it."

"Wouldn't they be protected by the same shields as the earthbound metallarians?" I asked.

"We will not know unless we try. I suspect that they cannot fire directed energy pulses without lowering their own electromagnetic shielding," *Orah* said.

I said, "If they can't lower their shields to fire, then how are the ground-based metallarians able to absorb that energy without lowering theirs?"

Mistress Diamond said, "The shielding is not a continuous stream. It is an energy loop of pulses and gaps. Sooner or later, we should make a hole. Eddie, who is no longer Eddie but *Yesod,* you will marshal a force of fifty. Split them in two. Half will fly east for two hundred kilometers; half will fly west for two hundred kilometers. From those points you will ascend to an orbit above the asteroids. Then proceed with your attack from above."

In theory, a tactically sound maneuver. In practice, a disaster.

We came in hot. Flaming meteors in our own right. The collisions were truly spectacular, visible, I suspect, from the ground as distant supernovae. Then as meteors falling scattershot. For myself, I cannot say which impact was the more humiliating and painful: the one in orbit or the one through the cottage. The former resulted in a hard ricochet; the latter a kinetic explosion that obliterated a homestead and the family in it.

One of my soldiers struck a gas station. The explosion incinerated the pumps, station, and everyone within one hundred yards. Most of my soldiers dropped head first into pavement and roads. The sight of wiggling legs protruding from the ground did nothing for my spirits. Nor did the few tangled in phone lines on collapsed poles, impaled—I cannot say how—on street lamps, and crushed by cars.

That death toll was not supposed to exist. Of the fifty in the attack, twelve survived. More or less. The news from the ground was no better. The metallarians had succeeded in infiltrating at least half the mechanized armor. Human soldiers inside the vehicles watched in horror as their own guns opened fire on the unpossessed tanks and APCs.

"This is a goddam rout. Maybe you were right, *Yesod*. We should have bombed them. I need a solution. Somebody, anybody!" Mistress Diamond cried.

"EM pulse. They affect metals in all kinds of crazy ways. That will buy us the time we need," *Orah* said.

"Anybody have a nuke or solar flare handy? No? I didn't think so," I said.

"There is a way," *Gikatila* said. "We carry within us the energy primordial. We can use our own life force to generate massive bursts of lightning. Those bursts will create a series of micro-EM pulses and overload the metallarians with electricity. The giants will drop like stones, and the backwash will put the asteroids out of commission."

Mistress Diamond seemed less than happy with the solution. Once they offered up their life force, she knew that most of her army would be killed. Since she now fancied herself a great general, even in defeat, such a pyrrhic victory did not sit well with her.

"Is there no other way?" she asked.

"No. Naturally, you and your second, *Yesod,* would not be part of this attack. You would simply observe and report back as to its success or failure," *Gikatila* said.

"Then let the remainder of my army gather itself. It will assume a position two hundred kilometers above the scrapyard, preferably in the clouds. It will lock hands. I will do the rest," Mistress Diamond ordered.

Our army was a bedraggled ragtag band of would-be angels. In spirit, beaten, bruised and bloody. But luck was with them in the form of ominous storm clouds. They flew inside and, in my mind, I saw them lock hands. I felt Mistress Diamond working their energy matrices like clay, shaping and smoothing it for a grand public release. When she was done, the bolts jumped from soldier to soldier, connecting all in a great energy web. A moment later, it discharged itself upward at the asteroids and downward at the metallarians. It was the great Northern Lights multiplied a thousandfold or more. From our vantage point, we saw exploding pinpoints of light above us as asteroid after asteroid burst apart. Below, the story was different. The metal giants stopped dead in their tracks and fell face first. As for the metal ghosts possessing the human vehicles, they tried to escape but disintegrated under the force of the super lightning. In one fell stroke, we had won the day.

Epilogue

In the days that followed, neither Mistress Diamond nor I showed ourselves in public. We ran the funeral parlor and cemetery from behind closed doors. It was only natural that we would grow closer. After all, I felt all the old emotions and drives even though I was a diamond entity. Somehow, she began to mirror my desire. A mystery to be sure, one that called for an explanation. However, Mr. Bits, who now worked for us, could offer none. We paid a visit to the site where we had encountered Kali and the *Alma de-Yihuda*. Despite our best efforts, none appeared in answer to our prayers. As we turned to go, a hooded figure emerged from the woods. When he walked toward us, he seemed to fade in and out of existence.

"I am *Devekuth* the mystic. I can answer whatever questions you have," the translucent creature said.

"Great. Why do we have libidos when, as diamonds, we cannot consummate?" I demanded.

"O but you can. My name, *Devekuth,* means ecstasy. The fulfillment you seek in the physical realm is hidden behind the veil. You two need only picture it to fulfill your desires. It is expected that such a union will produce mental offspring that can animate terrestrial rock and later be transformed into a neo-sapien. When we have enough neo-sapiens, we will move against the humans. There will be no metallarians to oppose us. We will take this world for our own. The humans will service us the way cattle, chickens and pigs service them."

With that he disappeared into thin air. Mistress Diamond and I sat against a tree, contemplating his words. She picked up a quartzite rock the size of a human infant.

"I think this will do. Are you ready, lover?" she asked.

"I think so," I replied.

"Then let us conspire to replace these creatures of bone and bowel with our own."

But there was no happy ending for us. As we mind melded, I looked up and saw metallarians as far as the eye could see. Nearest us stood a mishmash of scrap metal shaped like a man.

"I have never been one for public promiscuity. No matter. We let you win at the scrapyard to see what you could bring to the table. Nothing more than few electromagnetic tricks that we'll be ready for the next time. As for you, Fast Eddie Felson, you have been one of us all along. That war wound shrapnel in your spine stayed with you doing your transformation. It lets us control you. Now, kill that bitch beside you. You three scramble her brains while he dismembers her. Very good, Eddie. You will make an excellent fifth column for us. We have rendered your neo-sapiens army harmless. All that remains is for you to kill the facility's humans, alive or dead."

Like a good soldier, I did as I was ordered, for I was no "rotten soldier, soft as cheesecake." Now the only sounds would be bloody screams caused by rusty metal fragments carving up human flesh. Or those on a lower register made by captives as controlling metal fragments are forced into their spinal columns.

Rocks or metals make no difference. One conspiracy is as good as another as long as I am on the winning side. Mr. Bits would probably disagree. And Kali, well, she can't.

Metallicus Prime told me that she and her worm garden are dead. Not the happy ending I expected but it will do.

SHADOW AND LIGHT
By David Dean

William awoke, gasping and confused. This is how he had awakened most of his life. His wife, long dead now, had put it down to nightmares from his wartime experiences. They weren't. He'd never told her the truth about their origin.

Looking around the dim room for a moment, he wondered where he could be, then remembered both the answer and the reason. It was his kidneys, they were failing, and after several weeks of dialysis he had refused further treatment. Still, he'd been shocked at how rapid his decline had been—it had taken only days for him to end up in this place, which he now recognized as a hospital, though which one he didn't know.

Propped up in the narrow bed, he gazed out the single window as the light of dawn began to pink the edges of the horizon. From this vantage point he could see the outline of the back wall of a cemetery, the sharp points of its obelisks and vase-topped pedestals rising above it. The cemetery stood across a large lot of weeds and trash where several abandoned houses had been cleared away for some future project. Though he was looking at it from the wrong side and in bad lighting, he thought he knew the place, and a note of alarm began to sound in his head.

A tall, gangly figure of a man came into view and strode with purpose and speed across the empty lot. Upon reaching the wall, he scaled its ten foot height like a lizard, then stood and turned to peer in the direction of the hospital. William felt sure that he was looking right at his window. A moment later, the man dropped down onto the other side of the wall and vanished within its enclosure.

A tremor of terror coursed through William as he rang for a nurse. When she confirmed that he was in the hospice ward of St. Dymphna's Hospital, he asked for paper and pen.

* * *

"There you are," his son, Justin, said as William opened his eyes. His lunch tray was on the table positioned above his chest. Judging from the condensation on its plastic cover, it had been recently delivered. He realized that he must have fallen back to sleep after his morning of writing.

"You want me to help you," Justin offered, nodding at the tray.

William shook his head, eyeing it with distaste. "Take me out of here, son. I can't die in this place."

The pained look on Justin's face hurt him, as he had no wish to cause him any more distress than his dying was already inflicting.

"Dad," Justin said, forcing a smile onto his stubbled face, "this is the hospice ward of the best hospital in town. If there was more…time…we could work on getting you transferred to a residential place, but there's not. You know this as well as I do."

Nodding in agreement, William replied, "That's why I've got to get out. I don't have much time left."

Tears springing to his eyes, Justin leaned forward in his chair, hands clasped as if he might begin praying. "Dad! Please! This is hard enough."

"Help me sit up," William asked, and Justin, grateful for the interruption, complied, his father's shoulders and head rising to the accompanying whir of an electric motor.

Now on a level to look Justin in the eyes, William pulled open the small drawer concealed within the rolling hospital table and brought out the writing tablet he'd requested earlier. Placing it on the tray next to the food, he explained, "I wrote down something for you to read—not after I'm gone, but today—as soon as possible. Don't show it to any of the others, especially the doctors. They'll dope me to where I can't think anymore…or speak."

"Dad, you've already made out a will, remember?"

"It's not a will. Take it with you and read it. Then come back before dark and get me out."

"Dad you chose to take yourself off the dialysis machine. If it weren't for that you wouldn't be in this…"

"I did what I had to do, Justin. That was no kind of life for me. It's not suicide—Father Antony told me that. I simply chose to stop the treatment and let nature take its course." Pointing at the tablet, he added, "Read that…today. Then come back for me."

Rising, Justin picked up the writing pad and swiped the tears away from his eyes. "I'll read it, Dad. But as for getting you out, I can't promise that. I won't promise something that I can't deliver."

"You were always a good boy, son, and you're a fine man now." His hand shot out to grip Justin's own with surprising strength. "I can't die here."

* * *

That same evening, after a busy day at work in which he'd been unable to get to it, Justin took the writing pad into his home office and sat down. Once he'd switched on his desk lamp and put on his glasses, he opened it and began to read what his father had written:

Dear Justin,

I'm addressing this to you as my eldest child and because you have power of attorney over what happens to me. I also love you, which is why I want you—and only you—to know and, I hope, believe, what I've written here. If you do, then you'll understand why I can't stay in the hospital any longer, despite the fact that I'm dying. In fact, it has a lot to do with my dying.

This all began a long time ago—March 22, 1969. My eighteenth birthday had been the day before and I was on my way to the enlistment office. I'd made up my mind that I would join the Marines, in spite of the fact my parents were dead set against it. They wanted me to stay on and work the farm and I hadn't had the courage to tell them I was enlisting. So, I snuck off and began to walk down the road to town carrying nothing but a knapsack full of socks and underwear, thinking the Marines would supply everything else. Our little farm was about seventeen miles from the city proper and on a dirt road that fed into Highway 27. It wasn't even serviced by a bus company.

Though it was still winter, the day had struck warm and sunny, flocks of clouds scudding along on the breeze, blinkering the sun and casting alternate bars of shadow and light. I was walking fast because I wanted to make the highway before Pa, or any of the neighbors, came along. Once there I planned to hitch a ride into town.

As it was, I had the dusty yellow road all to myself with nothing but empty winter fields to either side. Occasionally, I'd come upon a stand of trees crowding round tumbled-down shacks gone grey with weather and neglect. When I'd been younger they'd housed sharecroppers and been filled with skinny children and roughed up women. Most had given up and drifted away to pick fruit or work in the mills. Seeing those deserted houses that day made me glad to be getting away. Life had been hard on us too. We'd hung on, but just barely.

Judging by the sun (I didn't own a watch), I guessed it to be an hour or so after noon and I was feeling tired and hungry. I fished out a biscuit I'd hidden in a clean handkerchief during breakfast and began to eat. It satisfied my hunger but made me thirsty. The day was growing warmer and sweat broke out on my brow. Patting my face with the greasy handkerchief, I rounded a bend where a shack sat close to the road.

I was so focused on making my way, that I didn't bother to give the place a glance—I'd seen it a thousand times during my short life—so the man's voice calling out shocked me to a halt.

Standing there in the bright sunlight, I shaded my eyes and looked toward the porch. The shack was no different than the others—a claptrap arrangement of grey, rotting lumber with a rusty tin roof, sitting up on a foundation of stacked stones. The porch roof, though sagging, remained intact and beneath this sat a figure leaning forward from a rickety chair.

"Hey there," he said again. "You look hot."

"Hey," I answered, squinting to see the man sitting in the deep shade of the porch. I could make out that he was tall and lean as a rake handle, but not much more than that. Still, I knew I didn't recognize him. "It's warm for March."

"Where you off to?"

I couldn't help but notice that the windows of the house were boarded up and I knew nobody had lived there for years. Still, there he sat—a man I'd never laid eyes on before, though most everyone along this road knew one another. So, I just gawped like the hayseed I was. "I'm heading on into town," I answered, and left it at that.

"Un huh," he replied. "Looks like you've been walking a ways; must be thirsty. Step on up here and I'll give you a dipper full of water."

Leaning a little to his right, he appeared to stir a bucket next to him with a metal ladle, then held it out for me, trickles of water spilling over its edge.

"Got a good well here," he remarked. "Clean water and cold as a well-digger's ass."

Another flight of puffy clouds sporting dark bellies came racing along, the road and the fields going dark, then light, the yellow broom grass bending with their passage. Off to the west, I could see the sky had grown crowded with towering banks of billowing grey sails.

I hesitated, though why, I couldn't say—I was thirsty enough.

The scattered flock of clouds fled, and I stood once more in the bright sunlight, he sitting in deep shadow.

"What'cha gonna do in town?" he asked, the dipper still in his hand, droplets flashing silver as they caught the light that stopped at the edge of the porch.

"Thought I might see a movie," I lied.

"Looks like you're running away to me," he responded with a smile that was white in the gloom. He nodded at me and I knew he meant the rucksack I was carrying. "Your folks know?"

I didn't want to answer so just stood there looking at that dipper of cold water.

"Well, hell, I ain't gonna tell nobody if you ain't," he went on. "You ain't have you—told nobody where you're going?"

When I gave a little shake of my head, the smile widened and he added, "Well then, come on up here and have a drink before you pass out. You got a ways to go yet."

Stepping though the gap in the sparse fencing, I noticed the yard was rocky and grown over with weeds. There wasn't a well visible, but I figured it must be in the back of the house. I could see the man more clearly as I crossed the few yards that separated us, his eyes glittering in the shade like an animal's. Even his teeth appeared sharp and glistening. The dipper rose a few inches at my approach, but the man holding it remained immobile, his large corded hand just beyond the reach of the sharp edge of daylight, his nails long, yellowed, and ragged.

"Go on," he urged me. "Take it."

My hand reached out even as I found myself staring at his face rather than the dipper. The face staring back into my own was lean and drawn, the features haggard and hungry-looking, the eager eyes peering into my own. Leaves were tangled in the dark hair of his head and the odor of the man was musky and rank. I no longer wanted the water but couldn't seem to stop myself. Before my fingers could close around it, he drew it back just enough so that it was no longer in the sunlight. I thought of my parents and friends, of how they would miss me, of how very lonely and lost I felt at that moment.

"Got'cha!" he cried, seizing my wrist, his nails digging into my flesh, even as the tin ladle clattered onto the dirty planks of the porch empty and dry.

With a scream, I yanked back, terror giving me strength. Caught off balance, the man was snatched from his chair so that the hand that clutched my wrist was exposed to the sun. Now it was he that shrieked, as his filthy hand blackened and blistered before my eyes, the burning climbing up his wrist like a fast-moving disease.

Releasing me, he drew back his hand and arm, hissing and stamping in fury and pain. I fell back against the rotted palings of the fence and slid down, watching him in horror, unable to get up and escape.

"I've marked ye!" he screamed, flexing the terrible fingers of his burnt hand which appeared to heal even as I watched. "You're mine now!"

I sat transfixed, aware of nothing but his raging face and the pain in my gouged wrist. Rising above the shack, I could see the summit of the great range of clouds I'd noted earlier peeking over the roof line. It occurred to me that if I didn't get up and run, they'd soon cover the sky above us, and the band of sunlight that stood between me and this creature—for that's how I thought of him—would vanish and he'd be released.

He, too, appeared to take notice of it, his pin-pointed pupils swiveling from me to the narrowing streak of light that stood between us.

Leaping to my feet, I made for the roadway, everything in my being focused on escape; on placing distance between him and me. Passing through the gateway, I turned left toward the highway a mile distant. I had no conscious reasoning for this but understood that my own home was much farther away than the busy highway, and that the great cloud bank would overtake us long before I reached it, overshadowing me the whole way. My only chance lay in the race to the highway and people—real people. Something told me that this monster would not risk revealing himself so publicly.

From the corner of my eye, I could see the man's hate-filled face, his swollen eyes focused on me in impotent fury, barely restrained at the edge of the porch. The band of light had already dwindled to half its previous width. I poured on the speed.

Ahead lay the undulating dirt road, yellow in the brilliant sunshine, a great wall of shadow sliding along it like a shade being drawn over the earth. Both my heart and legs were pumping furiously, and I bent everything I possessed—my will, my flesh, my mind—into winning the race. What he had planned for me I had no wish to know or even imagine.

Reaching the last of the tottering fence posts that marked the edge of the abandoned farm, I heard nothing behind me, no sound of pursuit. There was only the sound of my panting, the crunching of gravel and dirt beneath the soles of my shoes. Not even the rumbling of thunder that the clouds threatened.

Looking up I could see the thunderheads that stretched across the horizon, their boiling peaks like the crests of towering waves, their shadow preceding them. Even as I gulped down the now-humid air, the false twilight met and rushed past me, the chilling wind slowing my steps. It would reach the farmhouse within seconds.

Behind me, I heard his triumphant cry. The only thing I could liken it to was the scream of a fox, at once angry and lonely, and wholly inhuman. I risked a look back just in time to see him leap from the porch and into the yard, vaulting the low fence and gaining the road, his stride powerful and sure. I felt my heart quail and falter.

Far ahead I could see the trailing edge of the cloud bank that we were beneath, the premature twilight that it cast followed by the return of day. I had only to keep ahead of him long enough to reach it and I would live! Yet already the sound of his pounding feet began to reach my ears.

Something flew past my right ear with a whistle, followed moments later by something that struck my shoulder. I cried out in surprise and pain.

Glancing back again, I saw my pursuer—already within yards of me—scoop another stone from the roadbed without slowing or losing his balance and wing it at me. This time it hit me square in the back with tremendous force and I was knocked to my hands and knees, the sharp pebbles and coarse dirt lacerating my palms and tearing my trousers.

Without thinking, I snatched up a stone as well and rolling over onto my back hurled it as hard as I could at the man's triumphant face. Three years as starting pitcher of my school's baseball team paid off, the rock hurtling straight into my gaunt pursuer's left eye in an explosion of blood. He fell to his knees, clutching his wounded eye socket with both hands and howling in agony, black blood dribbling between his talon-like fingers.

Leaping up, I ran to the side of the road where larger stones had been pushed by the blade of a grading machine decades before. With both hands, I lifted a sizable rock over my head and staggered back to the wounded creature that still crouched and howled.

The uncovered eye, yellowed and bloodshot, regarded me with both fear and hate, even as he struggled to rise. I gave him no chance but brought the sharp-edged stone down onto his skull as hard as I was able. With a sickening crunch and agonized groan, he slumped down once more, his body slack, his features obscured by the dark blood that spilled from the crown of his narrow head.

Swaying and panting, I stood over him as he began to tremble the entire length of his frame, fighting the death that was stealing over him. As I watched, I heard him sigh and saw him grow still, his thin, angular face gone grey where the flesh showed through. He was dead.

I felt no triumph as I regained my breath, only a momentary relief that fled with an oncoming tide of guilt and uncertainty. What had I done? How would I explain this killing of an unarmed man in the middle of a lonely country road? What should I do next?

Feeling sick, I turned to see if anyone approached on foot or by car. The roadway lay empty in either direction—school not yet out for the day, the local farmers hard at work in their barnyards.

I seized the dead man by his feet and dragged his ragged corpse, bumping and shuddering, across the stone-strewn roadway, and rolled him into the drainage ditch that lay next to it.

My mind went blank, and I turned once more for the highway that lay beyond a bend in the road about a half-mile distant. All I could think about was the recruiting station and the distance it would place between me and the thing that lay in the trench.

The cloud bank that had been racing along moments before had stalled, its face grown dark and threatening, the land around me gone breathless and still. I stumbled on, a low growl of thunder rumbling across the countryside.

When it had subsided, I heard behind me the faint sound of tumbling rocks, the shifting of dirt and pebbles. As if in a waking dream, I turned to look back to where I had dumped the creature into the ditch, the scrabbling sounds grown louder, more frantic in the sudden stillness. A hand, white and long-fingered, shot up to seize the edge of the sluice, followed by another in the next second. Then its head rose up to regard me, the bleeding having stopped, the large, yellowed eyes glowing with hunger and fury. Flies danced about its face, eager to feast on the drying blood that remained there.

My legs became leaden, my mind fogged with terror. I stumbled on as if I were drunk. "God help me!" I pleaded. "God help me!"

Behind me came a hoarse grunting and the sound of scattering gravel. He had regained the roadway and staggered after me, reeling and lurching. I knew from having seen his hand heal that I had only moments to take advantage of his weakened condition.

Steadying my steps, I lengthened my stride and tried to even my breathing, concentrating on the great flood of light that lay at the trailing edge of the cloud bank. As if in answer to my prayers, I saw that the clouds had resumed their eastward movement, if only very slowly, a breath of air seeping through the suffocating humidity. There might be a chance, I thought, even as I heard my pursuer's own footsteps gain in strength and purpose. He, too, recognized the situation.

"My home lies just ahead!" he called out to me, as if the heeding of his breath were of no consequence. "Turn in when you reach it!"

I had no idea what he was talking about. No other shack or farm lay between us and the highway. Only the cemetery. Even as I recalled this fact, its obelisks and spires rose into view as I neared the curve it occupied. It had lain there since the 1830's, seeded with generations of families and grown to encompass several acres—a place I'd become accustomed to over a lifetime now filled me horror when I considered the creature's words.

"Turn in!" he cried again, laughing, as the pounding of his feet drew ever closer. "Many have!"

Thinking of all those derelict shacks behind us, empty now of their desperate occupants—folks so poor and unimportant that their quiet departures over the years had never been seriously questioned—a new and terrible explanation came to me.

Panting for air as I ran past the bricked wall, I redoubled my efforts, though I felt as if my legs might give out any moment. Behind me the sound of my hunter's footsteps were rapid and sure. The wind grew stronger, slowing my pace, even as it sped the flood of daylight it towed nearer by the moment.

The closeness of the chuckle behind me made my heart stutter and almost stop—I wouldn't reach safety in time, or it me.

Then I remembered the rucksack that I'd forgotten in all my terror.

Shrugging it off my shoulders even as I ran, I let the strap slide down my right arm and into my bleeding hand, then all in one motion, turned and slung it at my pursuer's ankles.

He was so close that I could see the surprise on his ghastly features as his feet stumbled over the bag and his ankles got caught up in the strap. With a shriek, he went down hard while I raced on.

As the sunlight met and broke over me, I fell to my hands and knees, too exhausted to run another step. When I looked back, it was to see the creature disentangle itself, springing to its feet, comprehending its peril.

"I've marked ye!" he cried once more, frustration and rage etched on his grotesque features. Turning, he fled, bounding like some animal, clambering over the cemetery wall to disappear. Moments later I heard the clang of something metal, then there was silence but for my panting and gasping. Daylight painted the graveyard with shadows as the cloud bank continued eastward.

I had made it.

You know the rest of the story, son. I joined up and served, came home and went to school on the G.I. Bill, became an English teacher, met your mom, married, and we had you kids. Dad died in a tractor accident while I was in Vietnam and mom sold up and moved into town, so I never had to go back there. I don't think I could've. I saw a lot of terrible things in the war, but nothing scared me like that thing did.

Yet, here I am, trapped in a bed overlooking the very cemetery where the creature lives…or exists, the city limits having crept out to the graveyard. It knows that I'm here. I've seen it standing atop the cemetery wall looking up at my window. I can't see it well at this distance, but the creature appears unchanged even as everything around it has. "I've marked ye!" he said, and he did. You've seen the three long scars across my wrist.

Get me out, son, before he comes for me.

* * *

Looking up from his desk, Justin saw the room had grown shadowy with dusk. He closed the small notebook.

It didn't matter that what his father had written couldn't be true, only that he believed it to be. It was that simple. He couldn't leave his dad, already sick and dying, to finish out his final days—possibly hours—waiting in terror for this terrible phantom of his imagination. That it was the result of the poisoning of his body by his refusal of dialysis was of no consequence.

Grabbing his jacket, Justin passed through the kitchen, pausing only long enough to tell his wife, "I've got to bring Dad home. He only has a few days left and he wants to be here. I know it'll be a lot of trouble and I should've discussed it with you before now, but something's come up, and there's no time. Please don't be angry."

Studying his face, she answered, "I'm not. You do what you think is right. We'll manage. I'll fix up the guest room for him while you make the arrangements."

Taking her by the shoulders, he kissed her and drew her close; then turned for the door, the sense of urgency imparted by his father's writings increased by his decision.

Arriving just after dark, he was greeted by the hospitality volunteer at the entrance desk, who signed him in and placed a paper admittance band round his wrist. "You don't have long," he warned Justin, glancing at the wall clock.

"Thanks," Justin replied, already heading for the elevator.

Stepping out onto the third floor, he noted a cluster of medical personnel around the nurses' station. The head nurse glanced up from her desk as he passed.

"Mr. Hall…excuse me, Mr. Hall!"

It didn't surprise Justin that she knew his name, as the hospice ward contained fewer patients than most, and its mission required a more personal touch.

"I've decided to take Dad…" he began.

"We've been trying to reach you, Mr. Hall," she interrupted him.

Justin patted himself down in search of his cell phone, finding nothing.

"I'm sorry," he replied, realizing he'd left it at home in his rush to get to the hospital. "What is it? Has anything happened?"

The other staff dispersed on cushioned soles.

She stood. "I'm sorry to tell you that your father has died. It was just a short while ago and his passing was rapid and…untroubled. If you'd like to wait a few minutes, we'll have everything ready for you to see him. The orderly hasn't had a chance yet to prepare the…your father. We've had a slight emergency in another room. Again, I'm so very sorry for your loss."

Feeling as if his lungs had been emptied of oxygen, he inhaled a deep breath of the sterile, yet sickly, air of the ward and managed to say, "Thank you, but I think I'll see him now—alone."

"Mr. Hall, as I mentioned, the orderly hasn't…"

Turning away, Justin strode toward his father's room.

"It can be a shock, Mr. Hall. It's really best to wait," she called after his retreating figure.

Rounding the corner, he noticed the fire stairs exit at the end of the corridor silently closing. Throwing open the door to his father's suite, he stepped into an unexpected gloom. The only light showing was that of a fluorescent bulb hidden behind a panel, its buzzing audible in the silence. This cast a faint radiance onto the ceiling above the bed where the shrunken figure of his father lay beneath a stained sheet. A stench filled the room.

* * *

Coming out of the hospital an hour later, wracked with grief, guilt, and no small amount of anger over the condition of his father's body and the baffled lack of explanation by the nurse, Justin shuffled across the near-empty parking lot. He didn't notice the man crouching by his car until he was almost upon him. He appeared to be sniffing the door handle.

"Excuse me," he said, "that's my car."

The man rose to his full and considerable height, his features masked in the deep shadows that lay between the ineffectual illumination of the street lamps. He didn't answer, nor move.

"What are you doing there?" Justin persisted.

Still, the man said and did nothing in response.

"Do I have to notify security?" he asked, beginning to feel alarmed as he took in the desolation of the large parking lot and remembering that he'd forgotten his phone.

"You're *his* son…" the figure spoke at last, "…*his* blood." The man took a step closer and out of the shadow. His chin appeared black and glistening, and there were dark patches on his clothing, which Justin could now see was ragged and filthy.

"Who're you?" Justin asked, as a tide of fear rose from his belly into his heart, making him feel light-headed.

Touching his chin with long, almost fleshless fingers, the nails sharp and streaked with dirt, the man held out his hand, palm out. "Poison," he said. "His blood was poison. It made me vomit."

"What're you talking about?" Justin asked, recalling the reek in his father's room, the inexplicable gouts of blood on and around his body.

He took a small step back from the tall, gaunt creature that confronted him, recognizing the terrible features familiar from his father's narrative, the huge, yellow eyes with their pinpointed pupils fixed upon him, knowing why a long ditch-like scar ran through its hairline from front to back.

"He won the race…" it went on, "…and then—all these years later—I find him dead and useless, his blood poisoned—that he's beaten me again."

"I'm getting security," Justin declared, backing away.

Unaffected by this threat, the creature answered, "When I claimed your father—I claimed his blood—*you* are his blood," then, pointing at the distant lighting of the hospital lobby, added with a hideous smile, "You look healthy to me, maybe you could make it. Shall we find out? I'll count to three."

With a small gasp of panicked understanding, Justin turned and began to stumble away, his legs leaden with the terror and inevitability of nightmare.

Behind him the vampire chuckled and said, "One…"

BAD THINGS

By Nikki Lynn Blakely

John David Lawrence was laid to rest on Saturday, June 20th, after a private morning service held for his immediate family. The rest of us—his co-workers, colleagues, friends, and acquaintances—had been invited to a separate afternoon service at the church, to be followed by a small reception.

The church, just outside the city limits, was in an unincorporated area of Hiscop Valley, a mile or so off the main freeway. If I hadn't been looking for it, I'd have driven right by it. Old and decrepit, it blended with its surroundings, like one of those insects resembling a leaf or a twig that would sting you if you accidentally stepped on it. It only looked harmless.

I had noticed the cemetery across the street, had seen it on my many drives from Hiscop to Riverton, my gaze always seeming to drift towards it as if pulled by an invisible magnet. Overgrown weeds and woody brambles crept silently over crumbling tombstones that had been defaced by the graffiti of bored teenagers, and discarded beer bottles lay broken and half-buried in the dirt. I had often wondered what sort of person might be buried there. Now I knew.

I'd been waiting in the parking lot for the past forty minutes, engine idling to keep the air conditioning circulating, spinning the knob on the radio trying to get a decent station. I wanted to be late enough to the service to miss the boring parts, but not so late as to draw attention. I'd have skipped it entirely, but people would have noticed, and then wondered, and the wondering was something best to be avoided.

Let's get this over with, I thought, as I turned off the ignition, grabbed my purse, and, shielding my eyes from the bright summer sun, headed inside.

I found an empty seat next to Matt and his wife, near the back, and slid in next to them. Alex, Renee and the blonde temp John had been banging were sitting a few rows up—I recognized the back of their heads—and of course Mr. Cullup himself was front and center. I also noticed some of my past clients, ones that John had *acquired,* which was a fancy way of saying stolen. I'd have to find them later and let them know I was both available and alive—*no hard feelings.*

Matt's wife reached over, grabbed my hand, and gave it a tight squeeze. I squeezed back.

"How are you holding up?" she leaned in and whispered.

"Oh, you know. Still in shock. It just doesn't seem real."

She squeezed again. "Such a shock. But they say he didn't suffer in the end, so at least there's that."

That would depend on how you defined the word suffer. At first, he'd have felt a little nauseous, and probably regretted the pizza he'd eaten for lunch, though it was nice of me to save him a slice. He'd said as much. There would have been vomiting. Lots of vomiting. Followed by loss of muscle control and difficulty breathing. Maybe even a seizure. Then heart failure and death.

"Yes. So glad." I smiled wanly at her. "Do they know what happened yet?"

"They think maybe a heart attack, which makes no sense at all. John was a total gym rat."

"Yeah, well, they can't always tell with things like that."

Monkshood is an almost undetectable poison. Someone would have to be looking specifically for it to find it, and there was no reason anyone would. John didn't have any enemies. Everyone loved John. Including me, in my own way. I just loved him more now that he was dead.

"So, I guess this makes you the top dog. Matt told me you were second in closings this quarter. I guess we'll be seeing your face instead of John's plastered on all the billboards around town."

"Huh, I hadn't thought of that."

Of course, I'd thought of that.

The minister instructed us all to rise then, to close our eyes and join in prayer, and I watched silently as everyone's chins dipped downward and they bowed their heads. Almost everyone. In the pew in front of me, an old woman with a flash of silver hair, who was still sitting, turned around to look at me. Her opaque eyes were the color of the moon, and as she stared, her mouth twisted wide into the shape of a silent scream.

"Amen!" shouted the minister, clasping his hands together.

"Amen!" echoed the congregation, and everyone bent to gather their belongings and began to shuffle from the pews. Matt and his wife pushed past me, and when I looked again, the old woman was lost in the crowd.

A dour-faced attendant ushered us down a narrow hallway to a large, open room. Rows of tables covered in plastic, white tablecloths were lined up, surrounded by gray metal fold-out chairs, and on the opposite wall a buffet had been set out with sandwich makings, fruit, and a platter of cookies. I filled a Styrofoam cup full of lukewarm coffee, grabbed a chocolate chip cookie, and surveyed the room, looking for the people I knew so I could say my hellos and goodbyes and get out. *Where did Matt and his wife get off to?*

As I scanned faces, I spotted the old woman in the opposite corner of the room, looking at me. I smiled and looked away. When I looked back again, she was still looking directly at me. *Did I know her?* Again, I looked away, then back again. She was staring, and scowling, almost as if I had the word 'murderer' written across my forehead, as if she knew. But of course, I didn't. She couldn't. That was stupid.

Get a grip. You're being paranoid, and that's when people make mistakes. That's how people get caught. Go over and introduce yourself, offer condolences. Maybe you remind her of her long-lost daughter or something.

Looking around one last time for a familiar face, and finding none, I made my way across the room toward the old woman.

She sat slouched in a wheelchair pushed up against the wall, her brown face leathery and shriveled like a rotten apple. And her eyes, clouded milky white and unblinking, remained fixated on me. Tufts of silvery hair floated around her face, and her thin lips were stretched taught in a sort of grimace. *Or was that supposed to be a smile?*

Sitting in the chair nearest to her was a dark-haired girl of about fourteen, her eyes glued to her phone, which played nonsensical music and emitted loud beeps as the girl punched at the buttons.

"Hi, I'm Christine." I bent down so I was eye level with the old woman and spoke slowly in the voice I reserved for small children and idiots. "I wanted to tell you how sorry I am for your loss."

"She can't hear you," the girl said, not bothering to look up from her game. "She's deaf. Blind too."

"Are you sure?"

The old woman was looking at me, not through me as a blind person would.

"Very. She's one hundred and three years old."

A low guttural growl emanated from the old woman, and a thin stream of drool spilled from the corner of her mouth.

I stood up, turning my attention to the girl.

"So. How did you know John?"

"He was my uncle."

"Well then, I'm sorry for your loss, too. It's so... tragic."

The old woman mumbled incoherently, words that didn't make sense, but didn't quite sound like gibberish either. They had a cadence.

"What's she saying?" I asked, looking at the old woman, then back to the girl.

"It's the old language. Just ignore her. She does that a lot."

"The old language?"

"Cree."

"Cree? Like an Indian?"

The girl finally looked up from her game. "We prefer Native American."

"Oh, of course, sorry."

I remembered hearing something about John being part Indian—*excuse me, Native American*. I had assumed it was something he'd made up to get more business. He was always working some angle, why not that one?

Angry words flew from the old woman's lips like bees from a hive, spittle spraying the air in front of her.

"What's she's saying?" I asked the girl.

"She says there's *Wetiko* hiding in your shadow."

"*Wetiko?* What's a *Wetiko?*"

"An evil spirit. It feeds on greed, misery, and death. And human flesh."

I laughed nervously. *Was this kid for real?* "What do you mean? Like a werewolf?"

The girl stopped playing her game and looked at me for the second time.

"No," she said. "Werewolves are fake. The *Wetiko* is real."

The old woman's voice grew louder, and a few people seated at nearby tables turned to stare. She gripped the sides of the wheelchair and leaned forward, her arms shaking as if trying to stand.

The girl stood and slipped her phone into her back pocket. "I think it's time for us to go. Nice to meet you." She grabbed the handles of the wheelchair and began pushing the old woman towards the exit.

"Piwa-pii Ksiistiko oonootoo i'himm! Wetiko! Wetiko!" The old woman's voice rose to a crescendo as she continued to scream and curse in the strange language.

"And that last part?" I called after them. "What does that last part mean?"

The girl stopped, turned, and shrugged. "I'm not sure. Bad things are gonna happen? Or bad things already happened?"

"Well, which is it?!" I called after her, but the wheelchair was already disappearing through the door, the old woman's voice still ringing in my ears.

* * *

Back at the office, I found everyone clustered in the conference room, drinking Jim Beam from ceramic coffee cups and picking at cold Chinese food that had been ordered in. The blonde temp's name was Marybeth, she told me for the umpteenth time, and explained that everyone had come back to the office right after the service, not bothering with the reception. I was thankful none of them had seen the spectacle the old woman had created.

"We needed something a little stronger than coffee, if you know what I mean," Marybeth said, and I did. I extended my cup, and she poured a generous glug of whiskey into it.

An oversized picture of John in a dark wood frame grinned at me from the middle of the large mahogany conference table. Next to the picture was the trophy Mr. Cullup awarded to the top salesperson each quarter, and next to that, in a manila envelope, was the quarterly bonus check.

I slunk down into a chair and rubbed at my right eye. There was a dark spot on my periphery, a shadow. The kind of thing you might see after staring at a bright light for too long, and I regretted leaving the house that morning without my sunglasses. I pulled out my phone and began to scroll, looking up now and then to feign interest in the conversation and to nod or shake my head at the right moments.

I could still hear the old woman's voice, high pitched and shrill, her words replaying themselves over and over in my head. What was it she kept repeating? *Wettico? Wemmico?* I typed it into the search bar but nothing hit. The shadow moved, and I rubbed at my eye again.

Ting. Ting. Ting. Mr. Cullup tapped the side of a ballpoint pen against his coffee cup.

"I'd like to make a toast. To John Lawrence, the best goddamn salesman this office has ever seen. He knew how to seal the deal. He was just like a son to me. He… he was… he…" Mr. Cullup's voice cracked, and Marybeth went and put an arm around his shoulders.

Wetiko I typed in, and bingo. An image popped up. A creature, tall, skeletal, with a hunched back and an exposed rib cage, standing upright on pointed hooves. Sharp, clawed hands hung limply at the end of long, sinewy arms. The face was not human, but animal, with a long snout and jagged teeth that dripped blood. And atop its hideous head, antlers, twisted and bent into a grotesque shape.

I read further:

Wetiko-an evil cannibalistic spirit summoned by greed and death. The spirit requires a human host to possess, then will transform them into a flesh-eating monster driven by an insatiable hunger.

"Jesus Christine, what are you looking at?" Renee stood over me, reaching for the fresh bottle of whisky someone had opened.

Quickly, I closed the browser and placed my phone face down on the table.

"To John," said Mr. Cullup, raising his coffee cup into the air, and then everyone's cups were in the air, their voices echoing, "To John."

"Heyyyy, I have an idea," slurred Alex, wobbling slightly in his chair. "Whyn't we take Johnny's trophy to him and put it on his grave?"

"That's a horrible idea," I said. "We've all been drinking. No one here is in any shape to drive."

"I am," said Matt. "I've not been drinking at all."

Fucking Matt.

"I think it's a great idea," said Mr. Cullup, staring me down. "If we are going to be passing the baton of top salesman to you, Christine, I think you could at least pay John this one last respect." He picked up the trophy and handed it to me. "Send me a picture of the trophy on Johnny's grave."

* * *

If John had been buried within the city limits, in a larger cemetery, we wouldn't have even been able to get in at all. Most cemeteries were gated, locked up at night for good reason: to prevent people exactly like us from doing things exactly like this. Or worse. But this one had no such gate, no such lock, and we were able to walk right in, undeterred.

I watched Alex weave in and out in between headstones, calling out names as he read them, until finally, one of the names that spilled from his mouth was John's. That's when I saw the shadow again. No longer just in the corner of my vision, it was now in plain view, hovering like a black mist over John's grave. I rubbed both my eyes, wondering if I was just as drunk as the others. But then I saw it take shape and move, thick and noxious as it floated towards me.

Instinctively, I backed away, stumbling on the uneven ground, then righting myself. The others didn't seem to see it. Alex was sitting atop a headstone, wearing the salesman trophy on the top of his head like a hat, and proclaiming himself to be king of the graveyard while Marybeth mock bowed at him. Renee and Matt were leaning against a tree, their faces lip locked as Matt's hand fondled her breast.

Before I could turn to run, the shadow was on me, and I felt searing pain as I absorbed it into my body. My skin stretched taut, my bones pulled and elongated, my body cracked as my back hunched, my chest split open, and my rib cage pushed though, and my teeth, so long and so sharp…

Renee screamed, pushing Matt away and pointing towards me. Then Matt screamed, and within seconds they were all screaming, running in all directions, and I was hungry. So very hungry…

I overtook Alex first. The sharp crack of his breaking bones filled my ears, then I felt the pull and snap of his sinew and muscle as it ripped, his yielding flesh tearing. There was a slick squelching sound, and the slurp of blood, and then, finally, I heard the wet gurgling of his last breath.

Then everything went black.

* * *

When my vision returned, I found myself lying on the ground, staring into the black, moonless sky. My tattered dress lay cold and wet against my skin, and a metallic, coppery taste I knew was blood filled my mouth. My fingers laid only inches from other fingers. A closer look revealed a hand severed at the wrist, the stump oozing blackish-red blood into the dirt.

I stood, my knees giving slightly as I stumbled forward, fighting down a wave of nausea. A flash of silver caught my eye—a small, beaded sandal on a foot, still attached to half a leg. Only a few hours earlier I'd complimented Marybeth on how well those sandals went with the blue-green dress she'd been wearing. If we had worn the same size, I might have bothered trying to find the match.

I squinted in the darkness, looking for a torso wearing the khaki slacks Matt had been wearing. When I found what was left of him, I fished the car keys from his pocket and made my way back to the parking lot. My tongue found a piece of gristle lodged behind a tooth, worked it loose, and I spat it to the ground.

I flipped the ignition just as dawn began to break, and I noticed the moon then, a thin fingernail of white cresting the horizon, and on peripheral, the shadow. This time, when I turned to look, it did not dissipate.

"Well, are you getting in or what?" I reached over and opened the passenger door and watched as the shadow filled the seat, then pulled the door closed.

I sped out of the lot, tires crunching on gravel and throwing clouds of dust, onto northbound I-80 towards Riverton. It occurred to me then that northbound 1-80 to Riverton went directly past Mr. Cullup's house and, despite the large meal I'd just eaten, I was still quite hungry. Ravenous, in fact, and so was my new friend. With any luck, we'd arrive just in time for breakfast.

GRAVE CITY
By Sinéad Persaud

Most of the bodies my dad disposed of were in relatively good condition. Gunshot wounds to the head or chest. Minimal cleanup necessary.

Hitmen and mobsters are calculating people. Cold and controlled, keeping their guns aimed true and their targets in clear sight. Mess is the mark of an amateur killer. Crimes of passion by those who still harbor some humanity in their depravity.

The first scene my dad took me to wasn't tidy. Looking like a small bundle of dirty laundry in my oversized black hoodie and giant leather gloves, I followed him as he made his way into the seedy bar, taking three steps for his every one. I carried a toolbox, and he hoisted a folded tarp over his shoulder.

The clientele barely glanced up from their cheap beers as we made a deft beeline to the men's bathroom. A handwritten "OUT OF ORDER" sign hung precariously by a lone square of tape on the brown, beer stained door.

Dad pushed the door in, but something large and dense obstructed the way. He motioned for me to stand back as he heaved his weight against the door, leaving room for the diminutive thirteen-year-old me to sneak inside the single-stall bathroom.

"Go in and move him so I can get inside," he said, blocking the view of the door from the uninterested patrons.

"Quickly please, so we can have our restroom back," the man behind the bar counter said, gruffly as though we were taking too long to order a drink, instead of covertly removing an entire crime scene. My dad threw a curt nod over his shoulder at the scowling bartender.

Once inside the space, I zipped the hoodie up over my nose to shield myself from the dizzying stench. The familiar scent of copper from my near-weekly nosebleeds could not be so easily blocked out. I took off one of my cumbersome gloves (a rookie mistake) and felt around the wall for a light switch. My fingers made contact with a sticky, cold, congealing substance. I hoped, with a churn in my stomach, that it was *only* blood on those walls.

My shaky hand found the switch, and the single bulb flickered on, accompanied by a deep buzzing sound. With a blink, my eyes adjusted to the gruesome scene before me.

Wedged between the foot of space between the door and the grimy, clogged sink were the remnants of a middle-aged man in a sleek, bespoke suit. I couldn't even tell what color his shirt had been as it was entirely soaked in quickly browning blood. What was left of his head betrayed a scalp of graying hair and tanned Caucasian skin. The entire face was caved in, white teeth hanging from pink gums, bringing to mind the Sarlacc pit that devoured Boba Fett whole. Last week's viewing of *The Return of the Jedi* was now forever tarnished.

"Hurry," my dad whispered from outside. His voice was, on the surface, unperturbed. But I knew to do what he said, and fast.

I crouched and shifted the man's lead-like legs in the direction of the toilet. His body lolled forward onto me and rivulets of blood dripped onto my hoodie. I shivered, despite the stuffy heat, sipping in shallow breaths, hoping it would suppress my urge to gag.

"Set!" I whispered, and my dad made his way inside and went to work. Once a surgeon back home in India, his tools were sharp and clean and utilized with dexterity. I stood by the door, listening as saw slid through bone.

Once the body was taken apart, we carried it in secured tarps to the van. Then we drove. A mile east of the local penitentiary. He'd already prepared the grave earlier that day.

The wide open space and heavy autumn fog made me nervous, but my dad knew what he was doing. In all his years in the business, he'd never been caught.

We buried the pieces of the bathroom man without speaking a word. When we'd finished, he drove the van to the public lot where we'd picked it up and got back in our family car, but not before laying down plastic wrap for us to sit on.

Home by 3am. Mom had left plates of food in the oven for us in case we were hungry. Lasagna.

I didn't think I'd ever be hungry again. Especially not for sheets of beige pasta over layers of meaty, red sauce.

We took turns showering and then scrubbed the tub with vinegar and baking soda. Freshly clean and feeling anything but tired, I stopped my dad as he made his way to his bedroom to join my snoring mom.

"What did he do?" I whispered, noticing a crusted line of blood I'd failed to scrub out from underneath my thumbnail.

"Owed someone money. Slept with someone's wife. Spoke out of turn. Ordered a drink with too many olives. Doesn't matter. We don't ask. We just bury. And you'll keep getting your piano lessons and mom will get to keep going to school."

"What do you get?" The question left my lips without my consent. So quiet, I wasn't even sure he'd hear me.

"A chance at living," he said with the slightest ghost of a heartbreaking smile.

The next few jobs that I tagged along on were far more palatable. If that's even possible. Gunshots, pools of blood in reasonable quantities that could be cleaned with a bottle of 409 and a roll of paper towels. Glassy eyes, frozen in that final expression of "What? Me? But I was your closest confidante!" Clean. Sterile. Easy.

We never buried in the same place twice. The state of Massachusetts is overflowing with historic cemeteries. The permanent resting places of the Salem Witch Trial judges, great authors like Louisa May Alcott, founding fathers like Samuel Adams, and revolutionaries like Crispus Attucks. But there was another cemetery: the cemetery cultivated by my dad and me. The final resting place of criminals, mob informants, moles, and swindlers. A graveyard where no loved ones could come and lay flowers down or run their hands over an engraved stone plaque.

Sometimes, to ease the bleak monotony of my apprenticeship, I would make up the inner monologue of our mark-of-the-night. "Oh, please don't take me to the ocean! I was born on the West Coast! My Dodgers-loving family would hate to know that I'm swimming with the Red Sox fishies over here for eternity!" "Ugh, even in death I have to listen to Mumford and Sons on the car radio? Yeesh!" "Indian food is too spicy for me and yet the only people at my funeral are an Indian guy and his scrawny daughter!? Life's funny that way."

Whenever we weren't burying bodies, life was normal. Or as normal as life could be for a thirteen-year-old with immigrant parents. Aside from the safe full of burner phones and secure storage unit of tarp and tools, we were a typical family. Mom went to night school for her physical therapy degree and I was third in my freshman year class. We ate dinner together as a family and I even went to the movies with my small group of friends on the weekends.

After a year or so, the shock of seeing dead bodies wore off.

One damp spring evening, as I licked my spoon clean, finishing a bite of mom's famous Key lime pie, a burner phone went off. Like the world's most loathsome grandfather clock. The ring of death.

An hour later I was boarding a private elevator of a high-rise Boston apartment building with my dad, tool kit in tow. The doors opened into a private penthouse apartment. A collection of limbs splayed out from underneath the grand dining room table ahead of us. A man in joggers and a Harvard sweatshirt watched a Celtics game on his 80-inch wall-mounted television, barely glancing at us as the elevator ding announced our arrival. A comical spray of blood on the floor to ceiling glass windows behind him didn't seem to cause him any concern either.

We went to work, and it was only as I was laying the tarp underneath the man's body with deft detachment that I realized how second nature this all was now. Was this how a brain surgeon felt as they drilled into a skull to prepare for surgery? Or a mortician as they brushed rouge onto the waxy face of a dead person?

As my homeroom teacher took attendance the next day, I pondered whether I was relieved or disgusted by how I'd reacted to the penthouse body. In movies when cops and homicide detectives are asked how they are able to get used to their grim job, the answer is always that they don't. Their constant sorrow and disgust are what keeps them human, keeps them good at their job.

I supposed I didn't need sorrow or disgust to be good at cleaning up dead bodies. Just discretion and a heavy-duty shovel.

My teacher said my name again, annoyance in her voice. She'd been calling it for a while.

"Sorry. Here!" I said, jolting from my thought coma and sighing at the ragged mess I'd made of my cuticles. Ever since I'd become my dad's shadow, it was a habit I couldn't shake. Violently tearing into my cuticles with my raggedy bitten-down nails. Red arcs lined each and every one of my nails like bloody, little crescent moons.

Years passed. Clients came and went. I'd respond to the late-night sound of a burner phone with Pavlovian obedience. Backpack of tools slung over my shoulder, sweatshirt zipped, squeaky clean boots with flat soles tugged on.

A sea of the dead loomed just below the surface of the earth. They spoke to me. Told me of their crimes. It was comforting to know where they were. That I could put them there and they'd stay. As foreboding and vile as these men were in life (and they were all men), in the end they were hacked up and tucked back into the earth by me.

My mom got her degree. Dad was able to find a job at a car dealership. I was accepted to Brown University.

But the night jobs never stopped.

"Why not?" I asked one night as we sprinkled damp dirt onto a handsome man who'd cuckolded a rich and powerful gambler in the Back Bay area. Rolling thunder boomed in the distance like a bowling ball getting closer and closer.

Dad continued shoveling, beads of sweat on his temple. He looked old.

"If I stop, we're a target. They'll come after you and your mother. If we aren't with them, we're against them. I know everyone's secrets."

"What happens next year? When I go to college?"

"You'll go. I'll keep digging. As long as I stay quiet, you're safe."

"Why did you start bringing me along?"

"What, you haven't enjoyed our father-daughter bonding?" he said, the closest thing to a joke I'd ever heard from him.

A moment of silence, and then: "I hated the idea of you finding out some other way. Families should be honest with one another, even if they have to hide from the rest of the world. You also needed to know how cruel the world can be. So you can make it better." He wiped his nose and patted the grave down with the backside of his shovel. "Plus, I needed the help. My knees aren't what they used to be, you know," he smiled. I chuckled. We shared a sentimental moment as rain started to fall on the freshly buried body of a man in a Tom Ford suit.

* * *

At Brown I stalked the crowded grounds like a phantom. Lectures on microbiology went in one ear and out the other, undigested by my distracted brain. Nights were an empty, endless hallway without the sordid alleys, concealed mob offices, and dimly lit parking garages. In an attempt to fill the void, I sought out the loudest parties, the edgiest people, and the most outrageous things I could put into my body.

On rare nights when I couldn't find anything noisy to immerse myself in, the ringing of burner phones seemed to come from every direction. A siren, an alarm clock, a movie in the common room. Sleep eluded me.

Academic probation came swiftly and with it, my dad's diagnosis. Brain tumor. Three months left.

He made jokes about how back in India he could have operated on himself and probably would have been okay. Mom was distraught.

"People might threaten you and your mother," Dad croaked from his home care bed. "Tell them you know nothing. The secrets of the city die with me."

The funeral was small and intimate. He didn't know many people. In his line of work, knowing people was a liability. Tears leaked from my eyes, rimmed with the telltale dark circles of exhaustion. I threw the ceremonial dirt on his coffin and thought of the dozens of families I'd deprived of this moment. I wished I could have telepathically reached out to them all to say, "Don't worry. A body isn't a memory."

The school found out about my recent bereavement and offered to erase my probation. They understood how the illness of a parent could cause someone in a new environment to 'act out.' I said I'd decide if I felt I needed some time away after the holiday break. Though I appreciated the leniency, something told me that academia would never agree with me.

* * *

Glistening turkey, cumulus clouds of garlicky mashed potatoes, and my favorite spicy green bean casserole stared up at me from the dining room table. Mom swirled the dregs of her wine before topping herself off. She tapped her foot to the Christmas mix I'd found online. The pom pom of my Santa hat tumbled into my face as I leaned forward to smear butter onto a warm roll.

We'd tried. Dad loved Christmas despite being Hindu. The bright colors, the carols, the presents, the clay-mation specials on television. He'd adored this time of year when people (for the most part) tried to be their best selves. So we decorated the house and wore red and green. Mom even stuck some lights on the ginkgo tree out front.

The holiday dinner was awkward. What did a mother and daughter talk about after their grave-digger-to-the-mob patriarch was gone and the daughter was hanging onto her education by a vodka soaked thread? But after dinner, three glasses of cheap wine in, the deluge of memories couldn't be contained.

"That one time your father tried to build a snowman and wouldn't stop until he'd chiseled Arnold Schwarzenegger's face perfectly?" Mom bashed her head lightly on the table, laughing. "It ended up looking more like Andy Richter!"

"Always the surgical precision with him!" I raised my glass to the heavens as though he were watching. "How about how he called The Beach Boys the Beach Bozos? I filled my glass up, emptying the body of Chardonnay.

"I'll never understand his hatred of The Beach Boys!" Mom shrugged, "They all seemed like nice fellows to me."

We reminisced until the clock struck midnight, signaling the end of Christmas. The end of our hearty attempt to make the Yuletide gay. My cheeks ached from the forgotten exercise of smiling.

I collected the dishes and set them in the sink to deal with in the morning. Mom took a sleeping pill and went upstairs to bed.

I shut off the living room lights on my way upstairs. The wine buzz started to wear off and a headache came to roost in its place. Angry silence and darkness closed in on me faster than ever. Immediately the phantom ringing of a burner phone sounded in my ears and I clenched my eyes shut.

The ringing didn't stop. I opened my eyes, colorful circles dancing in my vision. Sugarplums? No. Just the prelude to a migraine.

Ah, but it wasn't a phantom at all. The muffled ringing of a phone was indeed coming from somewhere in the house.

The safe. Still tucked in the corner of Mom and Dad's closet.

I crept upstairs, not worrying too much about the creaky stairs. Mom would be dead to the world after washing down her pill with a hydrating swig of wine. Pushing open the door to her room, I saw the rise and fall of her stomach from underneath the twisted sheet she'd managed to pull atop her.

The ringing stopped.

Did I imagine it? A traumatic cellular memory that I was doomed to have haunt me for the rest of my life?

I opened the closet door and knelt down at the safe. The same code as always sent the door flying open with a satisfying click. Four cellphones sat inside, silver messengers of someone's doom.

I picked one up and checked for missed calls. Two.

Surely everyone knew by now what had happened to my father. Surely they wouldn't still be calling for him to come to work. And on Christmas? Did the vengeful men of this earth not even rest for the birth of Jesus?

My finger hit the redial button. On purpose? By accident? I don't really know. But soon the phone was ringing.

Ringing.

And soon I was saying;

"Okay, be there soon."

Gerri Gray Photography

THE GARDEN IN THE GRAVEYARD
By Laura Green

The day had started slowly, only one morning funeral had taken place. Something about an unfortunate decapitation of a motorcyclist and a piano wire incident. All grisly stuff. Ted sometimes wondered how they put those unlucky souls back together. By the time the bodies made it to him they were gussied up in their coffins in their Sunday best. Hands laid across their chests, maybe with a rosary or a flower gripped in death's hands. They were dressed as if you could ignore the desecration that had happened upon their bodies.

Whenever there was a funeral, Ted stood back at a respectful distance. He was not dressed in black; he was always in his blue overalls. The denim fabric had blended so thoroughly with mud that even with a good scrub they never seemed to come clean. When it was time, Ted would appear from the wings and start shoveling the dirt over the mourners' deceased loved one. Their final resting place was in Ted's domain; he lived with the dead as if they were neighbors in the same apartment building. Not once did Ted have to complain about excessive noise or worry about overflowing rubbish in the communal bin area. The only rubbish they left were wilting flowers, turning brown with age and rot.

A sheen of sweat appeared on Ted's brow as he continued shoveling the dirt onto the coffin below. He put in a few more sprinklings of dirt, and once the grieving family became dots on the horizon, Ted reached into his pocket for his handkerchief to mop his brow. *It is mighty inconvenient that they must be buried six feet down*, he thought as he put the cloth back into his pocket. He raised his now empty hand up to his hair and swept back some fallen tendrils that had worked loose from his gelled, thinning hairline. As Ted brought his hand back down to his side, he noticed a tremor twitching at his pointer finger, which began gradually spreading to the other digits. The shakes had come on over time, but he noticed an increase in their frequency. Ted clenched his trembling hand into a fist and pressed it against his leg. He pushed with force against the denim fabric, willing his hand to stop. The tremor went away as quickly as it had appeared, and Ted looked down to his hand, feeling relived...until he saw that his untrimmed nails had burrowed deep into his palm. Small droplets of blood were climbing out from the puncture wounds. Ted reached into his pocket and extracted his handkerchief, wrapped it around his hand and tied the ends into a knot.

"Well, I could do with a break and there is no one around, apart from you! You don't mind, do you mate?" Ted called out to the boxed young man below.

Ted sniggered to himself. *They never answered back*, he thought. *How polite*.

Ted walked the thirty seconds from the grave to his small house, little more than the size of a generous outhouse. He poured himself a cup of coffee from the stale pot being kept warm on his coffee machine and took a large sip. Globs of liquid hung like dew drops on his straggly moustache hairs. Poking his tongue out of his dry chapped lips, he licked the stray drops. Turning his head, he gazed at the worn, broken down recliner chair and thought it would feel good for the stained fabric to be hugging his body as he laid down for a nap, but he had work to do in the garden.

"Work was never done for the living," Ted said into the musty air in his shack.

Ted's garden sat just behind his small house. It was his pride and joy: a vegetable garden where he toiled away to grow food for his table. The garden was surrounded by graves on all sides. Ted knew that people thought it was weird to grow vegetables in a graveyard, as they had told him as much, but he also knew that this was this was the most fertile soil around and more fool them who did not agree.

Ted dragged a hessian sack over to his crop of freshly planted potatoes. "Well, you spuds look like you could do with some goodness," he said lovingly to his plants as he reached his meaty hands into the sack to take out a handful of fertilizer. Ted smiled as he felt the wet contents of the sack, for he knew he was going to have the fluffiest potatoes he had ever grown. He spread a generous handful over the crop and stood to survey his masterpiece, the garden in the graveyard. He spied the carrots in the east corner and decided to give those some fertilizer too, then the parsnips. For the next half an hour Ted tended to each crop with care until the sack looked deflated. He peered into the bag.

"It looks like I will have to get some more fertilizer today, such a shame that it comes in the most awkward packages...but I guess that's where the fun is," Ted said softly under his breath as he popped a wad of chewing tobacco into his mouth. Ted had smoked up until a few years ago, but his lungs had been giving him trouble. Many a night he would wake up with the hacking cough he just could not shake, so he had taken to chewing his tobacco instead. In the graveyard he had the look of a cow chewing cud as he worked the dried leaves over in his mouth. His teeth looked like graves themselves, yellowing tombs with plant life stuck between them.

Mud-streaked and feeling slightly withered from the mid-afternoon sun beating down on him, Ted prepared for the second funeral of the day. The service was for a young woman whose untimely death was brought at the hands of her no-good cheating, beating husband. She had married young at nineteen, and with the blush of youth still on her cheeks, she was snuffed out like a fresh-smelling candle.

Ted watched from his usual polite distance as the mourners gathered at the gravesite. Grief was strong in the air; the feeling was palpable like a specter drifting past and tousling your hair. The service was full of the usual platitudes that Ted could recite in his sleep, and he often did so after consuming some of the high proof moonshine that he made in his bathtub.

After fifteen minutes the service was over, such a short amount of time to sum up even a short life. The bereaved were scattering away like summer's first dandelion pappus blown haphazardly on the wind. Ted held the shovel in his gnarled hand and walked towards the gaping mouth of the grave. If anyone were looking, they would have seen Ted carrying a length of rope over his shoulder and the pocket of his overalls bulging with the half-in half-out contents of a hessian bag, which had the sole purpose to carry fertilizer. What they would not see was the very sharp blade he kept strapped to his ankle.

Ted was getting on in age, but he still had a spring in his step where his garden and fertilizer harvesting were concerned. He crouched down and sat on the lip of the grave. It was six feet down, but he knew he would have stable footing and a secure landing point as the coffin was polished oak with gold accent handles, no expense spared for this poor lost girl. Ted slipped his buttocks off the grassy precipice and lowered himself down and landed on the lid of the coffin with the practiced softness of a cat jumping from a fence.

The lid came up easily with the swift jimmying with the shovel. The coffin opened to reveal the flaxen-haired corpse. She looked peaceful, Ted thought. The brutal way in which she died was not readable on her face, the eyes closed forevermore with eye caps full of spikes. Her skin had the waxy, heavily made-up quality the dead always had when they had an appointment with the mortuary cosmetologists makeup palette and tubes of glossy creams. With this makeover, they became creatures of the uncanny valley, seemingly human enough for their families to view before internment; but now in death they were like dolls, an idol, a replica of their past selves.

"You are awfully pretty, miss," Ted whispered to the still corpse as he ran his hand through a lock of her blonde hair. "Now if you do not mind, I have a favor to ask of you: I am all out of fertilizer for my garden, and it is imperative that I retrieve some more. What do you think? Nod once for yes, two for no, young lady!" Ted giggled cruelly. "Well, I shall take your silence and stillness as a yes." Ted touched the knife on his ankle, reassuring himself that it was there, and feeling the immense sense of power he could wield with it.

Ted placed the shovel beside the girl in the coffin and began his harvesting ritual. Ted was always respectful enough, he thought, when he was collecting his fertilizer. He solemnly thanked them for their donation to his garden and let the donor know that they would help grow the heartiest of root vegetables, the herbs with the deepest depth of flavor, and contribute to a hearty meal to feed him. As Ted bowed his head to the fastened eyes of the young woman, he saw a trickle emanating from her sweet, upturned button nose. It was blood, a slug-like trail that spilled over her pink lips.

Ted timidly reached out a shaking hand and touched her perfect, but seemingly cursed, nose. *How was her nose bleeding?* thought Ted. He hunkered down so close to her face that he could have kissed her dead lips. His stale coffee and tobacco-smelling breath seemed to make the light peach fuzz on her upper lip move. A drip of crimson suddenly appeared at the edge of her brittle, spider leg eyelashes; she was crying blood tears. Even though she was obviously dead, Ted checked her cold body for a pulse as he could not work out why she was bleeding. As Ted's fingers pressed against the girl's neck to feel for that unmistakable thump, the corpse turned her head. Her eyes began to open, the sound of her eyelids ripping as she pulled them free from the eye caps brought a torrent of hot, green bile into Ted's mouth, and he vomited all over his overalls. The girl looked at Ted with accusing eyes, her cloudy irises framed with spots of petechiae. Her lips curled into a smirk, and she began talking in a soft voice.

"What do you think you are doing, you pathetic man? You would not have been able to have me in life, but you come here and desecrate my body in death. I know what you have been doing…stealing the body parts of the defenseless. Hoarding them in sacks to scatter on your mediocre garden. Your favorite, I know, is the brain...the pink and grey spongy matter where all our memories lie. You keep that for yourself, preserve bits of it in old jam jars, and slice it up to have on toast. That is making you sick, Ted. You're dying even as you stand before me. You will pass in the most terrible way. Your brain will not even be able to comprehend it, and I will witness your passing. No one will attend your funeral, but your butchered dead victims will be waiting for you here. You should be scared. Ted."

The girl turned her head back to its original position and lay there peacefully.

Ted heard a high-pitched, animalistic shrill and he realized it was emanating from himself. It seemed to last forever and sounded unbelievably loud even though it was muted by the deep mud walls. Ted felt the tremors begin again, starting as always from his pointer finger, but this time no amount of clenching or pleading would make them stop. The tremors spread throughout his entire body. He felt as if he were shaking from his balls to his toes. A peal of laughter ripped itself from Ted's lips, and his whole body shook, racked with the tremors and his uncontrollable, misplaced amusement. The world began to swim around him, and no matter how much Ted tried to right himself, he could not keep his balance; he fell from his crouched position onto the corpse of the woman. His body, now in the fetal position, oozed blood, mucus and tears of laughter onto the pretty, pale blue summer dress of the girl who had issued Ted's death sentence.

As Ted lay there like an overgrown, grey-haired baby, the disembodied heads of his victims popped up all around him as if they were growing up through the earth. All the skulls had the unmistakable line all the way around the top where Ted had cut them open with a power tool and fished inside to pull out his delicacy. A bloody mess hung from the base of their heads, and they crowded closer to Ted, dragging their entrails over him, leaving road maps of gore. In the mouths of the heads were hessian sacks.

Ted caught a glimpse inside one of them and saw his very own face staring back at him from its depths, the look on his face was as if he had been lobotomized. Drool dripped from his scabbed lips, and his eyes had the same glassy appearance as those of the young girl's corpse. Ted tried to see into the other sacks, and the victim heads were obliging, reveling in the delight of what Ted was going to see as they drifted closer. In one sack was his left arm, hacked from his body; he knew it was his arm as it had the same Mum tattoo he had gotten while drunk as a teenager. In another sack was his right foot with the stubborn wart, and in the last sack he could see his shriveled member, curled in on itself like a shrimp. The foreskin baggy and grey, the pubic hair matted with blood. As Ted felt himself dying, he thought about the fact that he was still a virgin; his penis was neither useful nor ornamental throughout his life.

How fitting, Ted thought, as his addled mind struggled to remember which way was up in a six-foot hole, *that I will become the last donor to my graveyard garden.* A final laugh, more of a slight mirthless chuckle, eked its way from Ted's throat, punctuated by a strangled wheeze from his ruined lungs, and he died there atop the prettiest girl in the graveyard.

ROADKILL
By KN Gould

This time it was a raccoon. Good, raccoons were a more manageable size. It couldn't have been there for more than eight hours or so. Caleb imagined the busy intersection must have had a lot less traffic in the predawn darkness. The animal had almost made it to the safety of the other side of the three-lane road when the passing vehicle hit it, crushing its hindquarters in the process. Tire tracks were visible amidst the fur and blood. Death had come shortly after.

"Sorry, sorry. I'm sorry." Caleb worked carefully, sliding the shovel under the carcass a couple of inches at a time. He tried to ignore the looks of disgust he got from passing motorists. By now he should have been used to it. Caleb was only fifteen but he had already been doing this for a long time. This stretch of road, he knew from experience, had vehicle-animal collisions on an almost daily basis. There were no houses close by; he was on the border where the residential part of town turned into the industrial part of town. Open fields and bike paths ran along where this particular highway and road came together. This limited the prying eyes on him.

The raccoon died in the bike lane so at least he didn't have to worry about dodging traffic while he tried to pick it up. More than once he had had his own close call with a car doing fifty-five in a forty. Some of those, he was sure, were intentional. The last thing he wanted was to end up smeared across the road like this raccoon.

Caleb cringed with each scrape of the metal on asphalt. Since the animal had only been there a short time, it was easier to peel it off the pavement. The cool, mild weather also helped. During a hot afternoon in the summer, it was almost impossible to get the whole thing in one piece.

Once it was all on the shovel, Caleb carefully lifted it over to the little red wagon sitting safely in the grass off of the roadway. In the wagon was a cardboard box.

"Shhh, it's okay. It's all gonna be okay." Caleb spoke softly. The raccoon's eye stared lifelessly at the sky. Its tongue hung out of its partially open mouth.

He cradled the body in his gloved hands briefly before setting it into the box like a parent putting a newborn to bed.

"There you go, buddy." He stroked the fur as he whispered the comforting words.

Caleb closed up the box and placed the shovel next to it. Towing the wagon behind him, he headed in the direction away from the road, towards the closest bike paths. He would have preferred to leave the box open to the sunlight but doing so would have increased the chances of someone passing by and looking in. From time to time he crossed paths with a jogger or cyclist. Some of them were more so-cial than he was. Anyone seeing the raccoon might have had questions he didn't really want to answer.

He nodded politely when he did encounter people on the path. Caleb knew he was dirty and disheveled. That came with sleeping in a makeshift tent near the river every night. He also knew that he was small for his age so most people he ran into felt pity for him, not fear. Caleb was about as nonthreatening as one could be. That could change quickly if they knew what he had in the box.

The sun peeked through the clouds. It looked like the afternoon might be a nice one. You couldn't count on that, though. Spring in Oregon meant unpredictable weather. It wasn't uncommon to see someone walking around wearing a heavy sweatshirt along with shorts and sandals. Walking back to the Resting Place in the rain was unpleasant and Caleb appreciated the break in the clouds.

The rattle of the wagon behind him soothed him. Caleb hummed a melody to himself. Every so often he would turn back and talk to the cardboard box.

"We're getting there, buddy. We'll be there before you know it. Just hang in there."

* * *

Caleb was six when he first realized something might have been wrong. Not at first, of course; it took time for a boy that young to correctly interpret the looks the other neighborhood kids would give him. He heard things. Sometimes, a faint chirp or a whine he could ignore. Other times it was obvious and he would ask what that sound was. He found it odd, but not alarming, when they told him, time after time, that nobody else knew what he was talking about. He would just give a frustrated shrug and accept it like only a six-year-old could.

Caleb was an only child. Working two jobs, his mother barely had time to sleep while trying to keep a roof over their heads and food on the table. Her son's oddities didn't go unnoticed, but she grossly underestimated their importance. Maybe if he had been able to have a pet in the house, they could have figured it out sooner.

Rocky the cat died when Caleb was eight. The neighbor's dog–a mean and quick Doberman named Buster–was suspected, but guilt was never proven. Rocky belonged to Caleb's friend Jesse from down the street.

Caleb had heard the cat's yowls of pain from inside his house. His mother was in the back yard tending to the garden. He assumed that's why she didn't hear it. When the cries didn't diminish, Caleb opened the front door to investigate. Rocky was dead in Caleb's front yard, next to the driveway. His obviously broken back was bent unnaturally and his skin had been torn open in several places. Drying blood was spattered across his light gray fur. The cat lay completely still without even a hint of movement in his abdomen to show he was breathing. Despite this, the horrible screams that brought Caleb outside were still coming from Rocky.

"Rocky? Is that you? Oh, no." Caleb approached the cat slowly as he covered his own ears. This did nothing at all to block out the sound but he left them there anyway. Even from the front door, he could tell that Rocky was dead. He didn't know how the cat could still be making those noises. He just knew he was more scared than he had ever been.

Caleb struggled to push his fear away as he drew closer. He knelt down in the grass and tentatively touched the bloody fur. His hand instinctively jerked away on contact. He'd been expecting the cat to spring to life and scratch at him. To his relief, the cat remained still.

His fingertips touched the top of the cat's head before tracing a path down the back of his neck to his back. Caleb was careful to avoid the gaping wounds as best he could. The curious prodding turned to petting. His hand was streaked with red after a few strokes of the matted fur. He kept petting the dead cat. The screams slowly became less intense, both in volume and duration.

"I'm sorry, Rocky. That Buster sure is a bad dog. I'll get you back to your house. Jesse will be real sad to see you like this."

Caleb wasn't sure how long he sat with the cat, stroking its fur and talking to it. After a while, the only sound he could hear from Rocky was a low growl. The cat didn't sound happy but it sure was a lot better than before.

"Caleb, what are you-" His mother stood in the front doorway. Dirt stained her jeans and her hair had gone wild with her gardening hat removed. Her eyes widened as she took in the scene. "Get away from there right this instant!" The panic in her voice made Caleb afraid all over again.

"Mommy, it's Rocky. He got hurt but he's doing better now. I helped him."

She grabbed him up into her arms and sprinted back into the house. Before he could protest any further, she had him sitting on the kitchen counter, next to the sink.

"Oh, baby boy, that kitty's dead. You can't touch dead things, you don't know what germs they might have on them."

Now the tears started to flow. "But Mom, Rocky was crying, crying so loud and wouldn't stop. He's probably crying again because I'm not there." Sobs replaced words as his mother scrubbed the rest of the blood off of his hands and arms.

"It's okay, Caleb. Don't cry." She sighed and hugged him. "Mommy will take care of the kitty after we get you into the bath."

Caleb's mother ran the bath and got him into the tub. She left the water running while she went to tend to Rocky. It was almost overflowing by the time she came back. Caleb didn't ask his mother what she had done with the cat and she didn't offer up anything. What he did know, as he shivered in the warm bath water, was that he couldn't hear the dead cat's screams anymore.

* * *

The smooth, well maintained, bike paths crisscrossed the entire city. Caleb knew most of them so well he could navigate them even in the dark. In fact, he had done so on several occasions. The most direct route took him alongside the Willamette River after about a half hour of walking. Caleb's worn out shoes plodded along with the red wagon trailing behind.

At Steel Creek Park he faced his toughest test in avoiding people. Couples walked hand-in-hand while some kids that looked to be his age hung out on the benches near the bathrooms. A few fellow homeless guys sat smoking under a nearby footbridge. A couple of them looked familiar and Caleb avoided eye contact, hoping they wouldn't engage him in conversation. Two men sat, talking intently to each other. Neither of them looked up at him as he made his way quickly down the path. This was good; he was almost to his destination and he couldn't afford any complications.

Beyond the park, the paved path wound through the trees and brush. The river flowed close by, out of sight, but with the same steady, unmistakable rhythm it had a thousand years ago. As the path curved to the left, Caleb veered to the right, into the grass and mud. There was a path there, just not an obvious one. Looking closely, you could see the faint track where the blades of grass were just a little more worn than the ones around it. Most people didn't look closely, whether they were walking through nature or going about their daily routines.

Caleb saw it. He was the one who'd created the tracks in the first place over the course of a dozen trips. Low hanging branches brushed against his bare arms. The wagon bounced and jostled its cargo even more now that they were off the smoother surface. It wasn't long before he was far enough away; he couldn't see or even hear another person. He might as well have been in the middle of a forest instead of fifty feet from a popular walking trail. He parked the wagon, feeling comfortable that nobody would find it so far off the beaten path. The cardboard box was light but awkward in his arms as he carefully navigated down the hill.

The woods were thicker here, and Caleb had to hold the box out in front of him to keep the branches and blackberry vines from hitting him in the face. When he emerged, it was into a sunlit, grassy clearing. The slope was gentle and ran all the way to the rocky river bank.

"We're here, buddy," Caleb said, relieved. They'd made it safely to the Resting Place.

* * *

After Rocky's death, Caleb's mother kept a worried eye on her son. She was willing to overlook that first incident; children were prone to creating imaginative stories after all. Whatever she told herself to rationalize the disturbing image of Caleb petting a dead, blood-soaked animal couldn't comfort her when it happened again and again. Whether it was a bird lying in the grass at the park or a possum covered with maggots in a ditch, Caleb told his mother he could hear them. It got to the point where she would, at a moment's notice, cut across lanes of traffic just so she could turn and avoid the carcass on the side of the road.

The therapist seemed nice enough but he didn't believe Caleb's claims. Nobody did. It had to be the boy's way of dealing with his father leaving at such a young age, he told Caleb's mother. His coping mechanism, the therapist called it, was unlike anything he had ever seen before.

They saw each other once a week for almost two years before the insurance wouldn't cover it anymore. His mother couldn't afford to keep sending him so she convinced herself he was doing better and didn't need the weekly visits. Caleb was old enough to understand that his mother became upset when he talked about the animals. His solution was to simply stop talking about them, not just with his mother but with everyone. Whenever he would find one, he would close his eyes, sing a song to himself, and get past it as fast as he could. He thought he could hide it that way, that keeping it to himself would let him be more normal. Kids, though, have a kind of sixth sense when it comes to detecting weirdness in other kids. As a result, Caleb found himself with fewer and fewer friends as he went from elementary to middle school.

Caleb's uncle died when he was twelve. He'd been driving home from work after the graveyard shift and slammed right into a tree. The police said that he hadn't hit the brakes at all, leading them to believe he had fallen asleep at the wheel.

The funeral was on a Saturday in September. East Lawn Cemetery had the space for large gatherings but they only needed one of the smaller parlors for Uncle Bill's service. Caleb sat in one of the front pews, next to his mother. She didn't cry, he noticed. She had never cried in front of him. Two dozen other people, mostly work friends, took the seats behind them.

It was muffled at first, the voice that Caleb heard. It was crying softly and he couldn't quite make out what it was saying.

"Can't see…help…anyone…please," came through in between sobs. He looked around but, though the faces in the room looked sad, nobody was crying or talking.

Caleb was still searching for the source of the muffled voice when the pastor began to speak. "Friends and family, we are here today to pay our respects and remember the life of William Sturgill." A framed, blown up photo of Uncle Bill stood next to the closed casket and clergyman. To Caleb, it seemed that the face in the picture was staring right at him.

Suddenly, Caleb covered his ears with both hands. His earlier curiosity about the mystery voice was replaced with horror. A low whimper escaped him and he began to rock back and forth in his seat.

"Shhh." His mother, half-concerned, half-embarrassed, put her hand on his knee. "It's okay to be sad. We all miss him." Caleb barely heard her but he knew that she completely misunderstood. He wasn't upset because his uncle had died. He was upset because he could still hear the pleading voice.

It was coming from inside the casket.

Caleb rocked himself faster and started to cry through tightly closed eyes. The pastor stopped speaking and everyone in the room was staring at the child in the front row. Some of the looks were sympathetic, some worried.

"Caleb! Caleb, stop this right now," his mother whispered harshly. Her grip on his knee tightened. "You're being disrespectful."

With his ears covered and his whine quickly becoming a growl, Caleb didn't hear his mother chastising him. All he could hear was the voice of his Uncle Bill.

The boy's eyes shot open and he lifted his head, startling the funeral-goers. He looked over, not to the casket, but to the wall next to the photo of the dead man. His stare was intense like he was trying to see through the drywall into the room on the other side.

"What is that?" he asked through his own tears. "What's over there? What is making that noise?" He was yelling now, on the verge of losing whatever self-control remained.

The wall seemed paper-thin because Caleb could hear the screams through it all too clearly. Terror and pain that only he could hear filled the air. He couldn't make out any specific words, just mindless, guttural agony. Any normal set of vocal cords would have failed with such an expenditure, either going hoarse or giving out altogether. The howls ringing in Caleb's ears continued without weakening.

"Don't you hear that?" he cried. "Mom, make it stop. Why won't it stop?"

She picked him up and rushed him towards the exit, pushing through the small throng that had begun to respond with their belated concern. Caleb wrapped both arms around her neck with an iron grip. His mother used to carry him like that all of the time but the passage of time made it more difficult for her than in years past.

Leaving the parlor, she couldn't see where she was going. Her foot missed the single step outside the door and she staggered for a few steps before sprawling onto the asphalt of the parking lot. Caleb fell from her grasp and landed flat on his back. They both wept, together but for their own separate reasons.

Caleb sat up and wiped his eyes with his sleeve. He looked up to the sign hanging above the door a short distance from where they sat. The door led to the part of the building that existed on the other side of that wall, the place where those horrible sounds had come from. It read: CREMATORIUM.

The shrieks and wails wouldn't stop until he was in the car and they had driven a good distance away. Even then, they echoed in his head that night and for many nights after.

* * *

Caleb cradled the raccoon once again. He walked with it, searching for the right spot. The Resting Place held nineteen other dead animals. The new arrival would make twenty. Some, like the nutria, had been there for weeks and had decomposed to the point it was almost unrecognizable. There were others that looked so peaceful they might have been sleeping. There were cats, raccoons, mice, rats, birds, possums, and one dog. The largest resident was the deer. Caleb had spent most of a moonless night pulling it through the woods to get it to the Resting Place.

No matter the size of the animal or the length of time since they had passed, Caleb could hear them all.

This was not the first Resting Place, there had been others. His mother never looked at him the same way after

Uncle Bill's funeral. She didn't understand what was happening with her son and she was too afraid to dig deeper.

The first Resting Place had been in Caleb's back yard. He'd hidden two mice and a bird near the rose bush underneath the back window. Death, he figured out, didn't stop them from feeling the physical sensations they had always felt. Pain from their wounds was ever-present, but they could also feel the sun on their bodies or the kind touch of a person. Putting them in a place where they were safer and more comfortable alleviated the hurt and fear. Caleb didn't know if they could hear him when he spoke to them, but they always seemed to know when he was around.

His mother found the first Resting Place and disposed of the animals placed there. The argument that followed was full of nastiness and accusations, mostly from Caleb. It wasn't long after that he ran away from home.

He never did try to fully explain to her what it was he was doing with the animals. It wouldn't do any good, he thought. She wouldn't believe him and he would just end up going to see another therapist. The new therapist wouldn't believe him any more than the first one did.

Most of his time as a homeless teenager was spent just trying to survive. Scrounging or begging for food and money was his primary job. Whenever he could, Caleb sought out animals that needed his help. Nice, open areas with soft ground worked the best. Finding places that fit that description in a location secluded enough to avoid discovery proved difficult. Again and again, Caleb was forced to look for a new Resting Place after the previous one was found and the animals removed. He didn't want to think about what might have happened to them.

A patch of empty, slightly overgrown grass lay between a bird and one of the possums. Caleb knelt on the damp ground and carefully set the raccoon down.

"There you go, little guy. I know you're scared but it gets better. I promise."

Caleb stroked its fur and continued to talk softly. When he felt the raccoon was comfortable enough, he moved over to the next one. He spent a few minutes with each resident of the Resting Place, speaking to them reassuringly. One by one, he made sure to give every one of them attention. By the time he was done, his stomach rumbled with hunger and the sun was beginning to dip below the tree line.

"Okay, guys, I gotta go now. Don't worry, I'll be back tomorrow," Caleb said. He paused to look back for a moment before disappearing back into the woods. To others, the morbid tableau he had created here might have been disturbing, but it made Caleb smile. He was helping the dead animals in way that only he could.

His tent and meager belongings were at a spot farther up the river. It would be a lengthy hike to get there. Caleb knew of a quicker way but he still chose to take the longer route. The shortcut went right by East Lawn Cemetery. The moans and wails from the crowd who had unwillingly taken up residence there could reach Caleb's ears, even through six feet of soil.

There was nothing he could do for them.

THE CRONE'S COLLECTION
By Daniela Addamo

She had no idea where she was, how she got there, or more importantly, *who* she was. Her head throbbed and spun, until the young girl began to scan her surroundings and found herself inside a small pitch-black room with damp air sweeping over her body. Struggling to adjust her eyes to the dark void, she slowly reached out her arms until she felt a stone wall, cold to the touch. Before the panic alerted her stress hormones, bright yellow and blue flames burst from ornate, deteriorated brass candelabras with gilt paint peeling off, exposing an oxidized green patina. Her vision slowly became more clear as the flames besieged her with sharp shadows defining the curves and recesses of the sculpted stone architecture of the wood, winding in dramatic baroque fashion. She was confined in a space as small as a closet, which only brought about more confusion until she spotted a large corroded brass door knob. There was a skeleton key already inserted inside the keyhole. As relief washed over the young girl, she proceeded to turn the heavy key, listening to the loud sounds of twisting tumblers. *They must be ancient*, she thought. As she pulled the stone door with all her strength, she discovered it was a mausoleum inside a graveyard that seemed to go on for endless miles. Undulating hills with dilapidated tombstones made it impossible to see how far the graveyard actually expanded. Nothing but a forest of death.

Centuries-old, moss-covered mausoleums and tombstones, their names barely legible anymore, surrounded her as she navigated the graveyard. A faint murmuring arose. Perhaps it was the sound of an undertaker who could lead her to the exit, or perhaps, what would be much to her dismay, just a small animal scurrying about.

Tall weeping beech trees, with decayed gnarled trunks, cascaded its branches over her as she made her way to follow the sound, and she was certainly not dressed property for such an venture. The young girl wore a white short sleeved, ankle-length Victorian nightgown made of chiffon. Ruffles framed the bottom edge of the dress and neckline with a silk bow at the dip of the sweetheart line, a design far too elaborate for a nightgown for any ordinary girl, which did offer at least some clues as to her affluent background. Yet, even her lavish dress did not stir even the smallest memory of who she was. Her arms and legs grew cold from the biting wind, and every hit of the weeping beech trees' branches scratched her skin as she ran. Faint lines of blood began to trickle down from the fresh cuts on her skin. The sound grew louder until all hope of escaping was shattered when she discovered the source of the murmuring. A large mound of freshly shoveled dirt was covering a woman's body, with only her head exposed in front of a tombstone and a dirty shovel lying next to it. She appeared to be no older than in her sixties.

The woman's face was porcelain white, matte and lifeless, as perfect as a bisque doll that one might mistake her for. Her bordeaux red lips appeared almost separate from her face, plump and inflated. The only slight imperfection of her mien was her disheveled, nineteenth-century style, coiffured, blue-black hair, with particles of dirt interrupting her velvety locks. *Where have I seen that colored hair before?* the young girl thought. An instinct forced her head down to twirl a long piece of her own hair between her fingers–her blue-black hair. *Curious.*

Aside from the murmuring, the woman did in fact appear to be dead. Only...why was she buried so shallow and only partly exposed? In an abrupt instant, the woman's eyes opened, forcing the young girl to jump back in a fright.

However, she froze with more curiosity than fear. Zombies weren't real, at least not to her knowledge.

The woman too was startled by the young girl gazing down at her. She began to rise up from the ground, dirt descending down her vermillion hued dress, a favored color of the Gilded Age. She wore a high neck, satin, redingote bodice with gold-threaded frog enclosures leading down to a pointed princess line at the waist over a velvet layered skirt, with even more gold embroidery, draped over a large bustle. God only knew how many more layers sat beneath her costume. A large gold mourning brooch with four love knots around the rim was pinned to her lapel. Glimmering light reflected off the glass of the brooch, catching the young girl's attention. Upon closer inspection, the young girl noticed there was human hair knotted into a 'Prince of Wales Curl' behind the glass.

The woman then brushed the dirt off her dress and stood tall and stately. Though their memories didn't serve them well at the moment, they seemed to recognize each other as they moved closer to one another, squinting their eyes. At last, the young girl mustered enough courage to break the silence.

"Are you...ah...alive?"

"Of course I am alive, child. Why ever would you think not?" the woman snapped back with indignance that one might encounter from a woman who was born into wealth and lived a rather strict life.

The young girl blinked with confusion and replied, "So then...what were you doing underground like that? Did someone put you there?"

"I was sleeping," the woman said with a matter-of-fact tone, sounding bothered by the young girl's question to an obvious scene, or at least obvious in the woman's opinion. Each answer from the woman only brought about more confusion to the young girl.

"Why in heaven's name would you-"

"Wait a moment..." the woman interrupted the young girl. "Curious...you look rather familiar. Have we met before, miss..?"

"I don't know. Perhaps, though I cannot seem to recall...in fact...I cannot...I cannot remember my own name." Worry began to wash over the young girl's face when she was hit by the reality of this unnerving lack of information for the second time since her arrival at the graveyard.

With intrigued suspicion, the woman ran her eyes over the now dried blood on the young girl's pale skin from what looked like a bloody pattern of hairline fractures on glass.

"Have you injured yourself, child?"

The young girl followed the woman's eyes down to the cuts on her body.

"Oh, I was cut up by the branches of those trees," she said, pointing to the weeping beech leaves as they billowed in the wind with a sense of grace that seemed to mimic the woman's countenance.

"I see.." said the woman, as she studied the young girl.

"You did not answer my question. What were you doing *sleeping* under the dirt like that?"

The woman turned to look at the grave with a wistful mannerism, and for the first time since their encounter, the young girl was given some sort of clue as to the possible motives of this enigmatic woman.

"Well if you must know..." she said in a taut voice, then paused and changed her tone to one of melancholy. "I was visiting my daughter. She died from consumption many decades ago when she was just one and twenty. So young to suffer such a cruel fate."

The woman then pointed to her brooch.

"This is a lock of her hair. She had such beautiful blue-black hair. Well, she certainly took after my features. I come here to sleep above her coffin...and I can see her...in my dreams." Once she began, the woman seemed incapable of stopping her reverie out loud.

"When she passed away, I was stricken with grief. Life ceased to have meaning. I would have taken my own life if it wasn't for the fear of possibly never meeting her again in the afterlife. I was consumed, you see, with finding a way to be close to her. Even dabbled in séances that the new Spiritualists lot had begun to practice, though all proved to be a farce." She paused once more, shaking her head in disappointment.

"One day, a crone found me here laying fresh roses against her tombstone, as I had done every day at dusk since she died. At the time, it had been several months since my daughter's death. The crone told me how I could be with her. She explained every detail...burying myself under the dirt above her grave at dusk, but only if I began the ritual before the one year anniversary of her death, otherwise she would be lost to me forever. She left me with one last instruction, or a warning rather: 'One who lies with the dead, dies with the dead.' And that was the first and last time I ever saw the crone." The woman halted in contemplation of how her tale sounded when spoken out loud.

"At first, I found it ghastly and believed her to be mad. However...as the months passed, I was overcome with agony, more so every day. So I did what any grieving mother would do."

"You actually...buried yourself and slept here?" the young girl asked with wide eyes.

"Yes. The year was coming to an end. Only a few days before the anniversary of her death. And, I did not care for her warning. I would happily die if it meant I could spend as many years as I could visiting her in my dreams. What price would I pay if I eventually died here and then reunited with my dear girl? The crone believed it to be a curse, but I saw it as a solution. I have returned to her grave to sleep here every night since and have seen her...been with her for the past thirty-six years. The days feel long and numb, but in my dreams here, I find solace."

"And...no one ever sees you?" asked the girl, pursing her lips in suspicion.

"Not a soul. People, even the undertaker, walk about this place as if I am invisible. Perhaps it is some sort of enchantment. Admittedly, I have not a care in this world to understand why."

As the woman concluded her story, the young girl looked at her with swollen, sympathetic eyes. In less than a few seconds after her monologue, the woman was startled and gasped, frightening the young girl. She then reached her arm out slowly towards the young girl's neck. Immediately jumping back, the young girl tripped over an overgrown root. As she began to fall, the woman simultaneously grabbed a gold necklace hanging around the young girl's neck, breaking the delicate box chain, resulting in the young girl falling hard on the ground. Unmoved by what had transpired, the woman seemed almost entranced by the necklace, while the young girl moaned in pain from the fall.

"Where did you get this!" the woman shouted.

As she picked herself back up, the young girl looked puzzled. Winded by the blow, she replied softly, "I don't know. I told you. I can't remember anything."

"This was my daughter's. I gave it to her on her last birthday before the consumption took her. It was the very last time I saw her smile."

It was a round gold locket with a swag motif design around the edges and a seed pearl inside a starburst at the center.

"She loved stars...she would watch them for hours as they twinkled in the sky," the woman said, entering another reverie. Just then, she remembered she had placed an albumen photograph of herself and her daughter, taken when she was just a young girl, barely ten years old, inside the locket, and when she opened the locket, she discovered it was still there. A young doting mother, arms wrapped around her little girl with faint smiles. Her face tightened and her eyes widened as she lifted them from the photograph to the young girl in front of her. It was she, her daughter standing in front of her. Only, she was not the age at which she had died; she was *frozen* at the age she was in the photograph.

Twisting into an expression of shock and bereavement, the woman began to weep.

"How could I not know the sweet face of my own daughter?"

"Mama...is that you? I...I think I am starting to remember," replied the young girl as memories began to flood her mind with such aggression that she could barely keep up. Terrible, awful memories of when she fell ill, yet happy ones too, with her mother; for as Dante Alighieri once said, "there is no greater sorrow, than to recall happiness in times of misery."

"Oh my darling girl!" the woman cried out as she ran to embrace her daughter, and they wept in each other's arms. Finally, the young girl pulled away and smiled as her mother, wiped the trickling tears off her daughter's face, and caressed her hair.

"Mama...why could I not remember? Are you really here?"

A loud noise from a nearby mausoleum, similar to the one from which the young girl had entered the graveyard, interrupted their bittersweet reunion. A large stone door crept open from the mausoleum and the crone stepped outside. She was rather short, barely five feet tall and simply dressed, wearing only a tattered black cloak that fell all the way to the ground, covering her entire body. Her frayed white hair shrouded her face from the strong sudden gusts of wind.

In a menacing voice, the crone finally spoke, "You did not heed my warning, woman. You have slept with the dead and now you shall die with the dead."

"So let me die, you vile woman. Alas, let me finally be with my daughter," the woman pleaded with desperation in her voice.

With a creeping smile, the crone replied, "You laid here under the earth, stealing memories from your daughter that never came to pass, a future that was never lived. Spent years stealing time that did not belong to you. You have stolen your own life and it is mine to claim now. Oh, you foolish woman, how grateful I am for your invaluable grief. You *are* dead my dear. Just a few moments ago, you drew your last breath as you slept under the earth."

The crone paused for a moment, though soon realized she had nothing to lose by divulging the rest of her schemes, and relishing in it. *So proud. So..clever,* she thought.

"When I came to you all those years ago, I placed a remnant of your daughter's soul in an object that holds sentimental value to you. The locket you buried her in.It preserved your memories of her, but also your daughter's, as it belonged to her."

Frightened, the young girl hid behind her mother as the crone pulled open the left side of her cloak to reveal a trove of memorabilia. Lockets, pendants, pocket watches and the like, hung on the inside of her cloak, hundreds perhaps. A myriad of indistinct whispers slipped out from each piece of her collection.

"Mama...what is she going to do?"

"Not now, my love. She will *not* do anything," the mother assured, standing firm with the instinct typical of a protective mother, making them almost invincible. Though, however powerful her 'mama bear' aptitude grew, it could not possibly rival that of the crone, who was perhaps hundreds of years old, acquiring her own prowess through supernatural means.   And, in that moment, the mother realized how selfish her indulgence to grief had been, plagued with guilt she had never felt until now. She never cared who was affected by it during the entirety of the past thirty-six years, to a point where, over time, she had forgotten all about the rest of her family. One by one, each one of her other children and her husband had become estranged. Mourning over her dead child had only brought about more death. They were all absent from her life; they might as well have been dead too. *Oh, for God's sake, was this a lesson?* the woman thought. *But what good is a lesson if you cannot, well, learn from it? If you...have no chance of redemption?*

As if reading her thoughts, the crone responded, "Was it worth it?"

"Enough! You will not touch my daugh-"

Just as the woman began to protest, the crone's cloak sucked them both in and a new piece was added to her collection. Her smile was filled with gratification, shaping itself into a sinister 'V'.

"I did warn you, woman. One who lies with the dead, dies with the dead."

ACTUAL MALICE
By Phoenix Roberts

I watched the Grave Digger weep while he dug Rose Asher's first burial plot from the hole in my wall facing his workplace. His car's green headlights lit the ground for him. I knew it wasn't nice to stand at the window and spy, but the ripple of his shoulders stuck me there. The coyotes' howl broke the spell. I drew my curtains closed over the opening.

When the sun came up I let it in and looked across the way to admire the Grave Digger's work. I found Rose Asher's head poking through her plot with her arm stretched out before it, the nails pulled clean off her raw fingertips. Where the flesh of her face parted, I could see that her tongue was halved and jagged. Blood congealed where her neck met the ground, tufts of fur floating there like buoys.

The Grave Digger did not cry at her second funeral, delivering her eulogy.

"She didn't need to die," he said. "I won't have it happen to anyone else, either. In this town—from hereon out—if we're not dead, and someone puts us in a casket, we alert them that we are, in fact, alive. To that end…" He sought out the mayor. She nodded.

"To that end, we have installed bells with pulleys in every open plot in the graveyard. We're calling it the Rose Asher initiative."

The applause that ripped through the pews nearly deafened me. My hands stung from the effort of contributing.

We talked, in the weeks and months that followed, all of us, around water coolers, at mailboxes. Our words were careful at first, their meaning half-buried. No one wanted to be the first to say it outright. Trista Peters bit that bullet for us at the brick lottery afterparty.

The mayor called her number at the town hall, and she stepped forward from a throng of jovial laughter, banter, maybe-next-times. It wasn't a scowl I swallowed when I watched the Bricklayer bring her home ever-closer to complete. I'd just gotten some water down the wrong pipe, is all. It didn't matter to me that she was nearly a decade younger and had won so many times that she'd soon need no curtains whatsoever to hide from the coyotes. It didn't even occur to me to think in such terms.

"It would never be me," she said at the bar, after arguably one too many beers. She stomped a foot against the ground for emphasis, and not for the first time I felt heat at the back of my neck, looking at her shoes. Trista brought a collection of shoes with her when she moved into town. The pair that night were light, light pink, with a kiss of lace at the ankle strap. My only shoes were those made by the Cobbler, and he produced beige sneakers exclusively.

"If someone put *me* in a casket, I'd *make* them know how alive I was," Trista said as she stood in those shoes, "I don't want to speak ill of the dead, but—you have to admit, there was something seriously wrong with her, letting it happen."

We looked at her from our stools and tables, but really we looked at one another from the corners of our eyes, each of us trying to guess how the other might react. Color rose to Trista's cheeks. Her voice grew louder.

"Look—if you go around playing dead, don't expect my pity when someone believes you. That's all I'm saying."

Silence, silence, silence, and then—

"I'll drink to that." Dasa Priestly, who lived next door to me.

"And me." Ada Saltways, who no one liked very much, who grinned from ear to ear when I bought her a round to drink with from her brightly manicured hands. One by one, everyone at the bar drank to that. I was not the last.

Even so, for many nights, I stood by the gape in my house until much later than I meant to, rubbing the back of my neck. Some nights I opened the curtains. When I did, I saw a neighbor parked nearby, chewing their lips or grinding their teeth, and, like me, picking through the sounds of coyote howls for the metal call of the pulley-bells.

No such call came while I waited for it. Summer became fall, and every new death was verified by silence. So I stopped listening. I slept soundly, and for a long time, until the bells at last were put to use and jolted me out of bed.

I ran to the graveyard in my nightdress, only to see Trista, neither in a casket nor sullied by so much as a speck of dirt. I wasn't the only one who responded. At least half of the town were there.

"I think he was going to bury me alive," Trista said.

The Grave Digger stood a few feet away from her. He furrowed his brow, shook his head.

"I was not. We were playing hide-and-seek."

"Trista," said Ada, "The bells aren't for games of hide-and-seek, they're for genuine emergencies."

"We can't just go ringing the bells every time we're a little bit afraid," Dasa added. "I do understand, of course, that losing a game is pretty frightening. Or at least, I imagine it must be. I've never done it, and never would."

"I think you blew your situation a little out of proportion," I agreed. "Not very respectful of Rose's memory. Also, for what it's worth, in hide-and-seek, the goal for the hider is not to be found. You'll have a better chance of winning if you *don't* ring the bells."

Trista turned her head this way and that, looking for who-knew-what in the faces around her, until finally she apologized and we all went home. The coyotes woke me again later on. I rolled over and went back to sleep.

In the morning, I was the first to see organs strewn across the plot assigned to Trista like chew toys, drying blood and pus oozing from canine bite-marks. The ground was smooth in a Trista-shaped track for some ways leading up to her plot, which was half caved-in with dirt.

A shoe lay beside the place it cleared. Even through the mud clinging to it, I could see it was light, light pink, with a kiss of lace clinging still to the ankle-strap. It lay there in the sun, right where it fell when she kicked open the grave she had been buried alive in.

I brought the shoes in, and then I alerted the authorities.

We didn't talk very much in the days and weeks that followed. We tried not to look at one another.

The mayor called two numbers at the next brick lottery. For morale. One of them was mine. I lifted one foot, and then I listened to the people around me and heard only breathing, throats clearing, and I stayed right where I was. Without turning my head, I strained my eyes to see the cards closest to me, and I saw the second number there in a pair of hands with neon nails.

When I lifted my face to look at Ada squarely, I found her looking right back at me.

"Oh, this is ridiculous," she whispered to me. "It's very sad, what happened, but it's not our fault, really. We did the right thing, going out when we heard the pulley-bells. It was up to her, after that. She could have tried harder."

I felt a weight rise from my chest. The relief her remark had brought me was too much to contain. It swirled around my gut and emerged in bright, high-pitched barks. I laughed, along with Ada, and the two of us laughed and clutched one another, and we laughed, and we laughed, and we laughed, and we stepped forward to receive our bricks.

I waited after that. I waited and watched the way my neighbors held themselves. It wasn't until the most dead-eyed among them had a spring in their step that I began wearing Trista's shoes.

I listened, too, and for longer each night. I slept as little as I could, wore purple moons beneath my eyes, made clerical errors at work. When I did sleep, if I slept, I went to bed in running clothes. I bought a shovel.

The pulley-bells sang loud and clear the following summer, and I was out the door before even the first metallic note was done scraping. When I arrived in the graveyard with a shovel over one shoulder, Ada and the Grave Digger met me. The rest of the town filed in as I caught my breath.

Ada stood in the plot assigned to her. The Grave Digger's shirt was dirty. He leaned over her. His fist was closed around the bell-pull.

"She was trying to bury me alive," he said when he heard our footsteps fall near.

"That's not true!" Ada protested, "it's exactly the reverse."

"Ada," I argued, "You have to admit that it's him, and not you, ringing the pulley-bell right now."

"I was afraid to ring the bell. When Trista rang the bell—" Ada began. I shushed her.

"We've all moved on from that," I said.

We helped the Grave Digger away from the open plot. Dasa produced a blanket and a tray of cookies. I patted his shoulder. Ada pulled herself out of the grave and stomped off into the night, ranting and raving as she went.

"Like a petulant child," Dasa said. I nodded so hard I thought my neck might break. We let the evening swallow her before we returned to our homes. I did go to the hole in the wall when I heard coyotes later in the evening, but when I saw the green light of the Grave Digger's headlights move across the curtains, I knew he was safe. I went back to sleep.

Dasa wasn't there when I opened those curtains in the morning. I was alone when I saw Ada's bones, picked clean of meat and chewed at the ends, in a trail from her grave swarming with flies. The flies parted, just long enough for the sun to catch on the pile of skin neatly torn from her torso, neck, and face. At least her legs were intact. Those stood upright in her grave, dirt and rocks packed so tightly that she must have been unable to move when the coyotes reached her.

I drove to Dasa's house. I drove through stop signs and crosswalks. She didn't answer when I knocked, so I pushed aside her curtains and hoisted myself through the hole in her wall.

She sat on the couch. A news anchor spoke on the radio beside her, spoke softly of skin and bones at the graveyard.

"What?" she said, her voice cracking. "Why are you looking at me like that? I would have helped her, if she hadn't made it so confusing by throwing dirt on him."

I'd forgotten about the Grave Digger's dirty shirt. The memory tamed the feral energy which catapulted me into her home. She exhaled through her teeth watching my face change.

"You're right," I said. "She did go and make it all very confusing, didn't she?"

Dasa poured us lemonade. We listened to the news and we ate pastries.

I stopped listening for pulley-bells in the evenings. I put my running clothes in a box in the attic alongside my beige sneakers. I slept with earmuffs. Autumn came again, and one night a pair of green headlights flared on my curtains, pointing not at the graveyard, but at my own home. I opened the door when the Grave Digger knocked.

When he pushed me into his car, I did no pushing of my own. When he took me to an open grave, I didn't grab the bell-pull. When he dumped the first shovel-full of dirt into the grave with me, there was nothing left to do but lie down.

Gerri Craig Photography

BLACK MAGIC
By Thomas Grdic

Siegfried the Gravedigger had spent the last several minutes circling closer to the firelight, darting from ancient crypt to ancient crypt sinking into the soft earth that the city of Blackwater Watch was built upon. They were deep in the graveyard, close to the crumbling outer city wall. Long limbs of the twisted swamp trees broke the star-filled night sky with their jagged silhouettes. When the wind shifted one way, you could hear the distant nightlife of the city center. When it blew the other, it carried the sound of a thousand chirping insects, the howls of nameless things and the putrid smell of the swamp like a beast in decay. This noise helped Seigfried keep the element of surprise despite his large form. A full blooded orc, Seigfried stood over six feet tall, broad in the shoulders from years of working a shovel. He had grown a keg for a belly in his middle years, but otherwise his dark green skin rippled with inhuman muscle. In lock step beside him was his dog, Filly. She had been a constant companion for many years. Well-groomed, loyal and sweet tempered, the black and brown shepherd had served as a comfort to many a mourner when Seigfried's jutting jaw, fangs, and untamable salt and pepper beard could not. On nights like this, though, Seigfried was especially glad for her patience, and her strong bite.

Seigfried kneeled in the grass, barely breathing as he peeked around a stonework corner at the ritual. He had noticed strange goings on some nights ago. Figures moving around without light. He thought he was seeing things but Filly had barked at them. Other signs began to appear. Graves having been dug at, though not unearthed, strange symbols drawn in chalk, boot tracks and the remains of campfires. Part of him knew he should have called the guards, but this was his graveyard. If someone needed a lesson in respect, he felt he should instruct.

Five figures draped in cloaks of purple, so deep they were nearly black, stood around a small campfire. Strange paraphernalia was strewn about their feet. Amulets and wands, pocket sized altars, and bones. At a glance, Siegfried knew that these were old bones. Cracking with their years, still dirty from the rotting coffins or sepulchers from which they were pulled.

One of the figures raised one hand over the fire, throwing down dust that turned the flames a hellish black. With the other, they raised an old, leatherbound tome to eye level, and the group began to chant. Siegfried glanced about to make sure he wasn't being snuck up on and then sat back on his haunches. One hand on the grip of his shovel and the other patting at the fur of Filly's back. He could feel her heart pounding a steady drumbeat, ready to go, but Seigfried needed a moment longer to consider his next move. Two of the five had feminine voices, the rest were masculine. They sounded young, and some of them uncomfortably familiar, hints of the drawl that permeated the voices of the people here, so not outsiders. At least they were too distracted to notice him, and the leader had her back to him.

Taking a deep breath, Seigfried rose suddenly to his feet and loomed forward out of the darkness. Gritting his teeth, he gripped the shovel with both hands and slammed the flat of the blade square between the shoulders of the leader. With a sickening smack, she choked mid-chant and collapsed in a heap on the ground, gasping for breath, tome spinning away from her grip.

Seigfried leapt deeper into the circle, brandishing the shovel at each figure, his voice booming, "Your hoods! Off! Take them off, now!"

Filly stood beside him, hair on end, lips curled all the way back in the snarl of a creature that had not entirely forgotten its instinct to kill. In a moment, all the cultists revealed themselves, throwing their hoods down and throwing up their hands in a strange chorus. One cried out, "Don't hit me!" In a squeak. Another yelped, "Sorry!" A third whined that his mother was going to be very upset.

The leader lay groaning in the dirt, and Seigfried pressed the heel of his boot into the tender spot on her back when she tried to rise. The Gravedigger's breaths came out in ragged huffs of barely controlled rage. He pointed his shovel at each of these individuals in turn. There was spit in his beard. He recognized these "cultists," these children, most of them teenagers.

He pointed at one lad, gold piercings in his nose and ears, and blond hair styled just so. "Charlie Frye, do you want to explain to me what is going on here?"

He turned his steely gaze on one of the young women in this party "or what about you, Elisha Papley?" She was similarly decorated in the style of the children of the well-to-do. "Didn't I bury your sweet Grandmother on your family estate some two years ago?"

The young Papley turned a bright red and looked away. One of the teenagers began to babble something but quickly fell silent with the rest. Seigfried took his boot off of the back of the leader and scooped up the book as the fire returned to its usual shade of orange.

"What is this nonsense?" he muttered, turning the leatherbound tome over in one hand before moving to toss it into the flames.

The girl on the floor whipped up suddenly and grabbed his arm, "Wait! That's a copy of Irhaal Faepeiros' grimoire, the greatest necromancer to ever live! There are only three in existence!"

Seigfried stopped his movement and looked down at the girl sprawled out on the floor. Dark skinned, bushy red hair shaped into an undercut, showing the tall pointed ears of her Elvish lineage. They were pinned back like a cat that knows it's in trouble. Seigfried stared until the discomfort drew clarification.

She balled up a fist and slammed it hard into the earth, "Dammit! We just want something that is ours, our own power, ours. It's our right." she flicked her head back and stared daggers as best she could into the old Gravedigger, but withered under his unflinching scowl.

"Keenor Yinwarin," Seigfried growled, slamming his shovel into the ground so it stood upright. He hauled the half elf unceremoniously to her feet, "I should have known."

At this point, Filly had stopped snarling and was sitting at attention, watching the rest of the disobedient children closely.

"Know you nothing of your heritage? Irhaal Faepeiros means 'penis nostril' in High Elvish." Seigfried smacked the half elf on the nose with the book for emphasis. She recoiled and rubbed her face.

One of the others snickered but fell silent when Seigfried whirled around "Something funny Herberts Bottoms?" He scanned the lot of them. "I know living on the northside keeps your boots nice and dry, but you're all still wet behind the ears! Dabbling in black magic must seem like some new and fun way to disappoint your parents, but there are beasts that lurk among the graves. I guess being gnawed to death is certainly one way to disappoint them. Black magic is out there," Seigfried jabbed a finger over the walls of the city, "and people live and sleep out there in their villages every night while you curl up warm in bed. It is not to be found in human bones. And at least have the common courtesy to use the bones of your ancestors, and not the bones of the poor."

Seigfried tossed the tome into the flames, shooting up a shower of embers. The fear and courage had evaporated now, leaving only a heavy sense of shame. Seigfried let the feeling hang for a long moment.

"We're going to head back to the main gate, and there, I'm going to give each of you a hiding severe enough that you'll be limping all the way back up to Northtown rubbing your backsides. I expect to see either you or your parents some time in the next week to get this sorted out." The Gravedigger let go of the younger Yinwarin, picked up his shovel and brought Filly to heel with a click of his tongue.

"B-But what about the others?" Siegfried detected a sincere warble to Charlie Frye's voice.

Seigfried simply glared at them all until clarification once again broke through.

Keenor muttered "Some of us split off to find more bones, by the old tombs near the wall."

Seigfried felt his heart skip a beat and stared Keenor in the eyes, looking now for some sign of falsehood. He felt his cheek twitch. "How many?"

A puzzled look spread across the half elf's face. "Two. Erada Cobble and Marvolo Hewson."

The old tombs were built during the founding of the city and long before people had the good sense to cremate bodies before interring them in mausoleums. As the marsh shifted over the years, it split stone and popped tombs ajar. Seigfried did his best, but with little time and no payment for their upkeep, other duties often drew his priority. The best he could do was to seal the doors with silver chains and heavy wax, and get to them when he could on his quieter days. But he'd be in the ground long before he had any chance to win that battle against the Blackwater, and he knew it.

"What did they take with them?"

Yinwarin searched his gaze; her ears slowly began to pin back again. "Hammer, crowbars and lockpicks."

Seigfried slowly turned his gaze in the direction of the eastern wall. Everyone held their breath. The Gravedigger unclipped his lantern from his belt, lit it with a match, which popped and sizzled to life, and, kneeling down, held it up to Filly's snout. She bit down on the handle, holding it dutifully in her mouth.

He patted her head. "Gate," he whispered to her, "gate," and then straightened back up.

When a coffin cracks, in a town like this, it lets off a smell that can attract creatures for miles around. And they move quickly.

"As a group," his voice was like ice, "all of you are to follow the dog back to the front gate, and stay there until I return. Under no circumstances should you stray from the path, no matter who you might hear calling to you." He let the words sink in. "Go."

Seigfried watched carefully as the group shed their dark robes and began following Filly and her guiding light. He eyed the group and their nervous glances as they dipped in and out of view behind grave structures and willow trees.

Once they were out of sight, Seigfried turned to face the eastern wall, gripped his shovel and cursed that silly girl under his breath in Orcish before breaking off at a swift jog into the darkness. Her antics might finally have a body count.

* * *

Underneath the shadow of the city wall, even the silvery moonlight couldn't illuminate the tombs that deep in the graveyard. Seigfried felt his eyes twinge uncomfortably, and the world took on shades of gray. He followed the crowbar marks and broken picks on the ground by several of the mausoleums, and a pair of booted tracks leading between each in the gravel path. He saw in the distance a mausoleum with an open door. Seigfried slowed to a swift walk and approached the structure with his shovel in both hands. Nothing jumped out of the breach to meet him.

The silver-plated chain and padlock lay abandoned at the foot of the door. The wax that once sealed in the scent of decay lay in strips next to it. By this entrance, more movement had disturbed the gravel. Not made by boots, but by things that scratched and crawled. Steeling himself, Seigfried picked up the chain and wrapped it around his left forearm, held the heavy padlock in his palm, and squeezed the grip of the shovel in his right before stepping out in front of the doorway. He peered down the steep stairwell, held his breath and listened. Tombs should be silent, and the scratching sounds that echoed back up the yawning stairs set his hair on end. As he descended, the scratching grew louder, along with another sound.

Faint, muffled sobbing. When Seigfried stepped into the first room, his foot landed in something wet and sticky. He glanced down and followed the streak of blood as it tracked past the statue of a long dead figure and around a wall that separated the antechamber from the rest of the mausoleum. He checked each corner and shadowy place as he walked quietly, and he soon found himself in front of another set of doors that had been forced open.

On the other side, stone pillars held up a sagging ceiling that dripped fetid water into shallow pools on the floor. Against the walls. a half-dozen ancient coffins lay, some had their stone lids pushed ajar. The blood led to a final, double-wide sepulcher on a raised dais at the far end of the room, from where the sobs emanated. A coffin that crawled with three ghouls. They chittered and clawed at the gaps. Two more of the creatures lay between him and the sepulcher. Long pale tongues fell out from between their cracked teeth and lapped at the blood on the floor. They were small with hunched forms and were white like bloodless flesh. Their mouths wide and ragged, having chewed away their own lips long ago. Gray dead eyes bulged, and their veiny bellies were swollen with an unceasing hunger. The whole room smelt like dust, rot and the metallic tang of freshly spilt, human blood.

Siegfried felt rage rising in his chest again, and, slamming his shovel against the wall with a loud crack, shouted, "Corpse eaters!"

The chittering stopped as the ghouls whipped around to face him. For a moment, more of their foul venom foamed in their mouths. They swarmed forward, each of them letting out an ear-piercing screech that echoed in the small stone room.

The first one leapt with shriek as Seigfried swung the chain. It whipped through the air and the padlock caught the ghoul on the side of the head. Blackened blood sprayed out in a fine, hissing mist. Before the first ghoul hit the ground, Seigfried swung the edge of his shovel down at the shoulder of the second. Its arm smacked wetly on the stone. The creature let out a shriek of pain before it collected its arm and retreated into a darkened corner to gnaw on its final, still twitching meal.

One of the ghouls grabbed the chain as he tried to snake the weapon back, and it pulled with a strength enough to unbalance the Gravedigger. He barked out a curse as the lengths of metal wrapped around his arm crushed down hard enough to draw blood, and another ghoul leapt onto his back.

It screeched into his ears before sinking its teeth deep into his shoulder. Pain shot down his arm and across his chest as he felt the creature throb like a leech, sucking at the wound it had just opened. Its venom seeped into his bloodstream. The pain was like boiling lead in his veins. With a shout, he booted the third ghoul in the chest, sending it sliding back across the floor.

He dropped his shovel, reached back and shoved his fingers into the eyes of the ghoul on his back; the fleshy things exploding into cold jelly across the back of his hand. The ghoul roared into his body before it recoiled in pain, taking a chunk of flesh with it. He threw his back against the pillar behind him, nearly slipped on the blood that was running down his torso, and slammed the ghoul against the stone hard enough for something inside it to crack. Its limbs loosened enough for Seigfried to grab the creature and swing it over his head and onto his knee where another bone in its side gave out a sickening pop.

The sobbing grew louder, and Seigfried glanced up to see the lid sliding a little farther ajar. His eyes shot wide.

"Stay in the coffin!" he roared, before grabbing the blinded ghoul by the head and slamming it face first against the flagstone floor where it ceased moving.

The ghoul let go of the chain it had gripped and surged forward. Seigfried scooped up his shovel and slammed the point into its mouth, sending sheared teeth scattering across the floor like rain on a rooftop. It faltered for a moment before resuming its charge, taking Seigfried out by the knees. He fell hard onto his back, losing his grip on the shovel, which pinwheeled across the floor, away from him, with a ringing sound. The Gravedigger struggled to his feet again before the ghoul he had just kicked away leapt on his chest. It slammed its fists down on his sternum, forcing the air from his lungs. Before he could suck in another breath, the ghoul wrapped its hands around his throat and started to squeeze. The creature seemed to be laughing, its eyes wide. Blackened, acrid saliva dripped onto Siegfried's face, burning his eyes, as he battered its head with his fists. Once, twice, and then the other ghoul put all its weight on his left arm, pinning it down.

Seigfried realized with a start that the edges of his gray-scale vision were beginning to grow dark. He felt his lungs burning and his punches turning into limp slaps when the ghoul on his chest was suddenly wrenched away in a spray of blood. Its cackles turned into gurgling shrieks of pain as Filly dragged it away, growling, her teeth sunk all the way into the creature's neck.

Seigfried let out a triumphant bark of laughter as his dog pinned and finished the ghoul, before rolling over, shoving his wide hand into the mouth of the toothless ghoul and ripping its jaw out of its head with the crisp snap of tendons. Sucking in lungfuls of the sweetest tasting, musty tomb air, he leapt to his feet, and stomped on the screeching ghoul's head until it stopped trying to scramble away.

Seigfried leaned against a pillar and panted for a moment before he felt Filly pushing her snout into his numb right hand with a concerned whimper. He gave her wet fur a pat before picking up the cracked lantern and filling the horrors of the space with hesitant yellow light. Holding it up high, he marched up the stairs of the dias and slid the heavy stone lid off the coffin with a crash to the floor.

Inside, lying atop the well-dressed bones of a long dead noble couple, a halfling girl shrank away in fear. Beside her, a human boy, his limbs curled up like a dead insect, shaking, his jaw locked up tight and filled with vile foam. His arm looked chewed to pieces, but he was still taking shaky, irregular breaths.

"Up and out, come on," Siegfried said, softly but firmly, as he reached down to help the crying halfling girl. She sat down, quivering against the sepulcher. Carefully, he picked up the boy. He felt so light, and stiff as a board, and his eyes shone with the fear of someone far too young to die. He set him down on the soiled floor and, peeling back the fabric of his shirt to reveal his weeping, purplish wounds, racked his brain trying to remember the words to a healing incantation.

"Is-is he going to be okay?" The halfling girl managed to choke out the words as Filly wiggled her head into the girl's lap. She curled her fingers through the dog's fur.

"Hush," he murmured, holding his hand over the wounds. He whispered a few words before cursing in Orcish and trying again. This time, a white glow formed under his palm that sapped even more strength from him and made his head swim. The bleeding stopped, and the wounds stitched themselves into heavy scars. But the boy stayed locked up.

He put the boy over his shoulder, and thrust the lantern into the halfling's hands before scooping her up too. His shovel he could pick up later. "He needs an apothecary, but he'll be fine."

He hoped his words didn't betray his uncertainty.

* * *

"They blame me, you know." Keenor passed Seigfried a note, sealed with a wax stamp in the shape of the Yinwarin house crest. She looked as though she had spent the last few nights sleeplessly crying, heavy bags under her eyes. Seigfried reserved his sense of sympathy until she had done her due diligence.

Her ears twitched again and she looked away, casting her gaze over the graveyard now illuminated by the early morning gray light, "They'll be here though. They just didn't want to work with me. They'll come tomorrow. Marvolo is still in the clinic." Her voice trailed off.

Seigfried nodded, taking another drag from his pipe as he stowed the note in his back pocket. He passed Keenor the rake that was leaning against a pillar that held up his front porch.

"You'll rake the paths from there, to there," he pointed. "Make sure there are no footprints, and pull up any weeds you find. After that, come back here. We'll inspect your work, and then we'll return the bones to where they were found with all the appropriate rituals. The dead are like old gods. A lot of rules, and no forgiveness, so I expect you to be sincere."

The old Gravedigger sat down on the edge of the porch with a sniff beside where Filly was napping. "Go now," he said before cracking open the letter. He heard her footsteps crunching away through the frosted grass.

He noted with some sense of surprise that the apology was written with her untrained hand, but signed by both her father and herself.

"Yinwarin," he called out, and the girl stopped some steps away further down the hill, turning back to look at him, "where did you get that book?"

The half elf let out a short, bitter laugh, "From a trader, at Lucky's Tavern. I, ah, really should have known better."

Siegfried gave a nod, "That you should have. It was a shame for all of this to happen over a silly trick. But, after this long day, your debt to me and the dead will have been paid. The rest is up to you."

She nodded back and continued dutifully toward the graves. Siegfried waited until she was far down the hill before reaching under the porch and pulling up the tome, turning it over in his palms. It had scarcely been singed by the fire, and Seigfried had recovered enough bog bodies to know what preserved human skin felt like. He also knew enough Elvish to know that Irhaal Faepeiros absolutely did not mean 'penis nostrils.' That whole night had been a series of unfortunate coincidences, but someone in Blackwater Watch really was selling corpse magic to children.

Seigfried tossed the tome back under the porch and looked over at his sleepy Shepherd. Filly looked back through hooded eyes and let out what sounded like an exasperated huff.

"I know," he tapped out the ash of his pipe with one hand and patted her side with the other, "but we really do have business to attend to now."

Gerri R. Gray (also known as Madame Gray) is an American novelist, short story writer, editor, poet and lifelong aficionado of horror and dark humor. Her debut novel, *The Amnesia Girl!* (an outrageously dark comedy about the misadventures of two women who escape from a psychiatric hospital in the 1970s) was published by HellBound Books in 2017 and has since received favorable reviews by readers. Her work has appeared in a variety of print and online publications, including *Beautiful Tragedies*, *Coffin Bell*, *Dig Two Graves*, *Poetry Quarterly*, *Jitter Press* and *Night Picnic*. She is a member of the Horror Writers Association and Ladies of Horror Fiction, and one of her short stories was nominated for a Pushcart Prize. An antique dealer and former B&B proprietor, Gerri lives in upstate New York in an historic and decidedly haunted nineteenth-century house with her husband and a bevy of spirits. When she isn't busy editing and creating strange worlds filled with even stranger characters, she can often be found rummaging through antique shops, exploring haunted places, dabbling in the occult or traipsing through old cemeteries with her digital camera in hand.

You can visit her online at www.facebook.com/gerrigray13

OTHER HELLBOUND BOOKS

Goodbye Stranger

Another gripping noir thriller from the bestselling author of *The Gentleman's Choice* and *Dark Beauty*

Danielle Harrington has the life many women envy: She's beautiful, rich, has two wonderful children, and is married to the Preston Harrington - the handsome, charismatic, retired quarterback who won two Super Bowls.

Unfortunately, something is very wrong with Preston. Having suffered more than his fair share of injuries and concussions, he becomes quiet, withdrawn, and distant.

As Preston spends more time away from his family, Danielle begins suspect an affair without realizing her husband is involved in something much, much worse…

Following a series of tragic incidents and the return of an old nemesis from the past, things begin to spiral out of control for Danielle as Preston's dark side puts her and their children in terrible danger.

RK8

Mind the moon when you leave the theater! Road Kill: Texas Horror by Texas Writers returns, and Vol. 8 definitely goes Splatter-bump in the night!

It's a monstrous mosh of fallen angels, prepubescent prescience, tempestuous incest, intergalactic blues, a Gulliverian massacre, cynophile racists, murderous rodents, a prehistoric Devil Head, the return of Bram Stoker's forgotten hero, and so much more...

Featuring stories from the grand master of horror himself, Joe R. Lansdale, Emma E. Murray, Jae Mazer, Bret McCormick, Madison Estes, Chris Miller, James H. Longmore, Jonathan Louis Duckworth, Robert Stahl, Matt Micheli, Elford Alley, Iphigenia Strangeworth, Jacob Austin, R. L. Olvitt, Lawrence Buentello, Tom Bont, Bev Vincent, and the incomparable E. R. Bills.

Mice and Wolfmen

From the thought-provoking whimsical, the horrifying "what if," the wonderfully macabre, to the downright terrifying - Joe Pasquale delivers a dozen tales guaranteed to have the reader glancing over their shoulder as nighttime approaches, and those long, dark shadows begin to creep in.

Skulking within these pages, we have, for your ghoulish delectation, the blood-sucking undead, lycanthropes, the world's greatest escapologist, a restaurant most vile, a creature spawned in the very pit of Hell itself, and a warped version of The King of Rock 'n' Roll to chill the very blood in your veins.

Mr. Pasquale never fails to surprise - nor to shock, and every single one of his stories hits home, and hits hard. He writes as a lifelong fan of horror, of a childhood spent reading the greats - and it certainly shows here.

Enjoy...

Poe

A haunting collection of twenty-three terror-filled tales that pay loving homage to - and capture the very essence of - Edgar Allan Poe.

So, prepare yourself for blood-chilling nightmares as murder, madness, and the supernatural are masterfully blended together to create a delectably wicked potpourri of the macabre.

Featuring exemplary stories of horror from:

R. C. Mulhare, Scot Carpenter, Stephen A. Roddewig, Gerardo Serrano R., Greg Patrick, Drew Nicks, J. Rocky Colavito, Bernardo Villela, James Musgrave, Carlton Herzog, Barbara Jacobson, Guy Riessen, Jane Nightshade, Floyd Mcmillan, Jr., Jeanette Gibson, Bill Camp, J Louis Messina, N.D. Coley, Brett Knepper, Josh Poole, Jameson Grey, and the inimitable Gerri R. Gray

Splatterpunk

splat·ter·punk
noun
informal
noun: splatterpunk

Definition: "A literary genre characterized by graphically described scenes of an extremely gory nature."

HellBound Books are incredibly proud to present to you horror most raw and visceral, two-dozen suitably graphic, horrific tales of terror designed to churn the stomach and curdle the blood.

This superlative tome is an absolute must for fans of Richard Laymon, Clive Barker, Monica J. O'Rourke, Matt Shaw, Wrath James White and Jack Ketchum – all put to paper by some of the brightest new stars writing in the genre today.

Featuring stories by: Nick Clements, Carlton Herzog, NJ Gallegos, Scotty Milder, Steve Stark, Frederick Pangbourne, Cristalena Fury, Amber Willis, Kenneth Amenn, Erica Summers, Allie Guilderson, Cory Andrews, Andrew P. Weston, Shula Link, Carlton Herzog, DW Milton, Brent Bosworth, JD Fuller, Robert Allen Lupton, C.M. Noel, Julian Grant, Jay Sykes, Phil Williams, and the incomparable James H Longmore.

Crimes of Hate

"In compiling this anthology, it was my intention to focus on stories of crime motivated by hate. Not racially, politically, or religiously motivated violence, even though these are labeled 'hate crimes' in contemporary media.

Edgar Allan Poe's The Casque of Amontillado opens the anthology and The Interlopers by Saki (H.H. Munro) provides an appropriately hateful bookend as the final tale.

In between these two classic stories you will find seven very imaginative and original creations by incredibly talented contemporary authors:

Jennifer Trumbull gives us her take on what happens when a privileged young woman with everything going for her decides to kill someone in the aptly titled I Hate You.

Randall Smith cautions Don't Be Stupid in his disturbing tale of an eleven-year-old boy who's not quite right.

Psychopaths, Grieving and Timeslips is a most unusual novella from P.K. Kleypas. It deals with hate and the ensuing guilt it can arouse in 'normal' people forced to deal with psychopathic family members.

SF by Steven Purselley is a coming-of-age tale of profound darkness.

The Last Ray of Summer by Anthony Ferguson is another tale of family drama and the extreme measures required to end the acts of a sociopathic father.

Che Trujillo offers an inside look at the initiatory practices of an urban gang and a glimpse into the mind of a victim turned killer in Cherry Boy.

Crepuscular, my own contribution to this collection, tells of the lingering consequences crimes of hate can generate even decades after the fact.

So, immerse yourself in the strange situations and states of consciousness we have conjured for your amusement.

And, be cautioned against unleashing your own crimes of hate on the unsuspecting world."

Bret McCormick

A HellBound Books LLC Publication

www.hellboundbooks.com